To Have

M.L. Pennock

For Josie and Charlie

You're the reasons I breathe.

Table of Contents

Prologue: Stella 1

Chapter One: Stella 3

Chapter Two: Brian 7

Chapter Three: Stella 9

Chapter Four: Brian 15

Chapter Five: Stella 19

Chapter Six: Stella 23

Chapter Seven: Brian 29

Chapter Eight: Stella 33

Chapter Nine: Brian 39

Chapter Ten: Stella 43

Chapter Eleven: Brian 47

Chapter Twelve: Stella 51

Chapter Thirteen: Brian 57

Chapter Fourteen: Stella 61

Chapter Fifteen: Brian 67

Chapter Sixteen: Stella 73

Chapter Seventeen: Brian 81

Chapter Eighteen: Stella 89

Chapter Nineteen: Brian 95

Chapter Twenty: Stella 99

Chapter Twenty-One: Brian 105

Chapter Twenty-Two: Stella 115

Chapter Twenty-Three: Brian 127

Chapter Twenty-Four: Stella 133

Chapter Twenty-Five: Brian 137

Chapter Twenty-Six: Stella 143

Chapter Twenty-Seven: Brian 151

Chapter Twenty-Eight: Stella 163

Chapter Twenty-Nine: Brian 173

Chapter Thirty: Stella 179

Chapter Thirty-One: Brian 185

Chapter Thirty-Two: Stella 191

Chapter Thirty-Three: Brian 201

Chapter Thirty-Four: Stella 209

Chapter Thirty-Five: Brian 219

Chapter Thirty-Six: Stella 227

Chapter Thirty-Seven: Stella 235

Chapter Thirty-Eight: Brian 239

Chapter Thirty-Nine: Stella 243

Chapter Forty: Brian 249

Chapter Forty-One: Stella 255

Epilogue: Stephanie 257

Acknowledgments 261

About the Author 263

Prologue

Stella

"It'll hurt. It's going to be painful, girls, but it's worth it. You'll hear a lot as you grow up that whatever doesn't kill you, will make you stronger," Nana says to me and Steph. "Always ... always come out stronger."

She's talking about love, I can hear it in her voice, and it's something neither Steph nor I have any real clue about. I mean, we're not even out of high school yet ... hell, Steph's barely through junior high and I just turned 17, so really the idea of true love and being in love and understanding love is largely lost on us. Mostly lost on her. At least that's what "adults" would have us believe.

I've found it.

I think.

"I know what you're thinking, Stella. I'm sorry, sweetheart," she says, eyeing me cautiously and seeing right through me like she always does. "But, you're bound to get your heart broke at least once more. It happens to the best of us. This boy now, he's not the one. Deep down you know that. You're fortunate, though."

How fortunate could I really be if Keith isn't "the one"? I'm practically planning my life with him — the pictures of wedding dresses and flowers taped to notebook paper, a list of songs for the disc jockey all written out. I've drawn hearts next to the really important ones. The ones I'll dance to with him and my dad.

All those thoughts evaporate when she says, "Your first love was always a determined boy. He'll find his way back to you. Give it time, Stellie. Give him time."

Slipping into my thoughts, I pull my legs up tight to my chest and rest my head on my knees as I watch the wind rustling the leaves of the maple trees shading my grandmother's house. Breathing deeply, the scent of cinnamon heavy on the air, I close my eyes and open my heart ... and I see him.

It's not the one I've promised everything to, handed my heart over to so willingly; it scares me just a little how I could still feel so deeply for him. For Brian.

"Nana, how can you be sure he'll come back?" I'm not sure why I ask. I've never questioned her feelings before, but this time she's piqued my interest. Something just feels different.

She's picking at an old wound, one that took a long time for my heart to finally heal from. The scab is fresh enough a scar hasn't had time to form despite all the years between the injury and now.

In an instant, all that healing comes undone.

"He was made for you, Stella." She says it confidently. "That child was picked from the stars just for you."

Stella

Chapter One

My meeting was canceled. I came home early.

The look on his face when he walks into the room draws the conclusion for me. He wasn't expecting to see me.

"Where are you going? I didn't think you had any meetings out of town this week."

"I don't," he says.

I eye the cell phone in his hand as it plays a ringtone I've heard before. It's one I've been hearing more frequently.

"So, where are you going, then?"

The unmistakable notes of fear weave through the uncharacteristic anger I hear in my voice; it's like smoke clinging to the curtains after the toaster malfunctions.

The luggage set, a gift from my sister for our wedding, sits by the front door and I stand my ground right next to it hoping he might give me an answer. I'm silently urging him; just give me an answer.

I count the suitcases and realize every piece of clothing he owns is likely inside those fancy canvas boxes.

My entire life is packed in those bags. Probably folded neatly.

He likes his T-shirts tri-folded. That's how I've been folding them since college.

I shake the thought away. Take a deep breath. Try to make it make sense.

"Tell me what's going on. You're going somewhere. Where are you going, Keith?" I say it calmly, genuinely interested.

I say it like I have my wits about me; that's the furthest thing from the truth.

"I met someone," he says, giving me a pitying look. He pities me?

My mouth drops. I feel the air leave my lungs, but can't remember how to pull it back in.

"You what?"

He shakes his head and says quietly, "I don't expect you to understand right now, but I'm in love with someone else."

Rage. I feel it coursing through my veins, pumping wildly beneath my flesh. I want to slap his face, shake him violently, give him a swift kick to the balls, and lock him in the basement until he comes to his senses.

He's making a bed he has to lie in.

Lies. He's been lying to me.

And I feel the cold rush of panic wash over me.

"I'm sorry," he says, reaching for the doorknob.

It's all he says before opening the door and walking away from everything we've built together.

I wonder if she knows how he likes his T-shirts folded?

***

My sister answers on the third ring, happily distracted and finishing a conversation with someone in the background. Someone should just hit me with a bus or throw me in front of a herd of bulls on their way to pasture.

Stephanie still hasn't bothered to say hello and I have no patience left to listen to her conversation with someone else, especially someone as chipper as this person. I hear a lull in the conversation — "Steph, I need you."

That's all it takes to get her attention, thank God.

"Stellie, what's wrong?"

It's been our code since we were kids. Not a very good one, and not exactly cryptic, but still it's our code for "there's something more important to deal with than choosing which nail polish to wear to the dance and which suit to wear to the interview." And I feel the pain hit me in the chest again.

"He left." Two words. That's as simple as it is.

I'm met with silence, the unmistakable sound of a hand brushing over the mouthpiece of a telephone, the muffled voices as my sister excuses herself.

"Stell? What do you mean he left?" she whispers into the phone.

"My meeting was canceled so, I came home from the office between interviews and his car was in the driveway. I came in the house and the luggage was stacked by the front door." What isn't she getting? He left. That kind of sums it up.

My voice is way too calm. This isn't how people react when the love of their life walks out without a good reason and some high end couples therapy.

She's still quiet.

"Steph! Wake the fuck up! My husband literally just packed his bags, told me he didn't love me and walked out on me."

There's the hysteria. I'm yelling, finally. I'm a rational thinker and this is rational. Right? I'm supposed to be pissed off.

"Why?" I hear the pain in my sister's voice, in that single word. Keith has been like a big brother to her since we were kids. This is going to hurt her, too, and she's way more volatile than I am when she's been wronged.

I take a deep breath. I take another deep breath. I take one more ... and continue.

I was going to try to rationalize it all, but not knowing all the intricate details, his whys, his reasons for packing those bags, made it entirely too heartbreaking to attempt rationale ... I just couldn't fathom what was happening, but I wanted there to be a reason. A rational one, apparently.

"He wouldn't tell me anything other than he was in love with someone else. Steph, he left. He packed his clothes and deodorant and the cologne I bought him for our anniversary and he walked away," my voice catches and I sob my words into the phone to my sister. My shoulders shake violently as I try to hold my emotions back, but I just can't. I finally let them roam free. The tears and the anger seep out and run down my face.

It's been only a few hours, I tell myself, maybe he'll come back because this can't really be happening.

"I don't know what I did. Wasn't I good enough?" I yell into the phone between gasping breaths as the panic, the fear of being alone, grips me.

"Stella?" She attempts to get my attention. "Stell? Take a deep breath."

Breathe in, and out. Repeat. It feels like my chest is going to explode. I know it's my heart breaking into pieces and crumbling.

"I want to die. This is going to kill me, Stephie. This will be what breaks me."

Breathe in. Breathe out.

"You're stronger than you think. This is not going to break you," she says in that reassuring tone, the one we both seem to have inherited from our mom. "Tell me he at least told you who this whore is he says he fell in love with, because I'm going to hunt that bitch down and let her know she messed with the wrong set of sisters."

I listen to the words coming out of her mouth and wonder how I was lucky enough to have her land in our family. It's hard to believe she's my little sister. Isn't this how older brothers are supposed to react to their sister's lying, cheating husband walking out on a 20-year relationship? I guess that's not the case in our family, at least not where Steph is concerned.

Nope.

Little sister, big heart, bigger mouth. And she has a wicked right hook that goes with all of it.

Plus, we don't have an older brother. It's just us.

"Keith didn't mention her name, but I have an idea," I say. The pieces are starting to become glaringly obvious the longer I sit here on the stairs, staring at the closed front door in front of me. The signs I've missed. The nights I've spent alone. "He's taken a few business trips in the last couple months with the same coworker."

I choke on the words. I try to swallow, the bile slowly rising to the back of my throat. I'm going to be sick.

Brian

Chapter Two

"Mom, I'm thinking about moving back to New York." I'm standing in my parent's kitchen, cup of coffee in hand as I casually lean against one of the counters.

This feels like it's going to be a difficult conversation to have.

I'm not spontaneous. I'm logical and critical and a planner.

This is the first time I've bothered to mention the idea to anyone other than Greg, though, and I've already contacted a realtor and started shopping for a house. In Brockport. I haven't been back to the small college town since I started my freshman year at Syracuse. I just got in my car one day and got lost, leaving Central New York behind for a few hours. I wound my way through Rochester and felt the tension of being an undergrad in a strange city leave me as soon as I started passing nothing but cow pastures, corn fields, and apple orchards.

It was fall and there was one thing I knew for sure. This was home. I'd arrived home, to the hustle and bustle of country life for a single afternoon, and for more than five years I've thought about nothing but going back. Now that I've said something to my mom, I'm kind of panicking. Saying it to her makes it real.

She's staring at me wide-eyed. Oh, God, I'm going to break her heart. I was gone for college, came back for a few years, and now she's going to be sad again.

"Back to Syracuse?" she asks, a glint in her eyes that tells me she wouldn't believe me if I said yes so don't even think about lying.

So I don't.

"Actually, I'm looking for a place in Brockport. Greg and I have been talking about going into business and we think a small college town would be the best setting," I say in a rush trying to answer the questions I know are rattling around in her brain. I take a sip of my coffee, liquid courage of the morning variety. "We've been talking about opening a café since we finished grad school, but, you know, that fear of the unknown kind of kept me from taking that leap."

"Brockport?"

"Yes, ma'am."

"Do you want me to ask Jenny and Dale if they know of any places in town for rent?" A smile splits her face and I feel the uncertainty release the muscles in my neck. I haven't heard my mom talk about Mr. and Mrs. Barbieri in years, so it puts me at ease that she's still got connections back home, even though "home" was only our home for a handful of years when I was a kid.

"I didn't realize you still kept in touch with them, but, yeah, if you wouldn't mind asking her for me that would be great." I lean forward and plant a kiss on my mom's cheek. "You're not upset that I'll probably leave? I mean, this time it wouldn't be for just a few years and home on break, Mom, we're talking I'm going to uproot my life and go north again ... where it gets really cold and snow is a thing we drive in, not call in the National Guard to handle."

It's a conversation we've never had — the way I balked as a child when Dad's job transferred him to Tennessee and I was forced to leave behind the only girl I ever wanted to spend time with.

Stella Barbieri was it for me. I was five when we met, but still, for a five year old I was determined she was going to have my babies someday.

Then Dad got word they needed him to drop everything and come to Nashville. Mom held off telling me and Tommy until she had to, thinking she could rip the bandage off our childhood and we'd forget the pain with time and distance.

I never forgot that kind of pain. Stella had just turned nine when I found out we were moving. Two nine year olds made a lot of promises we didn't even know we'd fail to keep because to us, keeping promises was just something you did.

"I know you always loved it there. The Erie Canal right there to walk along, the atmosphere, the way the seasons changed. Come on, Brian, you can't hide love like that from your mother, no matter how long it's been since you've seen her or talked to her." She winks at me and pats me on the back as she walks out the door, calling back, "I'll send an email to Jenny and see what she can find for you."

I'm going home.

Stella

Chapter Three

Four months later

He was trouble from the first time I saw him. He wasn't safe. Keith Wells was a bad boy to the core and my mom had tried to tell me not to get involved, but he was new at school and I was twelve. What twelve-year-old wants to listen to their mother when they say not to do something?

We became friends within a few weeks of him moving to town and when we'd hang out it was like I found the new Yin to my Yang. Keith was in Mrs. Meyers' sixth grade class with me and his family had just moved in down the street, so I felt I should help him out. Being the new kid couldn't have been easy, not that I would really know. I've lived here all my life and everyone knows everyone else in this small town, but still I could assume.

After all, I was twelve, not a complete idiot.

We'd walk to school together, then he started sitting with me and my friends at lunch. Eventually, we were hanging out on the weekend ... and then holding hands.

"Steph, remember the first time Mom saw Keith holding my hand?" I stop trimming the rose bush in front of me and laugh at the memory of us snuggled on the couch under a blanket in front of the television on a rainy Saturday. We were just barely teenagers.

"You're laughing. Must be a good memory — was that when Mom and I walked in on you guys watching movies? I remember her freaking out because you were covered with a blanket, but I had no idea why," Stephanie says, licking the frosting off her spoon. "If we'd all been older, she probably would have thought something more was going on under that blanket."

My sister's uncanny ability to waggle her eyebrows at the best possible moment shines through and I can't help but burst into laughter, giggling like we're teenagers on a sleep over. Canned frosting, no cookies, and talking about boys.

"You're a perv. We were kids. When we were that age, things like that weren't going on," I say, shaking my head.

"But ..." Steph prods from her perch on the front steps of my house, chasing the frosting with a sip of wine.

"But he was a bad influence when we were kids, nonetheless."

"Are you sure this is okay? I don't think we're supposed to be here after dark. We're going to get caught," I giggle as Keith grabs my hand, pulling me closer to the fence, closer to him. The community pool closes at dusk and it's well past dark. There is no way we're going to be able to sneak in and swim without getting in trouble.

"You're always such a good girl, you know that, Stella? Live a little!" I wish he wasn't right, but I am. I'm the straight-A student, the kid who wouldn't know drugs if someone walked up and put them in my hand. I tried beer once, but my dad walked into the garage mid sip and put an end to that.

Stella, the good kid. That's me.

I follow Keith, laying my towel over the jagged top and sticking the toe of my shoe through a diamond-shaped hole in the fence to boost myself up. Swinging my leg over, I feel my heart pounding in my chest.

Stella ... the rule breaker.

"You know, I think I hate him. Part of me does, anyway," I say finally, squinting at the thought like that's going to clear up my feelings on the situation. "I've never hated anyone in my entire life, Steph, but he's hurt me just enough hate might be the only thing I feel for him. Is that wrong? We had a life together; shouldn't I still be wallowing in self-pity?"

The security of being in a loving marriage is gone, demolished in the blink of an eye. It's been four months since he left, but the sting is still fresh and every time I clean another box and find another card, another "I love you forever" signed at the bottom, it's like grinding salt in the festering wound.

"No. I don't hate him. I can't hate him. He's just bored with me. I'm boring. This is just going to prove to make me stronger, right?" I say aloud, trying to convince myself more than hold a conversation with my sister. "I want to cut his testicles off with my pruning shears, but I wouldn't call that hate."

Snip. Snip. Snip.

"Who needs therapy when you have rose bushes?" Steph says from behind me, arms crossed over her chest, sunglasses perched on top of her head. She's supposed to be here helping but instead she's eaten my frosting, drank my wine, and is now practicing the art of pissing me off.

I give her my most withering stare. It doesn't work.

"Rather than be a snarky bitch, why don't you make yourself useful and help me with these plants? Now that my marriage has fallen apart I finally have time to devote to these sons of bitches," I say gesturing to the dying rose bushes. They must hate how I've neglected them.

I pull my hair back off my neck and the sweat cools enough that I shiver. September just started but there's a chill in the air already, which means jack because this is Western New York and tomorrow it could be 75 and humid. Mother Nature's mood is as mercurial as mine lately.

Stupid New York. Stupid husband. Stupid life crumbling to dust.

Thank God Keith and I hadn't started a family yet. I don't think I could do this — have my life fall apart, that is — and try to keep up with kids at the same time. I can barely take care of myself right now. Caryn or Steph or my parents have been here with me or I've been at their homes almost every night since he left, just making sure I don't completely fall apart when the sun sets. Or I've been at the office. Work will set you free? Nope, work only reminds you the other side of the bed will still be empty when you finally fall into it too exhausted to bother crying.

"Stephie, I hope you know how much I appreciate all your support," I say, turning serious for a minute. I know without my baby sister I would have buried myself in the bottom of a bottle of wine every night just to ease the ache in my chest until my heart sewed itself back together. "You've kept my head above water. Thanks for having no life so you could be here with me," I tease. The moment got too tense and that's just not us. Even serious moments are filled with teasing and jokes.

"Shut up, I don't want to hear your sappy boohooing. Come help me get this sapling out before it takes root in the foundation of the house." She really just gets me. Steph's always let me say what I need to say and then we move on. When we were little our mom used to remind us in the midst of our arguments that we only had each other and that being sisters meant she'd given us each a built-in best friend. I know plenty of people that isn't true for, but for me and Stephanie it explains our relationship to a T.

"Have you been to that new coffee place in town?" Steph asks as she pushes her shovel into the dirt, trying to free the tree, and I'm so thankful for the change in subject. I really don't want to talk about the divorce any more than I have to.

"I went in with Caryn to check them out. She's planning a story for the business page to promote them since they just opened a few weeks ago. I use the term 'planning' loosely because I swear every time we go in all she does is flirt with the guy at the front counter. And we've been there a lot.

Like a lot a lot." My best friend is the biggest flirt I know. It's just her personality, she's naturally talkative and inquisitive, so she makes a great reporter. "If she can ever stop ogling his ass while he's making her lattes or whatever the hell she drinks maybe we'll get the story."

"A cute boy? And you didn't call me the moment you saw him? You're losing your edge." Enter Steph, the serial dater.

She loves to go on dates and spend time with people, but is afraid of commitment. No idea why, but it's turned her apartment into a figurative revolving door of guys who are good enough to settle down with until she decides they're *too* good for her and they get the boot. She's the exact opposite of me in the relationship department.

"Caryn called dibs. She knew you'd try to work some commitment-phobe voodoo magic on him," I laugh, remembering the conversation.

"Oh sweet baby Jesus in the manger!"

I'm cut off mid-sentence by Caryn's new favorite version of the typical "oh my God" — it's got a nice ring to it, I must say— and look up to see what's caught her eye. Tall, dark, and scruffy has caught it. And he's slinging liquid gold as far as we're concerned. Coffee. Hot, delicious coffee.

"The only thing that could be better than him making my coffee would be if he served it to me wearing nothing but that apron," Caryn whispers to me.

"You look like you're going to eat him for breakfast. Stop ogling or you're going to get the cops called on us, and I don't know about you but the only reason I want to see the chief is if he's giving me details on a case, so stop already!"

I sound desperate because it's embarrassing how she just stands there leering at the poor guy. We're in our thirties, not thirteen.

"Tell Steph I called dibs. She needs to remain hands off. He's totally mine." And judging by the look in her eyes, this is one dibs she'd put someone in a grave over. I don't have time in my life to be burying my best friend or my sister.

"Fine, whatever. I will let her know. Cross my heart." Placing a hand against her lower back, I shove Caryn forward with a hushed, "Coffee. Now."

Seriously, I need to figure out how to get a caffeine drip approved by the insurance company so I don't go through this on a daily basis since this will now be the only place we get coffee from per the "boys I like" portion of the Best Friend Agreement. Or BFA as it's become known to those in the know.

We order what would be our usual anywhere else, like Dunkin Donut or Tim Hortons, and while we wait I check out the scenery — it's trendy, but not so much so the community members who are here year round wouldn't fall in love with it and keep a steady stream of business flowing through. It's definitely designed like it belongs in a college town, too. Whoever owns it knows their shit and put a lot of effort into the aesthetics.

The books lining the walls on staggered shelves catch my eye. What's more is the variety of literature; genres are covered from children's literature to classic lit to literature from the 1960s right up through some more current releases. I wonder if it's the owner's personal collection or just for show. I imagine the hours I could get lost in here wading my way through Catcher in the Rye *and* A Clockwork Orange.

"Hey, Stell, coffee's up," Caryn calls to me. I've wandered off across the room, caught in my own thoughts.

I head back toward the counter, and notice a tall blonde man walking back through the door I assume leads to a kitchen. If I weren't miserable and ending a marriage, that's the kind of body I would want in my bed every night. Keith and I were comfortable with one another, but even getting to the gym or going for a run on a regular basis never gave him the kind of body that makes me go weak in the knees like this. Keith is handsome in a reserved way; not drop dead gorgeous but not below average.

I'm staring at the door as it swings shut and Caryn bumps my shoulder, shoving the coffee I ordered into my hand while I regain my composure. What the hell was that all about, anyway?

"Now who's being a creeper?" she gently scolds. "Stella, this is Greg, the Jumping Bean's manager. I was just telling him we work for the local paper and were interested in introducing the business to the community."

"So are they a thing? You said that was a few weeks ago. Maybe I have a shot now," Stephanie says, wiping dirt on her jeans. "More importantly, I want coffee."

"Not happening, kiddo. Well, coffee, yes we can go get coffee, but as far as Greg goes? Seriously, I don't want to have to break up some fight between you and Caryn over a guy. Not again," I say rolling my eyes. "It always gets too icky. There are plenty of grad students roaming the town for you to lure back to your lair."

Laughing, I grab my rake and the trowel, and head back to the garage so I can get cleaned up and recaffeinate.

Brian

Chapter Four

I've seen her come in a few times but haven't had the nerve to come up to the counter and talk to her. Instead, I find an excuse to go to my office or go bake something, anything to not break the magic of it maybe being her.

I've been wanting to ask this girl if she is who I think she is ... the grown up version of the little girl who stole my heart and never gave it back. I've been hopeful I would find her again for what feels like forever. Twenty years is a really long time to pray for someone to cross your path, and now I've transplanted myself to her hometown.

But she isn't why I moved back here. Not entirely. I came back because I remembered what I loved about this small town when I was a kid — close-knit community and a sense of security made it a logical choice when I was figuring out where to open a business, a coffeehouse no less, which this town desperately needed. Seriously, these people were drinking gas station swill before I came on the scene.

Knowing there was a chance she was here, even if just a slight possibility, only added to my need to set up shop. Her parents still live in the house she grew up in, so if she didn't live here there was the chance she'd visit.

That's what I told myself every time I saw a dark haired woman pull up out front or walk through the door.

Most mornings I'm in back working on inventory or going over schedules and payroll, so seeing Stella walk in for the first time a few weeks ago with a friend floored me. She looked just like her mom did when we were kids, so how could it not be Stella? I couldn't breathe just thinking it might be her.

Today's no different.

I'm peeking out from beyond the café doors in the kitchen, watching her like I'm witnessing my life in slow motion. I feel my breath catch as she turns away from the counter with her coffee, a smile breaking through as she says something quietly to her friend.

"Hey Greg, those two ladies you just served, any idea who they are? Names?" I ask my manager as he comes through the swinging door carrying coffee mugs to wash.

Greg Stevens has been my closest friend since college and when the chance to join me on this adventure arose, he came along for the ride as my right hand man and shop manager. We'd both focused on business and marketing in school with a concentration in entrepreneurship, so starting a business and putting our money where our mouths are just made sense.

It was modeled after a coffee shop we used to go to when we were in college. The place practically took all our money when we were working on projects or trying to impress girls with our maturity, because mature men drink coffee. It didn't matter at the time that maturity was a complete façade in hopes of being invited back to a girl's room. We could just as easily have opened a bar, but I wanted coffee and Greg wanted baked goods. It works, even for two manly men. We had to be the straightest guys on the planet who co-owned a coffeehouse and baked together. If some of our fraternity brothers could see us now, well, I really don't want to know what they'd say unless it was kudos and congratulations on a job well done for following our dreams.

The space we'd found was perfect for that coffeehouse atmosphere, too — little nooks worked for high-top tables, a handful of booths along one wall were perfect for people who wanted a little more room to spread out, a large open space near the front window was a selling point for us as we wanted it for open mic nights. My favorite additions to the space were bookshelves I'd made in my down time while waiting to close on the property. We hung the shelves randomly throughout the house for books, a lot of them novels I'd had to read for various literature classes I took over the years, even if they weren't part of my curriculum.

I'm a self-proclaimed nerd, so when I'm not working, I have my nose in a book unless I'm trying to work on another aspect of the business or clearing my mind in the woodshop behind my house a few blocks away. We encourage the arts and the people we attract to the coffeehouse come from all walks of life — teens wanting to feel like adults, adults wanting to feel young again, business types and artsy types. They all mesh well and I love seeing how vibrant they all are, together and separately.

When I think about it, this is perfection. Almost.

"Blondie is Caryn, and I'm pretty sure she calls her friend Stella or Stell or something like that. Caryn's that reporter I told you about like two months ago. She wants to do a story on the coffeehouse."

I remember him telling me, but I haven't been ready to call her. I haven't been ready to talk to anyone about the motivation behind this business and I know she'll ask, so I grunt and give Greg a non-committal, "Oh, okay" hoping he'll keep talking, say her name again and make it real.

"Honestly, I don't care what they call each other, as long as the blonde calls me tonight," Greg says with a crooked grin, breaking me out of my reverie. I must have looked confused, or maybe pissed off, because he started explaining himself and then I felt like a major asshole. "I slipped her my number. Is that okay?"

I should have told him it wasn't based purely on principle. It sounded like he'd been eyeing Caryn up for some time, though. Greg giving her his number is pretty minor in the grand scheme of things, plus getting angry about it would only make me a hypocrite. I would have done the same thing, but handed my number to the other woman. Greg was still talking, but all I could focus on was her name leaving his lips.

It was her. Stella's here drinking coffee in my shop. She comes here and has no idea it's me who owns it.

"Bri, what's going on? You look like you're going to pass out. You know them?" he says, eyeing me suspiciously, the same amused look he gives drunk people who turn into storytellers after a few too many. I haven't clued him in to the slight obsession I have with my childhood friend and I don't want to start telling him now. I don't think I'm ready to reintroduce myself to her and that's exactly what he'd try to get me to do. Or he'd say something to her because he's still a slick college frat boy on the inside.

"Later. I'll tell you everything later," I say cryptically, moving to the sink to run water for the dirty mugs he brought back as a tingle runs up my spine.

M.L. Pennock

Stella

Chapter Five

"Can I have a large black and one of the blueberry scones? Thanks," I say handing the barista money for my usual order. "On second thought, can you add a shot of espresso to the coffee? I could use the caffeine."

He smiles politely, and I'm sure he's noticing the shadows under my eyes. I don't think I've slept more than a few broken hours a night since Keith's bomb dropping and the subsequent flurry of paperwork and hiring of attorneys. What day is it? What month is it even? I can't remember. Just a few more days.

"No problem, Stella. I'll have your order out for you in just a sec. If you want to sit down, I'll bring it out for you."

It's become rather apparent I come here a lot, particularly since Greg was punching in my order before I even opened my mouth. I've gotten to know Greg over the last few months of flirty talk between him and Caryn, the type of flirting that made me realize my heart most certainly has started turning to stone. I've never seen Greg actually working with anyone else, with the exception of the elusive blonde who I've only seen from the back — and what a back it is — so it strikes me as odd there's another blonde guy standing back by the entryway to the offices watching me. Maybe it's the same guy; what would I know. I don't *think* I recognize him, though he seems familiar. Maybe it's the hair, or the glasses. I'd be able to tell if he turned around, I tell myself. Who cares — I'm tired, depressed and I just really need that coffee, and I need it now.

Greg knows where I tend to sit, so I make my way over to the small table in the corner and pull out my laptop.

And I sit staring at nothing in particular, fidgeting and rubbing my left ring finger with my thumb as if I'm twisting the band that no longer sits there. A tan line from working outside is all that remains of the ring that once symbolized a relationship that had lasted more than half my life.

I'm 32 and going through a divorce, I say to myself. *Don't break down here, Stell, that bastard isn't worth your tears. Just a few more days.*

"Stella?" I hear his voice before I realize he's set the coffee and scone on the table in front of me. There's concern in his voice and when I look up I'm wilted by the intense gaze in his thunderous blue eyes.

I'd know those eyes anywhere.

The last time I saw them in person, we were nine. And he left without even saying much of a goodbye.

"Brian, come find me! Count to a thousand and then find me, okay? No peeking this time!" I run away as fast as I can because I know he never actually counts to a thousand. He skips numbers, and that's not fair, but it makes it more fun for me. I have to hide as fast as I can before he looks up and starts searching the yard.

"One, two, twelve, thirty-seven ..." I hear his voice drift away as I run to the porch and slide between the house and a large potted plant. "Ready or not, here I come!"

I'm crouched down so he can't see me. He wanders close to the porch, but doesn't come up on it before turning and walking toward the swing set. I think he's giving up on the game, which isn't like him, but he must be. He's climbing up onto the swing as I scoot out from my hiding spot and make my way off the porch.

"Brian?" He's scaring me. We always play until we've found each other and he's never not found me before. Something isn't right; he looks sad. My Brian is never sad — he's the happiest boy on Earth, but right now he's crying and I don't know if I can fix him. "What happened? Did you get hurt?"

I'm just a little girl, but suddenly I feel the weight of the world crashing down on my shoulders as dread settles in my belly. It happens every time something bad happens, like my body knows before my brain does.

"My parents are moving. I'm moving away, Stella. Mom said something about a transfer at Dad's job, so we have to leave. We're leaving for Tennessee on Tuesday."

It's already Sunday.

My best friend is leaving me in two days and my heart is breaking.

He looks up at me, pain in his eyes, and the tears fall like rain from both of us as we cling to one another on the swing in my back yard.

I'd like to say Keith was my first love and my hardest loss, but I'd be lying.

It was Brian. It has always been Brian.

My breath catches in my throat as I suck in the shock and try to keep myself from falling apart.

"Oh my God." I stare at him, wide-eyed and disbelieving. This has to be a trick of the mind because there is no fucking way the boy from my past is the man sliding into the chair across from me. But I know it's him. I've seen the family pictures from the Christmas cards his mom sent to my mom for years after they moved, but for him to be here, now, has me a little baffled.

"How are you here?" I whisper, hoping he doesn't answer.

Am I breathing? I think I forgot how to breathe. I might be having a panic attack, I tell myself.

"What happened, Stell? You look so lost," Brian says as he reaches out to break off a piece of the pastry he set down just moments ago. Popping the sugary morsel into his mouth, he looks at me sadly. "The girl I knew always had a smile on her face."

I let out a stilted laugh. We were so young. We knew each other before we knew what heartache was, and now here he was entering my life again right in the midst of the second biggest one of my life without knowing he caused the first.

It feels like a daydream. He's not actually reentering my life with such minimal effort as if we've been sitting across from one another sharing pastries and coffee our entire adult lives. It can't be real.

I close my eyes against the hallucination and open them slowly.

Brian is sitting across from me and this just feels effortless. Maybe I'm in shock. This is what going into shock is like. It must be. But it makes it so easy to just tell him — offer him my broken, battered, and bruised heart on a platter and see if he can fix it like he used to when we were kids.

"The girl you knew ... she grew up. She grew up, thought she was in love, married him, and just found out he's a lying, cheating rat bastard who needs to be burned at the stake," I say quietly, feeling the hot tears slide down my face. Months of waiting for my paper marriage to finally end pool on the table in front of me. "My divorce will be final in three days. Friday. I just have to get through Friday."

Wiping the evidence of my failure as a wife from my face, I look up. I look into the most precious gift I could have ever been given in this moment and I swear I hear angels sing. God, that sounds so cheesy, but right now all I can think about is how he's found me and it's the first time Brian has found me in 23 years — it would be sinful to think there hadn't been some kind of divine intervention to bring him back to me.

He thoughtfully pops another piece of scone in his mouth, a thoughtful expression on his handsome face.

Reaching across the table, Brian takes my hand in his. It's the most comfortable I've felt since the day we sat huddled together on the swing set in my parent's backyard.

"Lying *and* cheating, you say? He never deserved you then."

Stella

Chapter Six

"Stella, wait! Can we talk for a minute?" Keith yells bounding down the courthouse steps after me.

"For what? What do I have to wait for? Keith, you took my trust, my love, my devotion and threw it in my face. You walked through our front door, packed your shit and left me. I've stood by your side since we were twelve. I was there through high school and college graduations, and your first job and the first promotion. We stood by one another through purchasing a home and building a life!" I realize I'm screaming at him and everything I've bottled up over the last several months is coming out now that we aren't in front of a judge. Instead we're in front of a courthouse and there are people looking at me like I've lost my damn mind. Someone will probably get a deputy from inside if I don't calm the fuck down.

I haven't lost my mind — I just lost a husband, I tell myself as I take a deep breath. "Tell me ... where did I go wrong?"

I need to know if it was something I did because as much as I want to put all the blame on him, I can't. This marriage was a work in progress from the time we were kids, and now, per the judge inside that courthouse behind my now ex-husband, that same marriage no longer exists. I finally feel free to ask the questions I haven't asked anyone.

"Please," I whisper to him. "Tell me what I didn't do right."

"That's just it, Stell. You were perfect. You just weren't perfect for me. I think after so much time together — our childhood and being a couple basically from the time we were kids right up through college — I think we followed the natural progression. We did what was expected of us. We graduated college, you went on for your master's, I started working, and then the next step was to get married. It's not what you want to hear, I know."

He's absolutely right, that's not what I want to hear. But, I won't cry. I won't do it, because he's right. It was what was expected after all those years being "Stella and Keith" to become "Mr. and Mrs." Too many people expected it and Keith and I for so long were in the habit of doing things to make other people happy.

In the end, making everyone else happy, that's what destroyed us.

"I get it, Keith," I say on a sigh. "I know and now you have an entirely new life. But you are part of almost every memory I have since I was twelve. Learning to move on from here is going to be and has been the hardest part because you were so ingrained in everything I did until six months ago when you walked away without so much as an explanation. I thought I at least deserved an explanation."

"She found out she was pregnant."

Stunned, I stand there. Did he really just blurt out that he got his mistress pregnant and that's why he left me? Maybe I didn't hear him correctly, so just for the sake of clarification I stutter through a "what?"

Taking a deep breath he begins, "Beth and I were just coworkers. There was nothing between us until we started working closely on a project for the firm. We were working longer hours together at the office and nothing turned into something."

What do I say to that?

"We started having lunch together most days, and then we were assigned another project and had to go out of town together about a year ago."

Why does he look devastated? As if baring his soul and making this confession is a consolation to me. It's not. It's been going on even longer than I thought and I was completely in the dark. My husband had been stepping out on me for over a year and I never questioned all those signs. There is something fundamentally wrong with me. It's the only logical explanation.

"About seven months ago," he continues. I'm supposed to be listening. Right. "Beth walked into work nearly hysterical and pulled me into the storage room and told me she was late. Probably not a detail you need," he says, wincing.

"This is why you didn't contest anything in the divorce? You didn't want the house?" Oh my God. So many questions are running through my mind, but my brain comes to a screeching halt when I realize he said "seven months ago." It's like getting a bag full of bricks to the face.

"You're going to be a dad. In a month?"

I can't keep the pain out of my voice, but I'll be damned if I'm going to start crying now after being so strong through all of this — his deserting me, the double life and the whirlwind divorce were enough to make my head spin — but he's about to be a father, too, and with that revelation he should have just torn my heart from my chest while it was still beating.

"Yeah. She's due three weeks from today," he says it quietly, practicing using his kid gloves already.

"I won't break, Keith. This won't break me," I say, hugging him briefly out of habit. "I'm glad you've found someone you can be happy with, but I can't have this conversation anymore."

I continue descending the courthouse steps, walking away from everything that used to be and confused about how I missed the fork in the road of my life.

Today, I tell myself pulling my phone from my purse to text Steph, today is going to require a lot of wine. Today I'm just going to get myself royally fucked up.

***

"I grabbed two bottles of red and three white, and a six-pack of cupcakes," Stephanie says as she graces my pajama-clad presence with her excellent timing.

I sigh, audibly, and the smile on her face falls.

"We aren't celebrating your divorce being final, are we?" She takes in the scenery — crumpled tissues, my hair up in a messy bun, the eyeliner streaks down my face — and cringes when she sees the photo album from our wedding day open to a picture of me staring into Keith's eyes like nothing else in the world mattered.

And on that day, nothing else did matter because I had been madly in love with him and we were finally starting our adult lives together as a cohesive unit. The dam breaks loose again and I choke back a sob.

"I swear, Steph, I was going to celebrate this. I was going to relish in my freedom, but it's a Friday night and I'm single for the first time since I was a kid." I shudder as I try to compose myself and blow my nose, again, in the least ladylike fashion. I'm just so done with the pretense that I am a lady.

I'm fucking miserable.

Unwrapping myself from the tangle of legs and blankets, I stand up on the couch and step down in my sister's direction holding out a hand — if she knows what's good for her, the cupcakes will come before the wine.

"No, actually, I want the whites, too," I say and gather them in my left arm as I head to the kitchen in the back of the house.

Sniffle. Sniffle. Sniffle. This has to stop. I can't let this control me.

"I took Monday and Tuesday off. There's no way I can go to the office after this and get the sympathy looks from my staff. They've been great to say nothing about it, but we've been busy, so there's been no time to poke and prod into my life," I say popping the cork out of a bottle of wine from the Finger Lakes.

"Would you like a glass, you fucking wino?" Steph cries out as I take a long pull from the bottle.

"I needed to make sure it was good." And it is. I blow my nose one more time and let out a breath I feel I've been holding for years. "Okay. I'm ready. Ask me what happened."

"For starters, I am so sorry I wasn't there with you. Mom and I would have both been there, but ... work. It fucks everything up," she unnecessarily explains. "So, tell me. What happened? Was he remorseful? Did you punch him in the junk? Ooh, was the whore there?"

Steph has wanted me to run Keith over with the car or punch him in the nuts or hire the mob to bust his kneecaps since I found out about his infidelity. But can I really consider Beth a whore? I mean, she didn't take money from him that I'm aware of, so in the literal sense it's doubtful she's a "whore."

"I need more wine," I say pouring a glass, shaking the English major thoughts from my head and taking a deep breath. "He got her pregnant."

And I wait for it to hit her, watching as the words slap her square in the face. This must be what watching a boxing match in slow motion looks like because I swear I see her face morph before my eyes from my sweet baby sister, who only wants to avenge my honor, to The Hulk. Stephanie just turned into the mother fucking Hulk in front of my eyes.

I cringe as she lets out an ear piercing, "He did what?"

"I'm just going to take these with me while you process that," I say, walking away with my bottle of wine and the cupcakes so I can plant my ass firmly back on the couch.

I've known this since this morning and I'm still trying to wrap my head around the idea my very recent ex-husband is going to be a father in less than a month.

Following me into the living room, Steph sets my glass down on the coffee table and takes a seat in the overstuffed armchair across from me.

"Ask," I tell her.

"How far along?"

"Due in three weeks." I take a long sip from my glass and top it off with more from the bottle.

"Work relationship?"

"Long hours. Put on projects together. Business trip to Pitt." Another sip.

"Due in three weeks."

"Yup."

"Fuck."

"My sentiments exactly," I say holding the package of cupcakes out to her.

"Here's to single ladies," Steph says raising her pastry. "May we be loud and obnoxious. May we forget our manners in spite of our mother. May we have a lot of filthy sex with men who won't break our hearts."

That was that. The toast to end all toasts. The wine began flowing and didn't stop until Steph decided sleep was more important and passed out on the living room floor, and despite my fairly drunken state I cleaned. It's been my modus operandi since high school — stress and alcohol turn me into a cleaning freak, so here I am, drunk at 10 p.m. and cleaning my house.

It doesn't matter that I hadn't slept well in the weeks leading up to the last day of our marriage or that I had enough wine pumping through my bloodstream to force me into a deep sleep for a month.

Sleep wasn't going to happen tonight.

Brian

Chapter Seven

Stella hadn't been back to the Jumping Bean since the day I sat down across from her and essentially ate my way back into her life. I love pastries. It couldn't be helped.

I spent the next couple of days trying to get her out of my head. The last thing I wanted to do was look like a stalker going after easy prey. I mean, the girl was going through a divorce and I walked back into her life after how many years? To anyone who didn't know we'd had a history — as innocent as that history was — they'd think I was setting my sights on the town's newest divorcee.

I wasn't, though. Maybe I was. I came back to this little college town specifically because I was hoping to find her again. I'll blame it on fate if I have to; I didn't know she was married, let alone getting divorced.

There was just so much hurt in her eyes. The pain was palpable. I was watching her eyes the day I told her we were moving all over again. It was that kind of pain. At least twice now she'd been put through this kind of agony. I hated seeing it on her. I hated seeing her hurt so much she couldn't even react to me sitting there.

She reacted, but it was to what was going on within her instead of me, my presence.

I just kept thinking, "It's been more than 20 years. Why isn't she happy to see me after losing touch?" I thought that over and over until she told me about the divorce and then my heart shattered for her. There was a storm brewing deep within her and because I'd kept my distance for months, watching her order up front and interact with her friend and sister, I was under the impression everything was on the up-and-up.

It wasn't and I just keep wanting to kick myself for not seeing that from where I'd catch my glimpses of her from the kitchen.

I was deep in thought Friday morning — the day she said her divorce was going to be final — when Greg snapped me back to reality with a towel to the back of my head. He's lucky I've known him as long as I have because anyone else would have been laid out on the floor and had their walking papers thrown out the back door after them.

"Dude. Seriously, what has gotten into you? Help me with these muffins or get the hell out of my kitchen," he said pulling open the oven door. It was half-past six in the morning and Greg was trying to get the baked goods ready for the display case, which meant a lot of cussing, swearing and hand-washing because he forgets we have to follow health department standards and constantly licks batter off his fingers.

I mumble a "sorry" and move out of his way like he suggested.

"This chick has you all jacked up," I hear him say as I go over the inventory list. I want to ignore him. I want to tell him to mind his own business. I want to find her and wrap her up in the warmest hug I can give her.

"She's not just some chick," I say quietly, a growl underlining my tone of voice.

I may have been a fraternity brother in college, but I was far from the loud raucous sort. I kept to myself, mostly, and was quiet. Trouble maker, I was not, and it was that quiet, reserved demeanor that's made me a decent businessman. When it comes to Stella, though, the protective side of me comes out. It always has.

"If she's not just some chick you're interested in, tell me about her," Greg says as he puts another tray of muffins in the oven. "You lurk back here waiting to hear her voice, Brian. You think I haven't seen you poke your head out every time another dark haired woman walks through that front door? I have. She's all up in your head and I have never seen you react this way to a woman. *Ever*. I've known you for a decade. Never."

He had a point. I dated in college but it was rare to want a second date from anyone. I was never excited over anyone back then, but I'm emotionally charged by the mere idea Stella might come in for coffee.

So I tell him finally. After the last few days of not having time to breathe, I start from the beginning, about how I'd been ripped away from my best friend, and while we tried to keep in touch, eventually being teenagers got in the way. It got more difficult to write letters or try to call when there was no end to the distance in sight. A family vacation to New York for me or to Tennessee for her could have kept that connection alive, but in the end we'd resolved ourselves to the Christmas cards our mothers sent one another each December. For a long time, those cards included the traditional family snapshot or school photos of me and Tommy, and Stella and Stephanie.

Eventually they were just the generic, "Hope all is well!" variety of Christmas greeting, and with that Stella and I had moved further from one another emotionally than we'd ever been.

It wasn't until I decided to apply to Syracuse University that I thought about finding her again. At that point we hadn't seen one another in ten years, and when I was actually accepted into the business program at SU, finding Stell was second and my education first. I couldn't look for her and offer her the world before I had anything to give.

I worked my way through college, was asked to join the fraternity, met Greg and then after graduation moved back home to start working with my dad because I needed a job, needed to apply myself. Then one day it just wasn't enough; things had gotten out of hand. There was no Stella in my life to ground me. It had been missing for so long, *she'd* been gone for so long and I just had to come back and find her.

"That's when I called and asked you about moving to New York and starting a business. I know I should have told you sooner that this was really all about 'some chick,' but I couldn't." This was not a conversation for two grown men. I felt my uterus growing by the second, I swear, but when I looked at Greg he had some shit-eating grin on his face and I couldn't even begin to predict what was about to come out of his mouth.

"You've been in love with this girl since you were nine? And you wait until now to tell me about her?" Did I say in love? I don't remember. Still, he had that look on his face. "She's really pretty, but she's going through a rough time, you know? Caryn's brought me up to speed."

How do I keep forgetting about that — the reporter who wants to do a story on the coffeehouse works with Stella. She probably drops a sizeable portion of her paycheck here each week and I haven't even called her.

"What do you mean she's brought you up to speed? Stella told me the other day she's going through a divorce, but I haven't seen her come in since then," I tell him. God, I wish she'd come in. I just want to know she's okay.

Greg starts telling me about all the sordid details about this guy Stella married cheating on her, but then the clock hits opening time and personal conversation comes to a standstill as a steady stream of students and people on their way to work fill the shop. If business keeps up like this, we might have to consider hiring someone to help out.

I go back to figuring out what supplies we need to order during the lull between the morning rush and lunch, and then place the order when we have a break in the afternoon. Greg closes down the kitchen, I wipe down the tables, and the dishwasher starts running as we lock up and say goodnight shortly after 10 p.m.

It's a Friday night and I'm about to go home to a house I bought and can't fill because there was no gentle laughter in its rooms, no soft floral scent wafting down the hallways, no auburn haired beauty waiting for me to walk through the door.

For the first time since moving back to Brockport, I truly feel alone and the rain pelting my ball cap is just one more reminder of how that loneliness feels — stinging and cold.

Stella

Chapter Eight

"What are you doing out here?"

I turn my head to see Brian standing on the porch, guarded by the roof and the front light casting a halo around him. He looks like an angel. Who the fuck am I trying to kid? He is an angel. He's my angel.

"I- I'm standing in the rain," I drunkenly stammer.

"I see that. Why are you standing in the rain, though? And, more importantly, in the rain in front of my house when you could just come in where it's warm and dry. I've got coffee on," Brian says pointing toward the door.

I'm standing, frozen out of fear that this is a dream and I'll wake up alone still, because if this is real I can't explain to Brian how I ended up here. I didn't even know he lives on this street until he walked out of the house I'm staring at. Why am I just staring at his house, at him? I should say something. What do you say to someone you've missed from your life for more than 20 years, though? God, how I've missed him. And now he's a man; last time I saw him, smelled him, touched him he was still just a little boy. But that's not right because I saw him the other day, but I didn't look at him.

He's beautiful. I say the only thing I can think of that doesn't sound absolutely creepy.

"I could use some coffee," and I follow him and his gloriously broad shoulders across the porch and into his home.

The scent of fresh ground beans permeates the layer of cold I'm trapped under, and as I shed my soaked sweater I welcome the warmth of Brian's home and his company. This house seems so familiar though I know I've never been here before. Its familiarity comes from the pictures on the walls and mantel, pictures I remember from our youth — the one of his parents at the neighborhood barbecue the summer before they moved; Brian and his brother, Tommy, standing arm-in-arm next to a car I assume the then teenage boys shared; a portrait of all four of them I remember seeing hang in his childhood home on the wall behind the couch.

They're all calling me back to a different time, a time when life was simple, when he was my best friend and my first love. And then one catches my eye and steals my breath.

Brian and I seated next to each other at the pool, our arms wrapped around the other's shoulders and a pair of "the world won't ever be able to separate us" grins on our faces. I remember the picture being taken but had never seen it. He moved a week later and his mom hadn't had the film developed before they left.

The tears silently make their way down my cheeks, leaving fresh drops on my already wet shirt, before I even realize they've escaped the confines of my eyes. Sighing deeply, I try to calm the panic in my brain and reach up touching the frame gently. It's the perfect snapshot of our youth.

"Sometimes I wish really hard that I could go back and be nine again." I hear the sorrow in his voice and know we're remembering the same time in our lives. "I was just a kid, but I would have begged them not to make me go to Tennessee if I'd known how far away it was from you. And when I was forced to go anyway, I would have never stopped writing to you. I'm so sorry I stopped sending you letters, Stella." This has been eating away at him for years. It's evident by the pain in his eyes, but we can't change the past; we can only take steps toward the future.

"We were babies. We thought Tennessee was the next town over," I laugh nervously, drunkenly, trying to keep conversation light. I don't want him to know how devastated I really am by everything that's happened over the last twenty-four hours, give or take twenty-three years. We really did think it was a short drive away. At least I did until my dad pulled out the atlas one night after dinner.

"Daddy, will you take me to see Brian tomorrow after you get home from work? I swear I'll get home from school and get all my homework done before we go." I'm so excited to see my best friend again soon and I just know if I use my manners like a lady I'll get to go. I want to see him. I miss him so much.

"Sweetie, going to see Brian would take a lot more planning than just getting in the car and going. Nashville is far away," my dad says.

I stare at him blankly until he takes a deep breath and gets up from his seat at the kitchen table, returning a few minutes later with a large book. He flips it open and thumbs through several pages until he finds what he's looking for.

"Stellie, this is a map of the United States," he says as if I'm completely unaware what a map of the continental U.S. looks like. "This is us up here in New York. And down here is Tennessee, where Brian and his folks moved to."

Instead of telling me I couldn't go see them, my dad gives me a lesson in how to read a map and use the legend and figure distance using a ruler. The lesson isn't pointless, I guess, but the end result is the same — I wouldn't be seeing Brian.

And my kid sized heart breaks a little more.

Brian hands me a mug of coffee. There's nothing in the cup but coffee. He didn't ask me how I take it, so I can only assume.

"You've been paying attention to how I take my coffee?" I ask tentatively, thankful my walk in the frigid rain sobered me up enough so I'm not slurring my speech.

"I didn't want to add the espresso in case you planned to sleep at all this weekend," he says, moving to a couch nestled in front of a crackling fireplace I hadn't noticed. "So. Are you stalking me?"

The question is riddled with humor and playfulness — I can't help but notice his personality hasn't changed much since we were kids and it's so easy to fall right back into that. It's almost like I'm nine again — I'm not the shy kid I was after Brian moved away. I'm the kid I was before he left.

"Why would you think that?" I laugh as I let the question leave my lips.

He lifts the mug to his mouth and takes a hesitant sip, and I wish for a moment I could be that cup. "You show up in my coffee shop and now you're at my house ... in the rain, Stella. You're soaked," he says taking in the T-shirt and jeans clinging to me thanks to Mother Nature's flawless timing. "Next thing you know, I'm going to find you hiding in the bushes outside the post office when I mail stuff to my brother."

"You forgot about the grocery store," I say, lifting the warm ceramic to my lips and breathing deeply before taking a sip, letting the steam warm my face and the scent calm my nerves. "I do my best stalking in the produce section, sometimes the meat department."

Silence settles on the conversation and when I glance at my hands wrapped around the warm ceramic, I realize just how soaked I am from the rain.

"My clothes are dripping on your hardwoods, Brian. I'm going to ruin your floor," I say, making a move toward the door. "I should go. I didn't mean to barge in on your evening."

Standing up from the couch, Brian makes his way over to me, a glint of fear in his eyes.

"Don't go. I've been waiting to see you for a long time. Come on, I've got a nice collection of hoodies and sweats from my Syracuse days," he says walking toward the back of the house where I assume a bedroom or laundry room must be.

"You went to Syracuse? It's a great school. I considered their master's program for journalism." Normal conversation. I can do this.

"I had a couple friends go to Newhouse. They loved the program, but I've lost touch with a lot of them since graduation. They just sort of scattered," he says handing me a pair of grey pants and a bright orange hooded sweatshirt. "Go ahead and change in the bathroom and just leave your wet clothes hanging over the shower to dry."

I slip through the door Brian pointed to and wait to hear the soft click of the latch falling into place before I let out the breath I'm holding. I sigh, deeply, before setting the clothes on the counter and stripping down to my bra and panties. The girl in the mirror looks strong. I wish I felt that way on the inside, but Keith's revelation at the courthouse may as well have crippled my heart. Part of me wishes I was still drunk and angry, but between cleaning my house in the middle of the night, the walk in the rain to clear my head while Steph slept, and now the coffee, I'm sober.

And sober is what I should be if I'm going to be here.

The sweats are loose and comfortable, the warmth enveloping my legs, and for the first time since walking through Brian's front door I realize how cold I was. Holding the sweatshirt to my nose, burying it into the soft fabric, I choke back a sob. I've tried so hard to close myself off and not feel. I did really well for a few months, after the initial shock wore off, until a couple days before we finalized everything this morning.

Now here I am, standing in a strange bathroom, sniffing clothes that belong to a man who is essentially a stranger. I'm sniffing his clothes.

They smell like Old Spice and cinnamon.

Breathe in. Breathe out. Repeat.

I pull the hoodie down over my head, wipe my eyes and, taking one more deep breath, open the door and step out of the bathroom.

Wandering back the way he led me, I walk quietly through an archway that connects the spacious kitchen and living room and stop in my tracks to take in the sight. Brian's sitting on the couch, his long legs stretched out in front of him with his feet stacked one on top of the other on the coffee table that sits between him and the fireplace, his left arm propping his head up in his hand like a kickstand.

I glance at the clock on his stove and realize it's going on midnight about the same time I hear him softly snoring, his breathing even and relaxed ... and it feels natural for me to be here after months of not knowing quite where I belong.

There's something unfurling in my chest and I can't put a finger on it, so I ignore it, and climb into the corner of the couch opposite him. Grabbing the mug I'd been drinking from before wallowing in Brian's bathroom, I take a sip.

"Ouch!" He refilled my mug with hot coffee while I was changing and now my slight outburst has ruined any chance to creepily stare at him while he sleeps.

"How did it go today?" His voice is quiet as he comes back to the waking world and pushes his face into his hands in an attempt to wake up. He asks the question like we've been in one another's presence for years, and it puts me at ease.

"It was ... the end. It's nice to have the finality of signed papers and my maiden name back legally, even though I've used it for writing purposes for forever, but it was still hard." I manage to sneak a peek at Brian while I fiddle with my coffee mug. "He stopped me on the courthouse steps and told me we'd basically just done what was expected — we grew up together, dated in junior high, high school, through college ..."

"So the natural progression of things trapped you?"

"That's how he feels," I shrug. "I can't change it now, but I wish I'd known he felt that way. Maybe then he would have kept his dick in his pants before divorcing me and wouldn't be starting a family in, oh, about three weeks," I say, purposefully looking at my watch. "He didn't even bother to mention it over the last six months of proceedings and lawyers."

His expression makes me giggle. It's the most adorable look despite the fact it's a mixture of disgust and horror and pain. God, he just makes things better.

"You're joking, right? He didn't actually get this woman pregnant and keep it from you? That's got to be the shadiest thing I've heard in a while," he says covering a laugh. "Stella, I don't mean to laugh, but ... wow."

"I can say one thing for certain. The man who divorced me is nothing like the man I married. I didn't even see how much he'd changed until he wasn't living at the house anymore," I divulge.

I attempt to stifle a yawn. Even with a crazy work schedule it was rare I wasn't in bed before midnight if I could help it. I had to take some time for myself and that time came in the form of a handful of hours of sleep if I was lucky.

"Are you warm enough?"

I barely hear the question as my eyes drift closed and I softly hum an "mmhmm" as a blanket is pulled over my legs.

Brian

Chapter Nine

She fell asleep in the middle of a conversation.

I could tell when she walked in the house she was exhausted and a little buzzed. She appeared to be surviving on fumes. And, if her consumer habits were any indication, she was subsisting on espresso and scones a lot more in the last couple weeks.

I refuse to wake her, so standing up from the couch I grab the blanket neatly resting along the back of the sofa and pull it up over her legs.

I push the hair off her forehead and gently kiss the creamy skin beneath it.

"I've missed you so much, Stell," I whisper into her hair.

My sweats make her look tiny, the dark circles under her eyes make her look frail. It's going to take all my willpower not to pick her up and carry her to my bed just so I can hold her for the rest of the night. That isn't what she needs. She doesn't need to think someone is already trying to make a move on her — least of all me. After having been gone for so long, only to show up as a chapter was closing on her life, I don't want to be someone she just falls into bed with.

Instead of reaching for her, I reach for the mugs, still half-filled with chilled coffee, and take them to the kitchen. It's well past midnight and even though Greg can handle the morning routine, I know the alarm will go off in a few hours and I'll feel compelled to go the couple blocks up the street to check on things. I always do.

I make my way back through the house, turning lights off as I go, and stop to watch her. It's hard to believe she's turned from the knobby kneed kid she was to the beautiful creature now lying on my couch. What haunts me is the way my heart wants to burst in her presence.

Stella lets a sleepy sigh slip between her lips as her breathing evens out a little more. Her head drops back to rest more comfortably on the pillow at the end of the couch and I hear the faint whimper a floor away.

By the time I'm to the top of the stairs, the sobbing has started.

"Hey, Bub, what's the matter? Bad dream?"

Britton clings to me as I seat myself on the edge of his bed and he climbs into my lap without so much as a word. Within a few minutes he's sound asleep again and I'm left smoothing the damp hair from his forehead. I place another kiss to his crown and breathe in the scent of watermelon shampoo.

I whisper "goodnight" while sliding him back into his bed and wrap his arms around the stuffed teddy bear he's had since birth — the only thing that remains of his mother other than a handful of photos.

***

"Britt, stop staring at her. Come on, your eggs are getting cold," I say walking back toward the kitchen. He doesn't budge. "Britton. Kitchen. Now."

The sternness in my voice gets his attention. I have no idea how long he'd been standing there watching Stella sleep, but if I hadn't walked in when I did I have a feeling he would have crawled up on the couch and snuggled right down with her. It's been a long time since he had a woman's attention other than my mom, so when he gets it undivided he soaks it up like a sponge. Apparently that goes for women who are sound asleep, as well.

"Daddy, who is she?" he asks as he climbs into his place at the breakfast nook. I don't miss the incredulity in his little voice. Britt's never seen me with a woman. I don't have lady friends. I don't do the dating thing anymore. I haven't dated since I found out a weekend fling during a friend's wedding extravaganza left me bearing the title "Father."

Dating was even more out of the question when Britt's mother walked into my parent's kitchen one morning five years ago with the baby, his diaper bag and a suitcase with all of his clothes shoved inside and said, "He's yours. I never wanted to be a mom."

She'd consulted an attorney, given up her rights and left town.

Three weeks old and abandoned by his own mother.

My son had no idea what it was like to have a woman's unconditional love other than what he'd gotten from Grandma Kathryn. His maternal grandparents probably don't even know he exists. I never met them, either. The entire relationship with his mom was because we'd created him.

I got the best part of the deal, though. I got him.

"That is Stella. We were best friends when I was your age and she came to visit last night," I smile at him. "Eat your eggs. We have to go check on Greg and make sure he didn't burn down the kitchen."

"But, why is she sleeping on our couch?"

"She fell asleep while we were talking. It's not a big deal, buddy. Eat your eggs." I'll tell my son it isn't a big deal, but it kind of is.

I hardly slept last night knowing Stella was just a couple rooms away.

Stella

Chapter Ten

I woke up with the feeling someone was standing over me but kept my eyes closed. I wasn't in my bed. This couldn't be good.

Then I heard Brian's voice and the sound of feet moving away from me.

When I finally feel brave enough to open my eyes, I'm met with the sunlight streaming in through a large bay window and eyes as blue as the Caribbean.

"What the ... ?" I sit up straight, knowing I sound a little manic. There's a miniature version of Brian sitting on the coffee table drinking a juice box, staring at me, wondering about me, who I am and why I'm here. I can see it in his eyes.

Why am *I here?* I wonder, too. Then I remember the night before — court, wine, cupcakes, the walk that still somehow mysteriously led me to this house.

"Britt! What did I tell you about staring at her? Leave her alone and get your shoes on," Brian says walking into the living room. As Britt stands from his perch on the coffee table, Brian quickly replaces him. The likeness is eerie, at best. They're identical, despite their age difference and the stubble lining Brian's jaw. I just stare at him as he hands me a mug of fresh coffee.

I take it, but I'm on autopilot.

"Let me explain," he says.

Autopilot breaks down and a smile, a real smile, cracks the shock on my face because I'm fairly certain I know what he's going to tell me. "Explain what, Bri?"

"I might have failed to mention during our visit last night that there was a creepy little dude sound asleep upstairs. Might have." A smile as wide as the one on my face releases the tension at his eyes. "This is my son, Britton — Britt. He's five."

That smile would have been enough to make my knees knock if I weren't still curled up on the couch, clutching my coffee like a lifeline and snuggled into the warmth of his sweatshirt.

Brian's a dad. How did I miss that? Oh, shit. If he's a dad, that means there's a mom somewhere.

"He's cute. He looks just like you did when we were that age. Is his mom going to be mad I slept over?" I'm used to asking difficult questions subtly, even though I haven't really been good at it lately because of the drama and preoccupation with my personal life. That's not to say my reporter instincts don't kick in when I need them most, like right now.

Brian lets out a strained laugh and I can tell this isn't a subject he really wants to talk about. Not right now at least.

"His mom isn't in the picture. It's just been me and Britt since he was a few weeks old," he says, and pride washes across his face as he leans to the side, looking over my shoulder to check on the little boy. "Have you got your shoes on, yet? Greg's probably wondering where we are."

"You have to work today?"

"I work every day of the week," he says with a sly grin.

"Isn't that illegal? They can't make you work seven days a week every week. Sounds like a story. I mean, I know the coffeehouse is new, but if your boss has you working that much, I doubt the labor board would be too pleased." I take a long sip of my coffee. There we go. The little bit of caffeine in my system has fully awakened the reporter lurking inside. He's grinning at me, though. I'm missing something.

"Oh yeah, my boss ... he's a real hard ass," he laughs. "Someone hasn't been doing her job, though. You didn't check the DBA for the newest business in town, did you?"

I open my mouth to answer him as my phone starts playing "Rhythm of Love" by the Plain White T's. Where the hell is my phone?

"Shit," I say standing up and heading toward the sound. I find my jeans from the night before — dry and folded — on the bathroom counter. Seven missed calls. All from my sister. My phone starts singing to me again from the top of the pile.

"Steph! I'm fine. I promise." I just don't even bother with normal greetings. She's not really a "hello" kind of person.

"Where are you? Oh my God, Stella, I woke up on your living room floor and you weren't here but your car is here. I kind of freaked out." Slightly dramatic for not even eight in the morning, but I get it. I would have done the same to her.

"I went for a walk," I say to her. It's not a lie, I tell myself. I really did go for a walk. "I'm going to call Caryn and see if she wants to go for coffee. Why don't you get ready and meet me at the Jumping Bean in like half an hour? Drive my car. I didn't bring my keys with me."

I finish the call, change out of Brian's sweats and into my jeans and shirt from the night before. My sweater is still damp and hanging over the curtain rod for the shower. I wonder if I can make it to the coffeehouse without freezing to death first, but realize we're still in Western New York. It might be 40 degrees outside right now and 70 by noon. Turning to leave the bathroom, I shove my phone in the back pocket of my jeans and grab the SU hoodie from the counter.

Brian

Chapter Eleven

Stella comes walking out of the bathroom looking like she belongs here. Her auburn hair is a crumpled mess around her shoulders after wearing it up all night. The shadows under her eyes are less noticeable.

It's taking all my energy to stay rooted in this spot by the front door. If I move at all, I know I'll walk in her direction, grab her, and never let her go again.

My heart clenches as my son leaves my side and runs to her, placing his hand in hers.

"Will you walk to work with us this morning?" Britt asks her, staring up into her hazel eyes.

This is what innocence looks like. And it's beautiful.

I want to freeze this moment because right now I'm seeing my past and my future collide.

"Sure, little man. I could use some coffee anyway. Want to sit with me and share a scone while I wait for my friends?"

Their conversation is so smooth and natural, and it hits me ... I'm raising a ladies man. Shaking my head and smiling, I open the front door and usher them out into the day.

***

"So, she slept over?"

"Yes."

"And no moves were made?"

"No. Greg, are you kidding me? Her divorce was final yesterday," I say gruffly. "Besides, I want to take her to dinner before I make any sort of move. The more important part of all this is Britt. I've never had a parade of women come through our home, and I'm not going to start now. Stella was my best friend when I was a kid and that's kind of where I want to start again."

Lies! All lies. What I wouldn't do to drag her back to my bed and make her understand how much one man can truly love and worship her. I don't want to just be her friend — I want to be her everything.

But "friends" is where it's going to remain until it evolves into something else on its own.

"You got this?" I ask Greg as a few more customers come through the door. Uncrossing my arms, I push off from the counter I'm leaning against. "I need to check on Britt."

Saturday and Sunday are the only days Britt is at the café with me, but this is the first time he's sat out in the gallery with someone other than me. He had a little time to sit with just Stella and I watched as he showed her his coloring books and talked to her about his favorite books. It amazes me how easy she makes things after all this time. Introducing the two of them wasn't something I had even thought about, but then again he's part of every part of my life so I've never put much thought into how people would react to my having a child. Even when we were living in Tennessee with my parents it was always me and Britt.

The only time it wasn't us was when Greg and I moved north to start the business in the spring. It was hard not having him with me all the time, but also made it easier to get our house established and the coffeehouse up and running before bringing him home.

The time he spent with just my parents was good for him, too. He was able to finish up the year in pre-K and had the summer to run wild and free before joining me in August to settle in before starting kindergarten at the beginning of September.

I walk out through the kitchen and see my guy in action. He and Stella have been joined by two more women, one I recognize as Caryn but I'm at a loss for who the other one is since her back is to me. One thing is clear though ... they're all wrapped around Britt's finger already.

Coming up behind the chairs, I fold my hands around the top of Stella's seat.

"Hey, Daddy! Stella's coloring with me, isn't that cool?"

"Yeah, buddy, that's awesome. Is she staying inside the lines?" I say, joking, and the three women at the table laugh at the silliness of it all.

I want to be part of this camaraderie. I want to take a few minutes to remember I'm not so busy. I pull a chair up from a nearby table and sit at a corner between Britt and Stella, but not before I notice the third woman gives Stella a look like she needs to introduce us.

But I already kind of recognize her. They both look so much like their mom it would be hard to miss the resemblance.

"Hi, I'm Brian," I say, holding my hand out for Stephanie to shake. "You probably don't remember me."

She takes my hand and shakes it gently, staring at me with a confused look on her face, as though she's heard that line before. And then she's looking from Britt to me to Stella.

"How do you know me?" she asks, realizing Stella isn't paying attention to us — she's coloring a picture with my son and ignoring the rest of the world.

I chuckle and say, "I moved into the house next door to you and Stella shortly before you were born. We only lived here for about four years, though, so you were still really little when we moved to Tennessee."

"That explains the accent. Yours and his."

"Well, I picked it up after we moved, but his ... Britt's is thick enough at times even I have trouble understanding him."

The boy has a drawl on him that will definitely attract the ladies if he doesn't lose it after being in New York for a while. It's obviously already being put to good use. I haven't even been acknowledged by Caryn and Stella is content with Britt's story telling. I could be satisfied if the rest of my day consisted of this right here.

Damn, my heart. This is almost too much to bear.

"So, tell me about the coffeehouse. Caryn said she was working on a story about it, but can't seem to get the owner to call her," Steph says, stirring her drink. "Seems to me, if your boss wanted to tell the community you guys are here, they would call her."

Have I not told any of them? I know I've been kind of cryptic about it, but I figured Greg would have told Caryn my name at least. They've had plenty of time to talk what with her coming in daily for her caffeine fix. I've seen her here every morning.

Realizing Britt and I are the only ones at the table, possibly in the entire coffeehouse right now, who know I own the business, I smile a real smile. I could have a lot of fun with this.

"Yeah, I should really kick his butt in gear and have him call her," I say turning to look at Caryn. "Can I get your cell number for that story you want to do?"

Caryn and Stella glance up at me as I pull my phone from the back pocket of my jeans, holding it just below the table in my lap, and wait for her to tell me the digits, then dial as she rattles them off to me. I hit send and wait to hear Caryn's phone start ringing.

She excuses herself from the table and heads for the door, going outside where it's less noisy and the clatter of cups and plates and Saturday morning chatter is just background music.

Stella and Steph exchange a glance, then both look at me.

"Probably a work call. We can't get away from them," Stella says explaining Caryn's quick departure while Steph gets up and moves over by Britt, picking up a crayon to give a Tyrannosaurus rex some color.

Once Caryn is at the door, I lift the phone to my ear and wait for the, "This is Caryn," as she gives her best professional greeting.

"Uh, hi. I'm calling about the coffeehouse you were interested in doing a story about." Stella's head whips up to look me dead in the eyes, like everything in the world just shifted slightly to the right and she was knocked off kilter. "If you're available Monday morning, stop in and we can talk then."

I finish my call telling Caryn to just have Greg get me from the back when she gets here, but don't tell her my name, then press the lock button on my phone and slip it into my rear pocket just as she comes wandering back through the door, a grin on her face.

"So weird that you were just asking Brian about the owner of this place, Steph. He called me. Like, just now. I've got to come in Monday for the story," she says.

"That's great. Can I put it on the budget for Tuesday or do you need a few days to get a wrap on the story?" Stella asks, stealing a glance in my direction but not letting on she might know my secret that really isn't a secret at all. It is something only Stella and I are privy to, though, and that alone — knowing I have that connection with her again so soon — makes it wildly intimate.

Stella

Chapter Twelve

It's half past midnight and I can't stop thinking about him. I've done nothing but toss and turn, flailing about in my bed like a damn fish stranded on the shoreline.

I don't like this feeling.

Aren't I supposed to be mourning the loss of my marriage still? I've slowly gotten over the shock, the divorce papers giving me some closure, but I still spent a few nights cutting up any clothes Keith left behind and made sure to burn anything I knew he liked enough to come back for in the months after he walked out. Sometimes in life you have to have the satisfaction of taking back that kind of power. I needed to take back something — anything — that he'd taken in all our years together. He knew me better than anyone else, but the look on his face when I told him I'd torched his best suit because he failed to grab it from my side of the closet was priceless.

More than priceless; it reminded me I had a backbone.

I'm not the Stella he grew up with — the girl he always made a point of making sound like a martyr — no, at some point between us taking our vows and him breaking those sacred promises, I had changed as much as he had.

And now I was changing again.

Brian.

How did he end up back in my life like this, walking into view from the haze of smoke wafting up from the smoldering ruins of my marriage? There's got to be some holy or divine reasoning behind this. Maybe I should start calling him Saint Brian. Seems he's been brought back to me to help save me from myself, so it's totally appropriate.

I stare at the ceiling until the faint sound of the fire whistle pulls me from my thoughts. I'm already awake, so I might as well make the best of it and go to work.

Pulling on the jeans I left lying in the armchair in the corner of the bedroom, I check my phone out of habit for messages. Seeing none, I toss it on the bed, pull a tank over my head, layer on a thermal shirt and pull my unruly hair up into a band I keep on my wrist whenever it's not holding my locks out of the way.

Phone, check; wallet and ID, check; keys, check. In less than ten minutes, I'm out the door, my camera bag slung across my shoulders. If it's a good one, I'll have some nice shots of the fire for the web. If it's not, I'll find something to photograph even if it ends up in my private collection of unused art.

Stepping out the front door, I hear sirens. Still. And they're piercing the chilled night air, breaking it apart into a thousand shards that stab straight through me. Sirens lasting this long can't be a good sign, and I jog to my beat up Chevy pick-up truck, tossing a heavy flannel jacket into the passenger seat as I jump in and start the engine in one swift, practiced motion. The door is hardly closed before I'm backing out of the driveway.

Twenty minutes later I'm pulling down a dirt road following a volunteer firefighter in a personal vehicle.

"Son of a bitch," I mutter to the dashboard as though the midnight radio personality can hear me at his end of the station.

This isn't just a fire. It's an inferno.

I spend the next several hours photographing from a safe distance, texting Caryn and writing down any details I can garner from the firefighters taking a break from the blaze that's quickly eating the timbers of an old farmhouse nestled along the edge of the Erie Canal.

I grew up walking the paths near here to get to the canal and now this small piece of local history will forever be gone.

The devastation is weighty because it was part of my hometown and as the sun begins to rise, burning the frost off a nearby cornfield, the wreckage is enough to make it hard to breathe. And I snap another photo of the sodden remains as smoke billows up from embers that slowly die away.

And I snap another photo.

"You could be doing so much more with your life, Stell! Why won't you at least call and see what they think of your portfolio?" Keith argues with me.

It's the same fight every time another big paper becomes his new obsession. A fight I refuse to have.

"This is home, Keith. This is where I grew up. This is where I'm comfortable."

"But what about the money? This little paper is never going to pay you what you're worth. Just send your resume. There's got to be at least one

larger news outlet that would let you name your price." It always comes down to money with him. He means well, but I'm not a journalist for the money.

He's never going to understand that.

"It's not the money. I'm here for the community, Keith. I do this job for our friends and our neighbors and to keep people informed. Please. Stop."

And I snap another photo. A firefighter in bunker pants, suspenders holding down what once was a white V-neck T-shirt, now tinged grey with soot and sweat. A helmet sitting on the rear bumper of a tanker truck. Three men on a line, spraying down more hot embers as they continue to control an element that can destroy in an instant. This ... this will be a full spread. This is community journalism and why I hate to bitch about what isn't in my paycheck.

I sigh deeply, reflectively, as a newer looking Chevy Tahoe creeps down the narrow country road and comes to rest a few car lengths behind the last truck.

"Who's that?" fire Chief Chad Thursten says using a bottle of water to point up the road as he walks toward me, his swagger slightly exaggerated from the exhaustion of beating down a fire for hours.

The words "not sure" almost leave my lips when I see a takeout tray pop out of the driver's door, followed by a strong tanned forearm, then a waffle-weave clad bicep, and a grin spreads across my face before I can stop it.

I lift my camera and snap another photo. This one is for me.

"Reinforcements, Chief." I look at his face and though he's less than a decade older than me, Chad's looking at me like a father would a daughter, a look that says he hopes I know what I'm doing, and it makes me smile even wider. "I'm going to go help him. If I know Brian, there are more coffee cups in the back of that truck."

Two trips later from Brian's Tahoe to the back of the chief's car, and a majority of the volunteer fire department is getting their first dose of caffeine since the alarms sounded more than seven hours ago.

"Chad, I'll stop down to the station later for details," I say shaking the chief's hand before he pulls me into a hug. It's a small town.

"You be careful, kid. Thanks for coming and keeping us company. Tell your mom and dad I said hi."

I wave to a few more guys, mostly men I went to school with or fathers of boys I went to school with, and head down the path to my truck.

"You make it a habit to spend all night at large structure fires?" His voice is thick with something I can't place and even though he's behind me, I can feel his eyes as they sweep across my body. "How long have you been out here, Stell?"

I turn slowly, propping my arm against the tailgate of my truck and brush the hair off my forehead, giving me a chance to peek at the watch on my right wrist.

"A long time. I got out here shortly after the alarms sounded in town. So ... almost eight hours?" God, it's really been an entire work day right here and now I have to go put in real hours at the office and meetings even though I was planning to have today off. "It's all part of the job."

Not really. I could have left after I got a few good photos, still gotten a full night of sleep and called Chad later this morning for all the details. But I despise missing things. I like being places when news is happening, so whenever I can I make sure I'm there with my notepad and camera.

"Are you okay to drive back into town?" He asks quietly, searching my eyes for something.

"Yeah." Pause. Deep breath. Shake away the cobwebs. "Yeah, I'll be okay. I just need to get home and grab a shower and some coffee and I'll be fine."

He was supposed to meet with Caryn this morning. Why is he here?

Brian grabs the tailgate with his left hand, standing to face me less than an arm's length away, and it's like he reads my mind when he says, "Caryn came in for her interview right when we opened this morning and mentioned you were out here. I wanted to do something to help but couldn't until we'd finished the interview." I take in the smoke billowing up like clouds, the sun breaking through and shining down on my friends still working to put out pockets of hot embers as they dig through the remains of what used to be someone's home. I feel thankful the house was empty when the fire started, but it's a detail I'll need to check on when I talk to the investigator. He breaks into my thoughts saying, "It looks like I missed all the excitement."

"Just a little," I laugh. "I got some really nice shots of the fire, though. I'll recreate it for you once I get the smell of soot and smoke out of my hair."

He takes in the sight of me — my disheveled hair, the flannel/thermal shirt combo I'm rocking, jeans with a hole in the knee — a slow movement of his head as his eyes rake back up my body and there's something primal in the way he seems to claim every inch of me and commit me to memory just as I am.

"Dinner?" I say tentatively. "You and Britt, come to my house tomorrow night for lasagna?"

"We wouldn't miss it for the world," Brian says, his voice gone husky. I close my eyes as the scent of his cologne hits my nose. I breathe him in and feel a feather light touch as he brushes the hair off my forehead and kisses me softly there. "Stop by the shop on your way to the office. I'll have your regular with a double shot ready so you don't have to wait."

I nod, my eyes still closed as I silently bask in the waves of heat working their way through my body, a feeling I don't even recognize because it's so new, and I suddenly wish I'd asked if he'd find a babysitter for Britt tomorrow night.

Before I can catch my breath and open my eyes, I hear his truck start and the crunch of stone as he turns the Tahoe around to head back to town.

Brian

Chapter Thirteen

Her eyes are still closed, a wistful look crossing her face when I pull my lips and hand from her smooth skin, the soft edges of a smile playing at the corner of her delicate mouth. I take the easy way out while she stands there and quietly retreat to my truck, walking backward in case she opens her eyes.

Please, God, don't let her open her eyes. If those eyes open, I'm done for. There'd be no going home for Stella to shower and get ready for the day. She'd have to call it a day right now. What hides behind those closed lids are bedroom eyes and all it would take for me to take her home — take her and show her how much I've never forgotten her — is one hooded glance in my direction.

I climb into the truck, watching her still form across the narrow gravel topped road, and bring the engine to life. One three-point turn and she's in my rearview mirror, looking exhausted and content.

The rest of the day goes by quickly once I get back to town and I'm so immersed in getting things done in the back of the building I don't even realize Stella's come and gone.

"Your girl ... she's looking better today," Greg says, leaning against the doorframe to the office hidden just off the kitchen and away from the rest of the coffeehouse. "I mean, on Friday she looked like someone killed her dog. Saturday, she was in here with the other girls and Britt and looked like a weight had been lifted off her shoulders. Today? Man. You must have magical powers."

I rhythmically tap the pen in my hand against my computer keyboard, contemplating what to tell him.

"She invited me and Britton over for dinner tomorrow night," I say. "I can't believe I missed her. She looked okay?"

Greg shoots me a confused look. "She had on eyeliner, a knee length black skirt and boots ... boots that came up to here," he says, indicating a spot just below his knee. "Yeah, I'd say she looked 'okay.'"

Shooting me a smug look, Greg turns on his heel and heads back out toward the coffeehouse.

"Like I said, Bri, you worked magic on that woman," he calls back over the top of the swinging café doors before I hear him greet a customer.

I lean forward in my chair, hands clasped together and elbows on my knees, staring at the floor. I run my right hand up over my head, mussing up my hair. I need to get out of here.

***

The sawdust flies up and scatters across my forearms, leaving the tan skin coated in pine scented flakes. I don't know what I'm making, but I needed to do something with my hands and pray it helps clear my head at least a little bit. I can't do cloudy brain right now, not with the business and Britt depending on me.

It's the very end of September, only a few more days until October hits and apple everything isn't the most coveted thing on the menu. Pumpkin spice will be on everyone's mind. I have to get the rest of my orders in for the coming week and yet, I really don't give a shit.

My brain feels like the synapses are set to "rapid fire" and someone else is holding the control. I take a deep breath and flip the switch, cutting the electricity. I listen as the motor on the saw dies slowly.

I stand staring at the blade as it slowly comes to a stop and the fog clouding my thoughts starts to clear.

She was at a fire all morning and hadn't slept. Stella looked like she'd been dragged through the flames herself, but was so content to be there. She was in her element.

When Caryn came in to do her interview this morning — and finally put two and two together that I was the owner of the Jumping Bean — she mentioned Stella had been out covering a fire most of the night, but I hadn't realized just what "most of the night" meant until I got out of my truck at the scene and walked toward her with a tray of coffee cups.

I didn't realize seeing her so close to something so volatile and dangerous would have the blood rushing to my ears and adrenaline pumping through my system. No matter how deeply I feel for Stella because of our time together as kids, I never would have thought the primal urge to protect her would surge through me like a force strong enough to stop my heart from beating in my chest until I was close enough to see she wasn't hurt in any way.

The aftermath of that feeling, it's almost more than I can handle right now.

I know she's in no position to give me her heart.

It doesn't change the fact that after just a handful of days having her back in my life, I never want to lose her again.

It's getting more and more difficult to resist touching her, even just in some small way, when she's close by. It doesn't seem like we've spent a lot of time together since I sat down across from her last week, but it feels like she's invaded every part of me. I smell her on the blanket on the back of my couch, I hear her laugh in the café. Seeing her cold and tired this morning gave me even more reason to want to protect her, hold her, get lost in her. I don't know if it was because she's Stella or if it's because Stella was in need and trying not to let on that she wanted someone to comfort her.

I'm getting really good at comforting her. I guess it's only fair. Before I stole her scone, the last time we saw one another it was her comforting me on that rusty swing set. We were comforting each other and hanging on for dear life.

I'm lost in my thoughts when I hear the school bus pull up out front and Britt's voice boom through the crisp air as he yells goodbye to his new friends. He's a social butterfly; everywhere he goes, people flock to him and soak up his amazing energy and enthusiasm for life.

I doubt he would be like this if his mother had stuck around and I catch myself wondering is Stella ever plans to have children.

"Dad! I don't have any workbook work to do tonight. Can we play catch?" Britt says as he bounds up the driveway to meet me in front of the barn where I'm waiting for him.

We won't have too many days left to toss the ball around before snow hits, so I grab the mitts off the pegs by the woodshop door and a ball from the rack underneath and spend the next hour catching up with my favorite guy.

"I saw Stella this morning." I toss the worn baseball to him. "She invited us for lasagna tomorrow night."

"She really likes coffee, Dad. Almost as much as you do! Can we take my crayons with us? She's a really good colorer," Britt says, lobbing the ball somewhere sort of in my direction. "And her sister is super pretty, but has no idea T-rexes aren't purple."

"But they could be," I counter. "Have you ever seen a real, live T-rex? Has anyone?"

He stops mid throw and gapes at me. "No ... but if they were purple they'd have no camouflage in the wild."

I can't stop myself from laughing at his logic, because it's pretty sound — especially for a five-year-old kid.

"So, dinner with Stella tomorrow? Would you like to go, then? Was the crayon question a yes?" I toss the ball gently to him again and he makes another solid attempt to catch it, almost getting it in his glove this time.

"It's a yes. As long as she has garlic bread."

"Deal."

I mentally take note that I need to make fresh bread tomorrow and let Stella know I have that part of dinner covered.

Britt and I head toward the house to put his backpack away before walking the short distance back to the café to help Greg with the afternoon rush. It seems like one of the busiest times of the day for us are those hours right after the public school closes down for the day and the college is prepping for evening classes.

"Hey little man! How was school today? Find yourself a girlfriend yet?" Greg teases when he sees Britton following behind me through the low-slung café doors on the way to the office. I dump my fleece and messenger bag in the chair, and when I'm turning to head back to the kitchen a piece of paper propped up in front of my computer monitor catches my eye.

In bold script, my name is scrawled across the front and in the second before I open the single-folded leaflet, I can smell her — the soft lilac scent that her mother always wore when we were kids, the same scent I noticed Stella wearing when she stumbled her way into my home last Friday night.

Brian,
Thank you ... for the coffee, for the company, and for finding me. Time after time, you've never not found me.
See you tomorrow night.
Stell

I head back out to man the counter while Greg takes a break, the smile never leaving my face. Suddenly, I feel like my entire world is falling together, and the force holding it in one piece is named Stella Barbieri.

Stella

Chapter Fourteen

"Fuck. Fuck, fuck, fuckity fucking shit." Stephanie sits at the island in the middle of my kitchen laughing as I let another string of profanity fly. "It hurts, Steph. Shut it!"

I burned myself. Again. I love to cook, but lately most of my appliances don't love me in return. This is only the third time in the last week I've burned myself on the stove and this time I haven't even put anything in it yet. I can't even fathom how I've kept myself alive this long.

"You're pretty preoccupied lately, Stella. If you ask me, you have too much on your mind and his name is Brian," she winks on the last word. "That man is just ... too much."

I can hear the sigh in her words, that thing girls do when they get all dreamy about a guy. I don't like Steph acting that way. I don't like the fact Steph has obviously noticed Brian.

"Whoa killer. Easy with the death glare," she snaps.

"What? What do you mean?" Caryn is the oblivious one, not me; I'm lost. I still have to get the lasagna put together and I have some serious calming down to do before they get here. And now I definitely have to kick my sister out before Brian and Britt arrive.

"You looked like you might leap across the room and gouge my eyes out. You've known this guy, what, a week?"

"Twenty-eight years, four months," I rattle off with ease, like I've been counting the days on my desk blotter. I haven't, but ... well, I may as well have been. "They moved into their house next door to us in May the year I turned five. Brian was already five when they came to Brockport."

I laugh at the memory of him calling across the way to me from his bedroom.

I am four and he just turned five.

His name is Brian and he has blonde hair and blue eyes.

My mommy says his parents are nice and I'll really like their little boy. They just moved in next door and I can see Brian's bedroom from my window. He's in there playing with his blocks and it looks like fun, so I turn to leave my room to go downstairs and find my blocks, too.

"Hey, want to play?"

I hear the little voice somewhere behind me coming in through the open window. He sounds nice just like Mommy said he was, like he could be my friend, but that's a lot of trust to put into four words.

I turn back around and walk to the window, coming face to face with the boy behind the voice.

"Earth to Stella?" Steph is standing in front of me, snapping her fingers in my face. "Where'd you go, sis?"

I blink at her. I've been zoning out a lot lately. Maybe I should look into taking a vacation.

"Before you were born I didn't have friends. When Brian moved in next door, I had this idea he wouldn't want to be my friend because he already had his built-in best friend — Tommy was almost three and the boys were inseparable." I look out the window as the sun dips lower in the sky, muting the fall colors on the trees along the side of the house. "But he wanted to play with me. The first day they lived next door, Brian and I sat on our front porch playing with Legos for hours while his parents unloaded and unpacked. We were practically joined at the hip from that day until they moved to Tennessee."

Her eyes soften, and I hope that look is her finally understanding without me having to come right out and say it, admit to someone other than myself that Brian was my first love.

From the first words he spoke to me.

The first time I saw his face.

I fell so hard.

I haven't told her much, but the little bit of information I've given Caryn has been enough to satisfy her curiosity — we grew up together, he moved, we lost touch, now he's back — but even with my best friend I've held back the new details ... where I feel myself falling hard for him all over again, but this time I have grown up feelings.

I leave out the details because I'm newly divorced and the last thing I need anyone in this little town to think is the local reporter is slipping into bed with the first guy to turn her head since the ink dried on her divorce decree. I just ... can't. I don't want to have to defend my life and my choices to anyone right now, so my mouth stays shut.

I just hope Steph can read between all those blurred lines.

I look at her and pray she can read my mind.

"So, this Brian guy. He seems like a rock star in the male species category. Successful businessman, seems to be a fabulous dad, his kid is great ... he's fucking gorgeous." Stephanie eyes me timidly. "Single."

"Single. He brought me coffee yesterday. Well, not just me. It was more like the entire volunteer fire department, but I think he was there for me," I say almost in a whisper, recalling the feelings he made me feel before he left me standing there practically panting from a simple kiss on the forehead. "And then when I stopped by the coffee shop, he'd made me my regular order with a double shot of espresso and wrapped up a scone for me."

"He's got it bad for you. Baked goods and coffee for you are like a normal woman's version of wine and dine and jewelry."

She's right. They are. And as strange as it is to admit, Keith never figured that out. I have more necklaces than I would ever wear from years of him not figuring out some really good cupcakes or a new coffee maker would get a bigger reaction out of me. Somehow, Brian got it right from the beginning, when I showed up on his doorstep in the rain.

I let out the breath I'm holding.

"Shit! They're going to be here in an hour and the pasta isn't even put together, and I look like hell. Help me," I say, grabbing Steph's hand and dragging her to the counter space where the ingredients are laid out.

Like clockwork, she layers noodles, I add sauce, more noodles, cheese, and in record time the pan is in the oven, a bottle of wine uncorked and she's got me sitting in a chair while she does something with my hair. I take the first sip of a perfectly chilled crisp vidal blanc and give myself permission to relax.

"You know, if you wanted me to, I could always come back later this evening after you and the boys eat and steal Britt away. Take him for ice cream or something? It would give you and Brian some more time to catch up."

Her tone is mildly suggestive, but innocent somehow. I stop mid-sip. "That's not a bad idea. But I kind of want to get to know Britt, too. Plus, I'm new to this whole single thing. Maybe a tiny chaperone isn't such a bad idea."

"True. You can't get into too much trouble with the kid here. Hair's done. I'm going to head out. Mom's convinced me to come do yoga with her, because, you know, we do yoga now," Steph says, rolling her eyes as I snort out a laugh.

"Good luck with that! Are you coming over tomorrow for our usual?"

"Maybe. Call me in the afternoon and see how sore I am from all this yogatastic stuff with Mom. If I'm moderately sore, it's a yes. If I feel paralyzed from the shoulders down, drink my portion."

Steph gives me a kiss on the cheek and walks out the front door. I turn and head up the stairs to change out of my dress clothes and into a pair of worn jeans, a white men's tank and one of my dad's old flannel shirts. Comfort comes first. Brian's seen me practically at my worst. Compared to that, I look like a model in this outfit.

I head back downstairs to set the table … and wait.

***

"After we lost touch, I never thought I'd see you again. I think I always held out hope that I'd run across you at some point, but stopped trying to look for you in every crowd," I say to Brian, handing him a plate to dry. Britt took his coloring books and crayons into the living room when we finished dinner, giving me and Brian a chance to talk more, the conversation coming easily after spending a meal talking about our childhood and all we've done since Brian moved to Tennessee — our educations and careers, our families. "I couldn't handle the heartache of never finding your face. It didn't help I was supposed to be loving Keith, and I did, but he wasn't you. Even when we were kids, Keith was never able to replace you."

I let the last sentence slip from my lips quietly, coming to audible terms that Brian has forever been irreplaceable. While Steph could see it in my eyes and hear it when she read between the lines earlier, I've just unwittingly outed myself. My heart may as well lay beating on the kitchen floor because it feels like every emotion I've ever had for this man just leaped from my body and, even though it's the last thing I should do, I want to say to him, "Here. Take this. Maybe you can fix it, put it back together and make it whole again."

I don't say it though. I've already said so much more than I had planned, more than I thought I'd be able to put into words.

The movement beside me comes to a stop. Before I can get my hands out of the soapy dishwater and turn in his direction, he's set the plate and towel on the counter and snatched me up, pulling me firmly to his chest. No words are spoken, but they don't need to be. Everything he wants to say is in his touch, the gentle strength with which he holds me, and I breathe him in deeply so I can make a new memory of us.

My suds covered hands rest at his elbows for another brief moment before I glide them up his arms, over his biceps to his broad shoulders and, standing on my tiptoes, I lean into him more. I need more of Brian — in my arms, in my life, in my heart — and my hands find one another, clasping at the nape of his neck as I rest my forehead against the side of his face, close my eyes and let him hold me a little longer.

This isn't a friendly hug. This is a touch that could consume me. There's a hunger in the way he grips my waist as though he's waited a lifetime for a moment like this one.

"At last," he sighs into my hair as he starts swaying us to some imaginary tune, one that I'm sure is saying everything our mouths can't right now.

We're in the midst of our music-less dance when I hear the refrigerator open behind me and Britt giggle. I'm not even sure how long Brian and I have stood like this, while he's been in the other room coloring and the dishwater has turned tepid. It feels like fate's pushed us together and reminded us we're allowed to *feel* despite heartache and past lovers no longer loving us, that regardless of how broken we may be as individuals we're each a half and together that makes us whole.

Color rises to my cheeks when I think about everything my body is doing to betray the exterior armor I try so hard to keep in place.

"Shhh ... go color," Brian says softly to Britt, and I feel a smile form on his lips as his cheek moves against my face.

"I have never seen my daddy look at someone the way he does when he looks at Stella," Britt says to ... someone? Maybe he has an imaginary friend. What kid hasn't had one of those?

"Yeah, well, Stella tends to look like that when she talks about your daddy, so I think the feeling is mutual," I hear Stephanie say. She must have snuck in when Brian and I weren't paying attention, which has been most of the hour since we finished dinner.

I lift my head and pull back to look at Brian. The air had a crackle in it when he showed up at my table in the coffeehouse last week; tonight it's an electrical firestorm.

"I haven't even been officially divorced a week, Bri," I say, not able to get my voice much louder than a whisper, as we stare at each other. "I have a feeling that doesn't matter much to you."

"No, it doesn't. But I won't push for more than you're willing to give me," he says as his focus dances between my eyes and lips as they part ever so slightly beneath his gaze.

"I'm willing to give you my entire world," I say, as his head dips dangerously close to my mouth, "but you're going to have to work for it."

Brian

Chapter Fifteen

"Work for it?" I lift my head slightly, my eyes falling on her mouth, a mouth so perfect da Vinci could have painted it on her himself, and I consider what working for it might entail. "I'll work for it Stell. I came back for you, I prayed every night for you, I wished on every shooting star I saw ... I wished for you."

Her breath comes out in a rush, caressing my lips like the kiss I'm anticipating — like I've been waiting for since I saw her for the second first time of my life — and it undoes me. My resolve to make her wait a little longer to feel my lips and teeth and tongue dissolves in an instant.

I won't let fate take all the credit for this, I think, catching Stella's full bottom lip between mine and feeling it quiver against my teeth as I deepen our first real kiss. Her breath hitches and a smile spreads across her face beneath my lips as she unhooks her hands from my neck and slowly, ever so slowly, slides them over my shoulders to rest on my chest and settles her feet flat on the floor.

She's nestled her body closer to mine and I can feel her heart beating against me, a steady and quick *boom-boom boom-boom* at my ribcage, like it's knocking, begging to break down any remaining walls to get to my heart.

Joke's on Stella.

Those walls came tumbling down the moment I saw her in my café. She may not know it yet, but seeing Stella again was the breath that brought me back to life.

I break the kiss just long enough to make sure she's real, reaching up to touch her face, her eyes dropping closed as she leans into my palm, her breathing heavy.

She's just as affected by me as I am by her and I can't keep my mouth off her another second. She breathes out a sigh, opening enough for the tip of my tongue to glide along her bottom lip, tasting of remnants of the fresh garlic bread I'd made just for tonight.

Dropping her head to the side, she gives me room to deepen our connection and I taste her, my tongue sliding along hers in a war of the senses, before pulling her top lip into my mouth and fisting my hand in her chestnut brown hair.

I kiss her like she means everything to me, because she does. And I kiss her with a passion strong enough to try to waylay my fears from seeing her at that fire, because no matter how safe she might have been or what good hands she was in, I couldn't function until I saw she was okay. I kiss her like it's the last time I may ever feel her lips against mine.

She feels so good in my arms, like she was made to fit against me, and I pull her as close as I can without crawling inside her soul to share the space.

Trailing my lips from Stella's mouth down along her jaw, I try to memorize the way her skin feels beneath mine, and as those gentle kisses reach the spot where her ear and neck collide, I feel her knees shake and a soft moan escape her throat.

"Should I work a little harder?" I ask, teasing without moving my mouth from the newly discovered oasis of flesh. The vibration from my words releases another involuntary moan, deep in her throat, and I can't help but wonder how long it's been since she's been touched like this, admired like this, as small a gesture as it is in this moment.

I can't help but wonder if he loved her like I want to.

"You're working?" Stella says quietly, dropping her forehead to my shoulder. "That didn't feel like you were even trying."

I hear the teasing in her voice, but my brain registers it as a challenge ... and I'm really good at winning.

I place another kiss to her neck and make quick work down to her collarbone, nudging her flannel shirt to the side with my nose to allow me access to the tender flesh hiding underneath. Walking her backward until we're pressed up against the counter, I place my hands on either side of her, caging her in.

"Sorry, ma'am. I'll try harder," I say, humor tickling the edges of my voice as I lift my head and smile down at her before capturing her lips between mine again.

It hits me that we're making out like teenagers in her kitchen ... right before I realize we're making out in her kitchen while my son is sitting a couple rooms away hanging out with Stella's sister. It's nothing we've encountered in his short lifetime —me being intimate with anyone — and I'm not sure how to talk to him, or what to tell him about what's going on between me and Stella.

I'll deal with it, I tell myself, *I'll deal with it when the time comes.*

Leaning my forehead against hers, I keep my eyes closed and try to reign in the emotion pulsing through me, attempt to calm the throbbing in my pelvis.

I breathe her in.

It doesn't help either issue.

I want to carry her out of this kitchen and up the stairs to a bed. I want to prove to her she's worthy of all the love I've secretly been storing away for her over the years. She's worth all those tiny rooms in my chest I've closed off to anyone else. She's worth every kiss I've missed exploring with her between ages nine and nineteen, every lust-filled glance I've reserved from fifteen to today.

But I can't prove any of that to her tonight.

Not tonight.

She's too fragile and I won't be the one to break her, but, Lord, how I want to bend her just a little bit at a time until she's ready for me. She'll make me work for anything she has to offer — I know her heart isn't going to be served to me on a silver platter.

And I don't want it to be.

I want to prove that every time I kiss her it's because I can't wait to kiss her.

"Hey, cowboy, did I lose you?" she says, brushing her hand along the day's growth on my face. "I feel like you drifted off into foreign territory. Come back to me."

"I'll always come back to you, Stella," I say, keeping my eyes closed, fearful she'll see everything I have to offer in a single glance. "I'll never not find you."

Even as kids she made me work for everything she gave me. I think that's what made me fall in love with her back then.

This is my chance to fall all over again.

We're still standing forehead-to-forehead against the counter when I hear the unmistakable sound of a throat clearing. I open my eyes and stare into the gold and green flecks in front of me, noting the way the skin at the corners of her eyes creases when she smiles, and she is smiling. She's grinning like a fool, actually, and I let out a laugh before chastely kissing her one last time and turning around to face the music.

"Hey Steph, how are you?" I feel the heat creep up my neck when I catch the smug look on her face and wonder how long she'd stood in the doorway before getting our attention.

She waits to say anything just long enough to make me think she might kill me for touching her sister. Steph was feisty as a toddler; the gleam in her eyes tells me not much has changed.

"Britt's got a sweet tooth so I was going to grab some ice cream to share with him," she says. Maybe she didn't see me kissing Stella after all. "I just didn't want to startle the two of you while your tongue was down my sister's throat."

Well, there goes that theory.

I drop my head into my hands to hide the grin on my face and hope neither woman thinks it's out of embarrassment. I'm far from ashamed I've finally tasted Stella's lips and I'd really prefer Steph turn around and walk away so I can show Stella just how much I'm not ashamed of our make out session.

Even still, how horrible this must look to Stephanie. The other day I was Mr. Nice Guy who visited with them over coffee and crayons; now I probably look like I'm preying on her sister. I should just collect my jacket and my kid and leave now. Save face and all that.

Chancing a glance at Stella, her smile hasn't faded and it feels like I can't breathe all over again. She lights up the entire room with the contentment and joy that's washed over her features. I'm still lost in her when I hear Steph laughing.

"Damn. Holy shit." And she's gasping for air in an attempt to calm herself down. "Stellie, I wish you could have seen his face from there. He looked scared of me for a second. I mean, I am scary, but ... you have nothing to worry about with me, Brian."

Stephanie is still trying to regain her composure when Britt wanders into the kitchen and silently takes in the scene.

"Did you find ice cream? Why is your shirt wet? Why is Stella crying?" He fires off one question after another without taking a breath and I start laughing because my little man is way too inquisitive for his own good.

Wait. Crying? No one was crying last time I looked around the room. The soft cries hit my ears and I turn to Stella next to me, seeing the tears running in rivulets down her cheeks. I gather her in my arms.

"Stell?" I say her name like a question, concern in my voice. "What's wrong?"

The energy in the room has changed dramatically in the last half hour and it's starting to make my head spin from all the emotions charging through my system. I brush the hair off her forehead, cupping her face in my hands, and I look at her — really look at her — and I swear she holds my entire history in the shimmery depths staring back at me.

Then she hiccups, and I fall a little harder.

"Nothing's wrong. That's just it. Everything is perfect right now." Steph and I look at her, confused. Britt's pulling a chair over to the fridge, likely in search of the ice cream. "This house hasn't been this happy in a long time." And she kisses me, sweetly brushing her lips against mine with the patience of a new lover, before wiping the tears that threaten to overflow again. The world moves in slow motion as we catch up to the here and now, before we have a chance to get stranded in one another and jump ship entirely.

"Here, buddy, let me help you," Steph says, taking Britt's hand while he jumps down from the chair, breaking apart the moment we were so consumed by.

Just like that the evening resumes, dessert is served and conversations are had about our daily interactions, schoolwork, the town.

It all goes back to normal, like my life wasn't just flipped upside down by this woman sitting next to me, the one I catch myself staring at when I think she isn't looking. My ice cream seems to taste a little sweeter, the pastries Britt and I made a little more buttery, but I think it has more to do with the company than the sugar and cream.

The evening moves into night and we finally pry an answer out of Stephanie about her impromptu visit. Once Stella threatens to call their mom for a reason why yoga night turned into Steph crashing our party, the poor girl sings like a canary.

"Okay, okay ... I wasn't doing yoga with Mom," she says, blushing. "I was supposed to be on a date with this guy from one of my grad classes. It just, ugh. It just wasn't working for me."

"What wasn't working for you?" Stella and I trip over one another to ask the question simultaneously.

"He wasn't. He's cute and all, but I felt like he was only after me for my brain," she admits sheepishly, like she wants to exchange "brain" for something else. "God, that sounds horrible. But really! He started quizzing me at dinner, digging around in my head like he was searching a textbook for answers about me. Weird, random questions, too. I'm surprised he didn't pull a highlighter out of his pocket. Pretty sure he had one on his person somewhere."

It throws me and Stella into a fit of laughter at the absurdity that Steph's date spent the entire date playing Twenty Questions. The image of her face covered in neon marker only makes us laugh harder.

Catching her breath, Stella's face falls a little. "Why didn't you just tell me you had a date tonight? You didn't have to scapegoat Mom, Steph. Kind of shady, you know?"

"It was more of a pity date than anything else, and I just didn't want you to think less of me for it. It seemed you'd ask way fewer questions if I told you I was hanging with Mom than going out for burgers with What's His Name," she says more to the coffee mug in her hands than to her sister — shy, like she's not telling the whole truth. "We got through dinner and I excused myself like a lady. I don't want to lead him on any longer. He's just not the type I like, you know? He was nice about it, I guess. Besides, I really wanted to come hang out with Britt. You're raising a great kid, Brian."

I look into the living room from where I'm sitting at the dining room table and watch the easy rise and fall of his chest. Snuggled under a blanket on Stella's couch, he fell asleep while watching a movie, shortly after finishing his ice cream.

"Yeah, I like him," I tease, eliciting a poke in the ribs from Stella. "Let's put it this way, if it weren't for Britton, I'd probably be working at a gas station wondering when my life was going to start instead of going out and fighting for my place in the world. His arrival and his mother's departure gave me some insight into what I wanted, for myself and for him."

"And what do you want for the two of you?" Stella asks timidly, watching carefully for my reaction.

"For us Stratford men to find love and success."

Stella

Chapter Sixteen

I lean against the closed door after watching Brian back out of the driveway and stay like that, listening to the quiet ... the blood rushing through my body and my nerves singing his praises.

It feels like I'm awake for the first time in years.

And it's scary. It's so scary I think running away might be the best option for me because I don't do spontaneous.

I can't.

My life is meticulously planned unless there's an emergency.

Take a little peek at my planner and it's all right there in black, blue and red ink. All color-coded depending on urgency and importance, from board meetings to charity events to family dinners.

Brian is a spark. He's giving me hope before I'm ready for it. Brian is not an emergency but I feel him in my soul and he's battling against my resolve with such force, such ... urgency.

Maybe, just maybe, Brian is an emergency.

But he's not one I'm ready to face — he's the freak storm on a cloudless day.

I have to run for cover.

I told him he'd have to work for it; I just hope I don't hurt him in the process. I still need to figure out who I am alone. Right now I don't know who Stella Barbieri is and I feel like I'm going to go crazy trying to remember.

I've had more than half a year to figure my shit out since Keith left. I didn't allow myself to dip too low into any sort of depression, at least not low enough I couldn't pull myself back up quickly. Maybe it wasn't low enough to give myself a chance to start healing.

I thought I'd started restoring myself the minute I accepted my fate, the looming title of "divorcee," and took back that maiden name. It made me feel powerful in the moment, to take that back and decide I'm my own person. In the end, throughout all these months, I think the only thing I came to terms with was Keith not loving me. I accepted that more than everything else.

I swept the rest of my feelings under the rug and consciously chose to ignore them.

And now I feel like, no matter how much fun we've had in the moment, it's going to hurt Brian because I just don't know how to deal with all of that shit I've buried. It's bubbling to the surface and I don't have the energy to push it down anymore.

Hanging my head, I let my body slide down the door as the sobs come wailing out of my body, screaming to get out, begging for release.

I cry for my failed marriage.

I cry for losing my best friend and because he came back to find me.

I cry because I'm falling in love and I never intended to love again.

I never want to hurt like this again.

This hurts.

It kills me that my own husband wouldn't talk to me about all the problems with our marriage and instead sought to comfort himself inside someone else's body. Maybe I was always just too busy to talk. He was too busy. Our careers took off and we were consumed by them ... until he was consumed by her.

I'm a failure.

If I had paid more attention I would have seen it all happening. Wouldn't I? There would have been something, like a neon sign indicating he'd opened his heart for business and kicked my love to the curb. I just don't know how I missed it all.

But maybe I just didn't want to see it.

I just didn't want to see someone else leave me after loving me for so long so I blocked it out. I ignored the smell of perfume on his suit coats, and made an excuse for the stud earring I found in his luggage. I blinded myself from the look in his eyes when he talked about work — about her — and tried not to notice how close they'd gotten.

I refused to see what was happening to my marriage, and for that alone I feel broken because only someone who is broken wouldn't recognize a failure in the making while holding onto the hope that every feeling that screams "cheater" is wrong.

I was hopeful.

Instead of seeing it coming, I became an expert sugarcoater with a workaholic complex and lost everything I thought mattered.

I want to call Steph, but I can't bring myself to tell her how this feels and try to release myself from the pain. It's not fair to throw all this at her, not when I've acted so oblivious to it despite the truth being right in front of me for so long.

"I ignored it and I should be over it by now," I scream into the silence. That's what I kept telling myself all those months and it made it easier to push the feelings down lower and lower for a while.

I'm getting them out now, and I think I've figuratively stomped the feelings into the ground and buried my hate and hurt. For tonight, at least.

My eyes grow heavier under the pent up emotion, the exhaustion from months of being "fine" — the one answer I give everyone when they ask how I'm doing,

I'm not fine.

I'm not broken, I didn't let that happen, but I'm finally falling apart.

And when all the parts of me crumble into a pile of dust, I pray there are some left over pieces large enough to start rebuilding me.

Reaching up from my spot on the floor, I lock the front door and pull myself up, stripping my shirt off as make my way up the stairs. I pull off my undershirt once I reach my bedroom, shimmy out of my jeans, pop my bra off. I reach for the first thing I can find to sleep in — a Syracuse University hoodie that's about three sizes too big.

I crawl into bed surrounded by the comfort of Old Spice and cinnamon, and the tears continue to come silently as sleep finally wraps me in its arms.

***

Friday night. Three days have passed since Brian and Britt came over for dinner and shook my life up like a snow globe.

Friday night. Four days since I've been inside the coffeehouse.

Work. That's all I've been doing. Working and begging Caryn to get me coffee every day when she goes to the coffeehouse just so I don't have to go in there and see him while I try to get my head on right, because work will solve all my problems. It's constant. There's always something to do, something to read, something to write about, a meeting to attend.

I refuse to have any down time. Down time is for wimps. Down time is for people who aren't serious about their career.

Down time gives the demons lurking in my mind a chance to wish and hope and think.

I can't afford down time right now. My heart can't handle it.

It's Friday night, nearing midnight, and I've been on the clock since 9 a.m. I don't remember if I ate lunch, but Steph stopped by with a chicken Caesar wrap around seven tonight, so I know I'm not starving.

The vibration on my desk pulls me back from the spot I was staring at on the wall. Caryn's name lights up the screen, along with the first part of her text. I unlock my phone and read the whole thing, and then I'm sorry I did.

Caryn: Why is your truck still at the office? Bitch, get home. You're doing it again.

Shit.

I drop my head into my hands, rubbing away the exhaustion. Or, at the very least, trying to. She knows all too well how I get with work when I'm blocking other things out, but usually I can persuade her to believe I'm just doing the job I love.

Picking up my phone again, I text Caryn back.

Me: Just making sure everything is set so I don't have to worry over the weekend.

It totally makes sense to hang out — at work — on a night we don't print. Totally logical. She won't question it though because for so long this has been my life. It was this way in college, too, when our friendship first blossomed. This is the Stella she's used to.

I need to sleep and as much as I don't want to admit it to her, Caryn is right. I am doing it again. It's my coping mechanism. One of them. Aside from wine and cupcakes, I work more when I'm stressed and it keeps me from realizing how truly depressed I am.

Work makes me forget my real life.

I did it a lot when Keith and I were still married and I wasn't able to deal with the out of town work trips. The problem was it would continue even after he was back from a trip and stay that way until an evening of plans came up and I was forced to leave the office before midnight. Dinners at his parent's house, dinners out with his colleagues, business events he needed to attend always seemed to crop up at the best times because they pulled me out of myself. Out of that darkness where I would hide.

But this time there isn't any of that and as fucked up as I am right now I'm looking forward to not being bothered with the dinners and the schmoozing and ass-kissing to bring me out of the funk steamrolling me.

At some point, I have to let the healing begin.

Another half hour has passed without me even realizing it. I'm going into shutdown. The weekend is going to be spent on the couch with ice cream and movies. Probably crying. If I give myself permission right now to break down completely this weekend, maybe Sunday I'll be ready to face Brian and be able to go buy my own coffee on Monday.

Maybe by then, I will remember my real life is better without Keith and I can allow myself to watch Brian look at me like I hold his world in the palm of my hands.

It just feels like my whole life hurts right now and I'm experiencing a different emotion every other minute — everything I went through with Keith and all the emotions thrown at me throughout the course of the entire divorce, and now these raging feelings for Brian that came from somewhere out of the depths like a giant squid on the hunt, it's gotten out of hand.

This is what turmoil feels like.

I shut down my computer, gather everything I might need over the weekend and put it all in my messenger bag, grab my cell and keys, and prepare to go out into the night.

Pulling the door shut behind me, I twist the key until I hear the safe sound of the deadbolt slide into place.

"Have you been avoiding me?"

I jump at the sound of his voice and slowly turn, my shoulders slumping with the weight of the question. How do I respond to that?

"Not intentionally," I say.

He's sitting against the front bumper of my truck, arms and ankles crossed, a Cleveland Indians baseball cap pulled down tight and sitting on his head backwards. I can see the fabric of a jersey beneath his unzipped Carhartt. He looks stunning. Can a man look stunning? Because, he does. He exudes country boy confidence.

"Stell, you've never been a good liar. Remember when we were seven and you broke your parent's kitchen window because you throw like a girl? You tried to get them to believe a flying unicorn hit the side of the house and its horn went through the glass."

I laugh at the memory. My mom was pissed.

He's not laughing, though.

"Would you believe me if I said I haven't been in the café this week because I told you you'd have to work for it?" I ask, pulling the corner of my bottom lip between my teeth. God, I hope he believes me.

Brian's eyes find mine and humor dances beneath his lashes in those dangerously deep blue pools.

"I might believe that, at least for tonight." He pushes off the truck and takes a step toward me; I have nowhere to go. I was already leaning against the door to the office when this conversation started. "I'll believe it for tonight, Stella, because I know you need time. The other night, when you started crying, I saw all those emotions play out on your face. I know you're scared. It's the first time in a long time you've been able to just be yourself. I won't stop you from having that."

How can he know me so well? He's reading me like an open book and has since the day we sat face-to-face for the first time in two decades. Other than my parents and Steph, no one has ever gotten that close. No one.

He takes another step closer. I could reach out and touch him. I could get over my insecurities, the fear of small town gossip, the idea that someone is going to think poorly of him ... I could just get past it all right now and make him take me home. With him. To his bed.

Like some lovesick schoolgirl, I sigh.

Another step and Brian's pressing his forehead to mine.

"Stella," he says, long and slow like he's making love to my name, breathing it out and pulling me in.

"You're going to ruin me for any other man," I say quietly into the night, closing my eyes and feeling the full weight of the moment on us, the sizzling and crackling of a passion that feels obscure and surreal and long awaited. The cool fall breeze settles a chill on my heated skin, skin I wish he'd claim again with his mouth, his lips.

"What makes you think I'm going to let another man have you?"

His hands reach for mine, gripping them lightly before his fingers begin blazing a trail up the backs of my arms to my shoulders. Turning his head slightly, Brian kisses my lips gently, sweetly, but he's not searching and not asking for me to give him anything in return.

My messenger bag slips off one shoulder, my purse from the other, and before I can react to his lips on mine, Brian is pulling away with my bags in hand.

"Come on. You can be a lady and drive me home," he says, reaching once again for my hand and leading me to my truck. "I walked."

The fog lifts. Something is missing. Not something. Someone.

"Where is Britt? You didn't leave him home alone, did you?" There's panic in my voice. I drop Brian's hand as he opens my door so I can climb in.

"I'm only a few blocks from home. I'm sure he's fine. He's a tough kid. He can ward of anyone who tries to break in," he says, deadpan, and I'm not sure if he's serious or just really good at sarcasm.

I narrow my eyes and he flashes me a smile while closing my door.

"Actually," he says, opening the passenger door and hopping into the seat, still holding my bags, "I was watching the game with Greg tonight and we were still hanging out when Caryn called him upset because you were still at the office. He's at the house in case Britt wakes up."

"Why didn't you just call me and tell me to go home? That's what Caryn did, but I imagine you would have been nicer about it."

"And miss the look on your face when you turned around to see me standing there?" His laugh brings a smile to my lips and I can't believe I kept myself away from him for three days. Romantic feelings aside, I like spending time with Brian. He's fun and amazing and beautiful. "Besides, I missed you. Just a little. This way, too, I can convince you to come inside for a cup of coffee."

"Beer and it's a deal." It's been a long week.

"Beer it is."

Brian

Chapter Seventeen

"What do you mean you haven't read the story yet?" I'm laughing at Stella. A few beers in and she's coming unglued, but in a good way. She needed to unwind. "You're the freaking editor, Stella, and you didn't even read her story about me?"

She lets out a groan — a melodic little version of a groan deep in her chest that makes her ten times sexier than she already is because it shows how not superhuman she is — and covers her face.

"I know, I know. I suck. A lot. I've just been in my own world this week," Stella says into her hand, the other clutching her bottle of beer.

I can't decide what's more enticing, the fact she drinks beer or that she walked into my kitchen and climbed up onto the counter to visit like she used to when she'd come into my parent's house. Or both.

We got back to the house and, when Stella walked in behind me, Greg made a quick departure even though we'd told him to hang around. It may be after midnight, but he was more than welcome to have a few more drinks with us.

Instead he slipped out the door telling us to enjoy ourselves and that he'd take care of everything at the coffeehouse in the morning.

I'm not immune to the fact he didn't necessarily want to leave. We both need time to relax and just do the brotherhood thing without the business and things related to work getting in the way. We want to spend a Friday night drinking and watching baseball. It's what we do, and we've always been really good at it.

But Greg also knows my history — or lack thereof — with love. It doesn't exist. I looked for it a lot in college, but no one ever compared to what I knew I wanted. Even Britton's mom never measured up. She was the furthest thing from my "dream girl" and before finding out she was pregnant she was just going to be a fun memory to revisit on lonely nights.

When Stella walked into my life? It was over. And Greg knew from the moment I told him about her. So, his quiet exit tonight, it's welcomed.

It's time she reads that story Caryn wrote.

"Okay, you might suck but I'll be the judge of how much," I say, and I know by the blush that colors her cheeks she's listening to my words but hearing the double entendre, so I wink at her and take another sip of my beer. "You can make it up to me, you know?"

Her mouth drops open. Laughing I reach across the space separating us and push her jaw closed.

"I'm more of a gentleman than that, Stell. You can make it up to me by reading the article. I smell kind of like a foot after being in the kitchen most of the day. You read. I'll shower." That should do it.

Grabbing the paper from the breakfast table, I sidle up to where Stella's sitting on the counter and push my hips between her jean clad knees. Taking the beer from her hand and setting it next to her, I place the paper on her lap.

"Read it, like you're just a regular person enjoying the story. No playing editor tonight. No fixing grammatical errors someone else didn't catch." My voice is low, an authoritative growl that causes her breath to stumble as it falls from her lips. "I want you to enjoy this story like you forgot how much the written word means to you, to who you are."

She's watching me — my lips, my eyes, the crease in my right cheek knowing it hides a dimple that makes her sigh when I smile.

"Kiss me. Please? And then go take a shower. Because, you're right, you smell."

The dimple comes out of hiding and the unmistakable sound of her sighing hits all my senses as I dip my head toward hers, sliding my lips over to her ear a split second before they can connect with hers.

"Read first. Kisses after," I whisper. Turning on my heels, I high tail it to the bathroom before she can object again.

Standing there any longer would have left us both breathless, possibly naked. Naked could be really good, but I want her to read Caryn's story first.

Pulling my jersey and undershirt over my head as I walk through the bathroom door, I hear the rustling of newsprint and smile to myself knowing I got my way. I love getting my way.

As quickly as I can, I pull my jeans and boxer briefs off and throw everything in a pile next to the hamper. Jumping under the warm spray of water, I try as hard as I can to not think about Stella in the other room.

I can't help it.

"Seriously," I scold myself. "What the fuck. Are you fifteen?"

It's like my penis just caught up with my brain and realized there's a girl in the other room. A girl both are attracted to. A girl who goes cross-eyed when she's kissed like she deserves to be kissed, and I plan to kiss her like that all night long.

I bite my tongue to keep from crying out as I twist the temperature gauge on the shower from hot to holy-Christ-that's-cold in hopes I can get my anatomy under control. The last damn thing I need is to walk out of the bathroom with a raging erection. I want her to see how much I care about her, not how much I'd love to take her to bed.

Right, don't think about beds, Brian. Don't be a dumbass.

Shutting the water off, I start running numbers for inventory and figuring up how many pounds of flour we need to order — the absolute least sexy thing I can think of — while I towel dry my hair and wrap the cloth loosely around my hips.

I only get the shower curtain pulled halfway open before I stop myself.

"You came back ... to find me?" Stella's leaning on the doorframe, one arm crossed in front of her chest and gripping the opposite bicep; the newspaper dangles from her fingers.

Sometime in the eight minutes that it took me to shower, she took her hair down and made herself look even more delectable, probably without realizing what she did.

I know I'm staring at her, but I just can't tear my eyes away. I'm not just naked in front of her, I'm splayed open and my heart is beating for her. And she knows it.

"It seemed like a good investment," I say, finding my voice.

I'm still standing in the bathtub, and now I'm not sure if I attempt to hold her or get dressed in the clothes I'd laid out before Caryn called Greg and I went off in search of Stella. My brain is at war with my body again, so I reach for the clean boxer briefs on the counter while I step out of the tub and slip them on under the towel.

She's looking. She's watching. Taking everything in and I'm praying I haven't just overwhelmed her. Not again, not after how she's been all week from what Caryn told me and Greg — scatterbrained and living on coffee.

I toss the towel over the curtain rod and pull on the pair of sweatpants I'd set aside.

"I came back to start a business. The bonus was the possibility of rediscovering you," I say. "I knew your parents were still here — your mom helped my realtor find this place for me before I moved back — but I was too afraid to ask her if you were still here. I was scared to death you wouldn't remember me. And she didn't say anything about you being here."

I inhale deeply, trying to prepare myself.

"I knew if I found you before I was ready, before you were ready, you would have run from me. As it was, I came back around the time you found out your husband was leaving you, and my fear of asking about you turned into a blessing in disguise. It — without my knowing what happened to you — gave me a good reason to wait. I couldn't just approach you the first time I saw you, Stella, because that first time I saw you all I wanted to do was pull you into my arms and keep you for myself, so I took my time getting used to the idea that you ... you're still here."

"You came back to find me." She repeats herself, but isn't questioning it anymore. How could she?

"I always told you I would never not find you," I say quietly. "It just took me a lot longer than I planned this time."

"Well, I'm right here." There's fire in her hooded eyes and a quirk to her lips as she drops the newspaper and takes three steps across the expanse separating us. Wrapping her arms around my neck, she whispers against my lips, "Are you ready to find me now?"

Pulling her in closer, my hands find her ribcage and I slowly slide them along her body to her hips and, turning her slightly, I reach down and grab her thighs just above her knees and lift. I need to feel her against me everywhere. I lift her enough to place her bottom on the bathroom counter and push myself between her legs, my hips colliding with her roughly as I take her face in my hands and look at her, barely contained lust streaking through her hazel eyes.

And I kiss her. The kiss she nearly begged me for earlier totally obliterated by the animalistic need rushing through my veins to consume her, make her mine and let her own me in return.

It's a battle of tongues and lips as we come together and fall apart in the frenzied act of removing her shirt and bra to finally feel the heat of skin on skin contact.

Stella reaches behind me and grabs my shoulders, trailing her nails down my back until another thread of control snaps and I grind my hips into her, feeling the pressure start to build as my cock gets thicker, harder. Her breath hitches and I move my mouth from her perfectly swollen lips to her bare neck, giving her the attention she seeks while my hands slip beneath the waistband of her jeans.

I pop the button and reach for the zipper as she lifts her legs and wraps them around my waist, pulling me into her again, a whimper slipping from her sweet mouth as I simultaneously push against her and drag my teeth across her nipple.

Her hands are in my hair, urging me to stay as her breathing becomes more labored. Holding her in my right arm, keeping myself pressed tightly to her still clothed core, I reach up and gently roll the nub on her other breast between my fingers.

"Brian," she breathes my name out like it's the most important word she'll ever say. "Please."

She slowly begins pushing my sweats down my hips, over the swell of my ass, and pulls my mouth back to hers.

"Please. Don't make me wait for this," she says, her lips a fraction of an inch away from mine, a look in her eyes that tells me if I don't give into her request she may just take what she wants from me. I'd be okay with that, but our first time I want it to be me giving her everything she needs.

Her pleasure is my pleasure, and I can't wait to get mine. I crush my lips against hers and pray I don't tell her I love her ... yet.

Grabbing the top of her jeans, I push the waistband down until she lifts her hips and I slide them as gracefully as I can over her backside and down her thighs until I have no choice but to give up my place between her legs to work them clear off her body. I take a step back and toss them in the pile with my dirty clothes, catching sight of her sitting in just a pair of navy blue cotton panties, legs dangling, full breasts and the mouth of an angel who's been roughly and thoroughly bitten and kissed.

"God, you're beautiful. You're gorgeous with clothes on, but right now ... Stella, you're more perfect than even my wildest wet dreams could have summoned." A shy smile spreads across her lips.

"Yeah, well, you're not so bad yourself," she jests. "Get back over here."

There's no reason to object. I haven't been with anyone in years, and I wonder if it was all leading me to this moment, to Stella wrapping me up in her legs and arms.

"Lose the pants, country boy."

And I do, right before I press my body back against the safe haven she's providing me. Pushing her hair away from her face, I can't help but thank my lucky stars that her ex-husband was such an ungrateful asshole to give this up, because I'm going to love her better than he ever could.

Our lips collide once more, but it's not as needy and standing there in my bathroom, I map out Stella's body with my lips and tongue until she's whimpering again and her eyes are glazed over in a just-fuck-me-already haze.

I need to slow down. I need to know if this is what she wants, if she really wants it as much as I do.

"I don't know, Stell. Do you think we should? I mean, I'm game if you are, but —"

"Don't you dare, Brian Alexander Stratford. I've wanted this moment from the minute I watched you turn and walk your sweet ass through the café doors — before I knew it was you. Don't you dare make me wait longer." She's authoritative. And bossy. And I can't get enough of her, so I reach for her face to pull her lips to mine again as she reaches into my boxers, pushing them down off my hips.

Concentrating on the gentle, firm strokes, I lose myself in the sensation and forget everything but the feel of her hand on my flesh.

"Panties," I grunt, smiling. "I can't do anything if you have those on."

With one hand still stroking my cock, she uses the other to shimmy out of that pair of little blue underwear. Kicking them off, she pulls me back into her personal space, a sanctuary that exudes strength and femininity and I can't wait to sink myself into all of that.

Pulling her hips forward on the counter, I slowly press myself into her, trailing soft kisses along her jaw as I feel her stretch around me, enveloping me in her slick folds. I thrust into Stella to the hilt, and hold myself there, unhurried in our lovemaking as I lay my forehead against hers.

"You feel so good," I say, and regardless of how cliché it is, it's the truth.

She nips my lip with her teeth, clenching her muscles around me and wiggling her hips until I groan and have no choice but to move. I pull out and leisurely pump my hips back into her until we find a rhythm. The methodical thrust and pull turns feverish and frenzied again when we start chasing our orgasms, racing one another to the finish line.

So close, I think, *I'm so close,* as Stella arches her back, holding herself up with one arm as she brings her right hand between us to slowly stroke the beautiful bundle of nerves nestled at the apex of her thighs while we dangle together on the precipice.

I feel the waves begin crashing over her. I focus on the moans escaping her throat and follow right behind as her orgasm sets off a chain reaction inside me. Holding her waist, I slam my hips into her as that telling tingling sensation creeps up my back and the final swell and eruption shudders through me, my body throbbing and pulsing with the release.

I pull her tightly to me, afraid to let go or pull away from her body.

Stella's lips find mine, they find my stubbled jaw, my earlobe, my neck … and I feel like I'm finally home with her in my arms.

My heart is still pounding when she looks up at me, a content smile on her face.

"Bed?" I ask, because I don't want her to leave tonight. I want to hold onto her.

"Snuggling?"

"I wouldn't have it any other way."

"Then take me to bed."

M.L. Pennock

Stella

Chapter Eighteen

I pull Brian's dirty Indians jersey over my head and find my panties, slipping them up my shaky legs, while he tugs his boxer briefs back into place. I don't think they made it down past his knees.

Sex has never been like that for me — fast and slow, giving and wanting. My cheeks are starting to hurt from smiling. It's the first real smile I've had on my face since the last time I spent time with Brian.

Maybe he's the common denominator in my happiness, to reminding me who I am.

Brushing aside the thought, I catch his eye again. We keep sneaking glances at one another in our hurried attempt to get dressed and upstairs.

And do so as quietly as possible.

"You don't think we woke him, do you?" I ask in a hushed voice because my paranoia is certainly taking its toll on me now.

How could we have been so stupid? I think to myself. *Britt is sound asleep a floor away and Brian and I just went after each other like a pair of hormone-driven teenagers. In his bathroom, with the door open.*

Bending down to pick up my jeans, I chance a glance in Brian's direction again and catch him staring at me.

"What?" I ask, biting my lip. "Why are you looking at me like that?"

He shakes his head, a smile climbing into the corners of his mouth, and takes a quick step in my direction. Wrapping an arm around my waist, he pulls me to him, pressing me against his chest in a hug that allows my heart to speak directly to his.

"You know," I say into his neck, a giggle escaping my mouth, "this is kind of how things got out of hand a little bit ago."

"I'm okay with that if you are," he says, grabbing my hand as he pulls away and leads me out of the bathroom.

Brian stops at the fridge on our way through the kitchen and grabs out bottled water and a container of cannoli I didn't know he was hiding. My mouth starts watering at the thought of that sweet, cheesy filling. I reach for the container, but he pulls it out of reach.

"No, ma'am. These are all mine, you'll have to find your own," he says.

"That's not fair, Brian. I have loved cannoli since birth. You have to share. I'm your guest and you have better manners than that," I spout off and turn away from him, sticking my bottom lip out in a mock pout. "And if you don't share, I'll call your mom and tell on you."

A Cheshire grin forms on my lips when I hear him gasp dramatically.

"You wouldn't."

"Oh, I would, Bri. Remember all those school lunches you promised to share? So many cookies! And you usually gave them to the other boys you sat with. I totally told your mom about that, too." I turn my head slightly so he can see the humor in my eyes.

The playful look has been erased and replaced with a very serious one; his bright eyes now cloudy like the sky when a storm is rushing over the horizon.

"Do you know why I used to give up all those cookies to the other boys?" Setting the water and container of cannoli on the counter Brian reaches for my face, caressing my cheeks and tucking my hair back behind my ears. I don't know where he's going with this, and I know I shouldn't speak, but he has to know what I'm thinking.

"They were just cookies. I'm not mad anymore," I try to say, but he touches my bottom lip with his thumb and shakes his head at me, quieting the thought before I can say anymore.

"It was a bribe. They all thought you were pretty and wanted you to be their girlfriend — hold your hand before school started in the morning, walk you to the bus circle, all that — and I wouldn't let them."

His eyes dance between my lips and eyes, above my head to something on the wall, and back to me.

"Even in second grade, I wanted you to be mine. You were my Stella then, and I'm back here to make that happen now, again," he says quietly. "So, if sharing this container of cannoli with you will keep you from calling my mom and telling on me, I guess I can do that, too."

He gently kisses my lips and before he can break away, I reach over and snag the container off the counter.

"Come with me and I'll show you what I can do with these treats," I say coyly, walking back toward the door that leads to the front of the house and the stairs that no doubt will take me to his bed. I catch a glimpse of the hunger in his eyes as I round the corner, the bottom of his jersey lightly brushing the backs of my thighs with each step, and a shiver creeps up my spine.

I find the stairs in spite of the darkness shrouding the room, and begin my ascent to the second floor. Nearing the top of the stairs I hear the creak of a foot stepping near the bottom and my heart begins to race.

"First room on the left," he whispers, and I quickly disappear from his view as I step into what, at first glance, could be described as a dimly lit man cave. My eyes adjust quickly and I see how wrong I was to assume it would be a cavern of dirty laundry and unmade bedding.

You can tell a lot about a person by the appearance of their intimate space.

This is not a typical man's bedroom, but Brian isn't like most of the men I know, past or present.

Centered between two north facing windows is a queen size bed, perfectly made to military precision — the bedspread taut and firm — with four pillows stacked along the headboard.

A large homemade quilt covers the sheets. I recognize the pattern right away, an intricate rendition of the Irish chain, done in a variety of blues and greens.

"Wow," I whisper, as I run my hand over what must have taken months of work to complete. I'm marveling at the hand stitching when I hear him approach from the top of the stairs across the hall.

"My mom made it," Brian says, his voice thick with emotion. "She started working on it when I told her I was moving back north. Said she needed to make sure I'd stay warm if I was going to live somewhere it snows seven months a year."

I laugh because it's both mostly accurate and sad. We do get a lot of snow.

"But all that snow just means more snuggling, right?" I say as his arms come around me from behind. I close my eyes and lean back into him, enjoying the closeness of a man, something I haven't admitted to anyone has long been missing from my life. Long before Keith left.

"How about we get that snuggling started now? You know, practice makes perfect. By the time it starts snowing for the season we could be experts," Brian says softly close to my ear and my legs weaken at the huskiness in his voice.

I place a knee on the bed and swiftly move to the center, waiting for him to join me.

***

"So, let me get this straight, he left you six months ago but you guys hadn't been intimate in almost a year?" Brian's incredulity at the situation is endearing, and a little unnerving. I don't respond right away, instead taking my time to suck the filling out of another cannoli.

Sitting cross-legged in the middle of his bed, Brian's lying next to me on his back staring at the ceiling as I slowly polish off my half of the container. I refuse to attempt eye contact after my admission. Yet. The vulnerable feeling is going to pass eventually, but it's still kind of raw and to openly admit there was nothing happening in my bedroom for longer than anyone could have imagined rubs that rawness back to bleeding.

"Yup. Crazy isn't it?"

He lifts his head to look at me, wide-eyed. "Crazy doesn't even begin to explain the things wrong with that man."

The silence is heavy. I don't like it and I can't help the need to fill that void.

"Between his business trips and me always working late — either out of need or because I didn't want to go home, I'm not sure — we just lost that part of each other. When I was home early, he wasn't. When he was home early, I wasn't. When we were both home early? I just stopped waiting for him to come to bed."

The truth hurts. It's painful, like a thousand shards of glass are being shoved under my skin. But the pieces of me are already starting to get glued back together and I can look at the situation a little more clearly. It certainly doesn't hurt as much as it did two weeks ago; six months ago feels like a blow I took forever ago.

"Let's put it this way," I say, lying across Brian's chest to look at him closely so he doesn't miss a word of what I'm about to say. "My marriage started out filled with love, or I thought it did, and mostly ended with me sharing a last name with a roommate. I can see that now, and I still probably wouldn't admit it to him, but that's what it feels like the last few years have been. However, if it hadn't ended? This" — I motion to the minimal space between our bodies — "wouldn't be happening."

He sighs, the deep rise and fall of his chest lifting me along with it, and he pushes his fingers into my hair, tipping my head to look into my eyes, searching.

"I know. And we may have been able to have a friendship if he hadn't left you, but, still, just a friendship? I don't know if that's something I could have survived. Not without wanting more. I've loved you for too long," he says, his mouth going slack and his eyes widening, like he realizes he just said something he didn't mean to.

"Loved. Like, past tense?" I ask, staring back at Brian, because it's entirely possible to want someone without loving them still. "As in, you used to love me?"

His tongue darts out, leaving a glistening trail in its wake along his bottom lip.

"No. As in, 'I have loved you for too long.' As in, you were my best friend and I loved you then for being by my side when we were kids. Present tense. As in, you've only been back in my life a couple weeks, but it's that feeling multiplied by thousands," he says slowly, softly, sensually. "I love you in the present tense, Stella."

I kiss him. His hands in my hair and a half-eaten cannoli in my hand, I find his lips like they're the lifeline I need to make it back to the surface — he's been a beacon in the dark and I know he's a safe harbor, so when I come up gasping for air I focus on him time and time again.

"Don't get cannoli on this quilt. My mom will kill me," he says, lips still connected to mine, and I feel him smile underneath me as he slips his hands down the front of the jersey and pops the top button free.

"Then you need to let me move so I can get rid of it," I say back to him as he drops his head onto the bed.

"That right there is about the sexiest thing I have ever seen. I can't believe you just shoved that entire thing in your mouth," he says, releasing another button as I struggle to sit up and straddle his hips, feeling him thicken between my thighs.

I chew enough to swallow without choking. "I don't waste food. Family rule."

"Well in that case we should definitely eat the rest of these," he says reaching out to grab the container. The empty container. "Did you eat all of those?"

"Maybe. You can make me more tomorrow. You're supposed to be kissing me now. There might be a little sugar right here," I say pointing to the corner of my mouth.

"Right there?" he asks, pulling me down to his lips.

"Yeah, right there," I reply, breathily, as he licks the crease of my mouth before taking my top lip between his, pulling it in with his tongue to deepen the kiss.

I feel the jersey start to slip off my shoulders and tighten around my body, holding me snug within the fabric, as Brian lifts his hips and rolls us over so he's settled between my legs and taken control.

His kisses land gently on my jaw as he works his way back down my neck, nuzzling under my ear, setting off a reaction that leaves my back arching and a low moan escaping my throat.

"Stell, not that I want to stop," Brian says, trailing his nose from my ear down my neck. "But ..."

He doesn't even have to finish.

"Fuck. We ... oh my God."

"You're not on any birth control, are you?" he asks, timidly, and judging by his reaction to my reaction he's already aware of the answer.

I cover my face with both hands; I can't even let him look at me.

"I can't believe this is happening," I say into my hands after a moment of trying to pull myself together. "I was on the pill for the longest time and then it just seemed pointless, so I didn't renew my prescription. Brian ... I'm so sorry. This is all my fault."

I can feel the tears welling up behind my eyelids and I will them to go away. I'm so tired of crying about everything; I'm stronger than this.

"No it's not. Nothing is your fault. I was down there with you. I remember it well," he says with a smile, then dropping a kiss to my lips he moves to lie beside me. "I'm just as responsible as you are. I wasn't exactly using my brain, so I think it's safe to say we have chemistry since I don't do much without thinking it through all the way. Nothing trips me up like you do."

He has a way of putting me at ease. I laugh through the tears because he's right — he probably thinks before he acts with most things and plans everything out — and turn into his chest to feel his warmth.

"I've destroyed any mood there was now, haven't I? Is the option to snuggle still open?"

"For you, it's always open," he says sleepily, setting his hand on my hip and cradling my head in the crook of his elbow on the other arm.

"Brian ...?"

"Mmmhmm," he hums quietly, drifting off.

"I love you in the present tense, too," I whisper, hoping my words make it home through the haze of sleep.

Brian

Chapter Nineteen

This is going to be the longest three weeks of our lives.

Her period is due around Halloween.

We're giving it twenty-one days to show up before we panic.

That's twenty-one long ass days that are going to move by slowly until we know if we've accidentally created a little person.

It's only Saturday afternoon and I already feel anxious — we made love once twelve hours ago and I seriously want to go buy her a case box of pregnancy tests. Just in case she's as anxious as I am.

What am I thinking? Of course she's anxious. She has to be. It's her body this is going to happen to if it happens.

What kind of asshole am I to not have condoms? Or to not even think about needing one? As if being celibate for damn near six years is reason enough to not have any stashed away. This is what happens when I let my penis do the thinking for me.

"Bride's side or groom's?" I ask, holding my arm out for the blonde stepping into the church.

"Uh ... bride. And you are?" Her voice has a hoarseness to it that tickles something in my brain, it's sexy and unique and doesn't quite fit her face and body.

"Brian. Friend of the groom and usher," I say as she wraps her arm around my elbow so I can show her to a pew. "I'm at your service ..."

"Emily. Emily Long. Since you're in the wedding, I assume you'll be at the reception. Can I also assume you'll save me a dance?" She asks the question like I have the option to say no, and I don't want to. It's been lonely being back in Tennessee and I plan to have as much fun tonight as I can.

"Well, Emily, I think that can be arranged," I smile as she takes her seat and I head to the back of the church.

I was thinking with my penis then, but used protection that failed and resulted in the best gift ever. I may not have been in love with Emily, but there was a reason Britt was brought into our lives — into my life — and I hope I'm just overthinking things. Or thinking about how different Stella is from Emily.

I put three scoops of beans in the grinder and hit the button. The machine comes to life, the café fills with the whirring sound of the blades and the aroma of fresh ground coffee seeps into my pores, calming my nerves as I move through the motions.

"Hey, man, you okay?" Greg comes up behind me and I jump.

"What? Yeah, I'm fine. Why?"

"You were standing here staring at that machine like you could control it with your mind. Did you turn into a Jedi overnight or ... something's up. Something happened after I left your place last night. You're different." Greg cocks an eyebrow at me and I try to play it off like nothing's out of the ordinary with a shoulder shrug. "No. None of that."

He leans in close, smells me, and stands up straight again.

"Nope. Kitchen. Let's go." He pushes my shoulder until I've turned and we start walking toward the kitchen, my fresh ground coffee in hand.

"For real, Greg, nothing's up —"

"Liar. What are we, fifteen? I smell a girl on you. Stella stayed over, didn't she?"

There's no use playing around with Greg; he knows me way too well and was the master of knowing who in our fraternity got laid any night of the week even if he hadn't been to the house or at the same party. It's a gift, really. I fear for his daughters' boyfriends if he ever has any kids.

"Yeah, she stayed, but please say nothing to anyone. Especially Caryn. If she wants her best friend to know she spent the night with me that's her business," I say, realizing just how horribly this could end if he says something and Stell isn't ready for people to know about whatever it is we are right now. "And nothing in front of Britt. No innuendo, no frat house routines, nothing. Please?"

"I wouldn't ... okay, I would, but I won't. So, what happened?" He wants information. He always wants details. I should have lied.

"You left. She stayed. Things got crazy. We went to bed. Slept. She got up early this morning to shower, left the house in a pair of my sweatpants and a thermal shirt before Britt woke up and could ask about our sleepover," I hurry through the abridged version. "We agreed we want to take things slower in front of Britton to let him get used to the idea of a woman being in my life since she's the first since, well, since his mother. He's a really smart kid, though, and I'm not sure how long we'll be able to keep up any sort of charade, so really, keep it to yourself."

My cellphone starts ringing and gives me a way out of the conversation before he can dig further, so I excuse myself and head back out front to brew more coffee, answering on my way through the café doors.

"Hey, you, what's up?" I ask after seeing Stella's name on the screen.

"How late are you staying at the coffeehouse today? I'm making dinner and want to know what time I should have it ready if you and Britt are free to join me," she says it nonchalantly, but even nonchalance sounds heaven-sent coming from her mouth. "And if you're going to be late, I figured I would just come grab him and he can help me make dinner."

I finish adding water to the machine and turn to watch Britt sitting at a table near the counter coloring. The kid deserves to go do something other than keep us company and color all day.

"Let me ask him," I say into the phone before pulling it from my ear. "Hey, Britt, Stella wants to know if you want to go to her house and help make dinner? If you want to, I'll be over after Greg and I shut down."

I barely get the question out of my mouth before he starts throwing his crayons into his crayon box and packing up his papers.

"Uh, how fast can you get here?" I ask into the phone, laughing at the genuine excitement from my boy. "I'll be lucky if I can get him to sit still until you do."

"I'm on my way then. He can hit the supermarket with me to get groceries while we're at it," she says, a smile on her voice.

***

She walks in and it's like the whole world stops for her, just for a moment, and I'm the only one who notices.

"Is he ready?" Stella asks leaning over the counter looking for Britt.

"He's in the office waiting for you and I set his seat in the entryway," I say, reaching for her. I can't stop my hands from touching her face and I pull her to me as she leans further across the marble slab, kissing her quickly and whispering in her ear, "I missed you this morning after you left."

She smells like lilac perfume and my Old Spice body wash. It's an interesting combination, one I could get used to everyday for the rest of my life.

"I missed you, too, but I got lots done around the house now that I'm out of my funk. Thank you for that, and the cannoli. Sweets always help." She brushes another kiss across my lips as the café doors swing open and

Britt comes barreling into the coffeehouse and straight out toward the front door. "That's my cue. See you in a few hours."

I leave one more quick kiss on her lips before she turns to catch up with Britt.

"You're staring, lover boy," Greg says behind me.

"It's kind of hard not to. My whole life just walked out the door."

"I've never seen you like this over a girl. A woman," he exclaims. "Shit. Stella is a woman. I have never in my life seen you so won over by a woman, Brian." He's leaning against the back counter between the grinders and other machines, arms across his chest and watching my every move.

"I told her last night I love her."

"You did what? Man, you move fast. Weren't you the one who was all 'Oh no I can't tell her how I feel because she just got divorced'?" he says, mocking me.

"Yeah, that was me. It kind of slipped out. We were talking about her ex-husband and what wouldn't have happened between us if he hadn't left her," I admit. "I could never have just been friends with Stella. She was my entire world when we were kids, and now? I can't deny I am completely in love with her as an adult. I just can't."

I step away from the counter, away from Greg and any ridiculous confrontation he's going to attempt to have with me.

"I get it. I completely understand, Bri."

My feet stop and I turn my head to look at him quizzically.

"I'm falling for Caryn. It's hard to stop it when it starts, it's hard to wonder how much it could hurt if she doesn't feel the same. That girl, though — Stella — she loves you as much as you love her. I don't care how new her single status is. That chick is one hundred percent yours," he says quietly in the lull of café goers. "I want that."

It's an even more quiet admission, and not something I think he's ever wanted before.

"If you want it, you need to work for it," I tell him with a wink before pushing through the swinging doors to the kitchen.

Stella

Chapter Twenty

It's been nineteen days since the unprotected "it" happened.

We haven't fully panicked yet, but anytime Brian and I have been near each other since that night and the idea of being intimate has come up, we've made sure there are condoms somewhere close by. The glove compartment of his Tahoe. My purse. His office at the coffeehouse. The woodshop behind his house. My nightstand. My bathroom. His bathroom.

Holy shit, I haven't had this much sex in years.

And since we've been careful every time since that night, if there's a chance I'm pregnant we can basically pinpoint when it happened. But it hasn't stopped me from using every Internet search engine and pregnancy website to research what might be happening with my body. In case I'm pregnant. Because I'm aware it could have happened. My animalistic attraction to Brian could have triggered an egg to jump ship early and — BAM! — pregnant.

Maybe.

More than likely not, but I seem to attract the unexpected.

Two more days for my period to show up before we hole ourselves up in my bathroom or his and I pee the scariest pee of my life.

***

"The salad forks do not go in the same slot as the dinner forks, Steph." I yell it. I yell it loudly. And then I burst into tears.

It's been twenty-two days and nothing. And Brian and I haven't had a minute to discuss the implications of this thing not showing up. It's probably late because of stress, stress from thinking about the possibility of my uterus incubating a little person.

"Crying? Over forks?" Steph walks into the kitchen as I wipe my eyes again, trying to stop the tears. I feel like all I do is cry — first because of Keith's infidelity and then because of Brian's everything and now this. It's hard to stop the tears because of the "what ifs" clouding my brain. It's a

Saturday night and normally I'm drinking like a lush. I'm not tonight. "Have a glass of wine and I'll fix the damn forks, you weirdo."

"I'm not drinking tonight," I say, realizing I didn't want to say it out loud a second too late.

"That's hilarious. You not drinking on a Saturday night is unheard of. The only thing that would stop you from drinking is if you were pregnant." The color drains from Steph's face on the word "pregnant." "Oh. ... Oh my God, Stella."

"I don't know. I'm due, like, now. Yesterday, today or tomorrow. Dates have been hit or miss since I went off the pill." I glance at my sister and she has a questioning look on her face. I never told her I went off my birth control. I look down at my hands, still holding the forks I've taken out of the drawer she had put them into when helping me with dishes earlier, and take a deep breath.

I start. "So, things weren't good with Keith long before they weren't good."

"How long before?" Steph asks taking the bundle of silverware from my hands and sorting it back into the drawer.

"He left, what, seven or so months ago? So the good stopped happening more than a year and a half ago," I say with a sigh. These are things I could have opened up to my sister about long before now, but I figured the last thing she would want to hear about was my sex life or lack thereof. "My birth control refills ran out and I just didn't bother to get a new prescription because nothing was happening. I figured there was no reason to take it if I didn't need to since there was literally nothing but sleep happening in this house."

"So why the freaking out? If it's been that long since you've had sex, freaking out over your period should be null and void if nothing has happened to make it late. No point in getting anxious when there's no reason to, right," she says, putting the last few forks away, like the matter is cut and dry — I wasn't having sex with my husband so I can't possibly be having sex now. It's like she's forgotten I could maybe be having sex with someone else, but she doesn't seem invested in this conversation enough to figure that out.

She's aloof and it's weird.

Something is up with her that I'll have to figure out later, once I get through this whole "could be pregnant" concern.

I respond by biting my lip. I shift my eyes. She's got that questioning look on her face again as she closes the silverware drawer and then she sucks in a breath. Bingo.

"Brian?" she squeals, whipping around to face me. It's high-pitched and hurts my ears, so I back away from her a little more. We really need to have a conversation about how to use our inside voices. "I didn't know you guys had, you know, done anything. When did that start? Are you guys dating? Is this, ooh, is this your first real relationship ever?"

"Stephanie, I was married. No it's not my first real relationship." I try to say it with conviction, but the grin breaks out on my face without warning. "It's my first relationship I get to start as an adult. So it's kind of the same thing."

"But ..." she prods before I have a chance to tell her more. She's kind of nosey. I love her for it even if she is scatterbrained lately.

"But we got ahead of ourselves the first time and now we're kind of," deep breath, "in the waiting game."

For the next couple of hours Stephanie drinks while I talk. I talk incessantly about Brian, what he's like now that we're both grown up, how amazing Britton is, how not shocked our mom was when I showed up with the two of them in tow one evening to visit and how Dad just kind of acted like Brian was the son he'd never had.

In all the years Keith and I were together, Dad kept him at a safe distance and didn't exactly express any sort of trust in him. I guess now I know why and it's a relief to see how my father is with Brian and Britt — like they belong with us.

Everything has come so easy with them, though, and it's a little surreal.

"It's like we were meant to find one another again, with a little push from him. Did you know he and Greg specifically moved here to open the café because Brian was hoping I was still living here?"

"It sounds a little like a fairytale, Stell. Or like he's a really cute stalker. Either way, better hold on tight to him."

"I never wanted to let him go in the first place. The first school year after he moved was the hardest one I'd ever had, and that's saying a lot considering I hadn't even hit puberty and acne and peer pressure yet."

"So, what's keeping you from taking that test today?" Steph asks, pouring the last drops of wine from the bottle into her glass. "I mean, if you were technically due yesterday you're already late so if you are a test should light up like a light bulb."

What is keeping me from doing it now? I really don't have a good answer, other than if it is positive, I really want Brian with me so we can know together. Something in me doesn't want to tell him if I'm pregnant; I want him to find out at the same time I do.

The explanation is simple enough and Steph understands my reasons, at least she says she does, though her eyes speak a different story.

"I want to be here for you, too," she says finally, quietly tapping her index finger on the top of the empty wine bottle.

Getting up from my seat at the counter, I walk over and give my sister a hug. Not just a hug, an embrace. I wrap her up in the warmth of my arms and try to take away the forlornness that's fallen like a curtain across her features.

"I want you to be here, too," I tell her as I reach for my cell phone and send Brian a text asking him if he's free to come over when they close tonight. Reading from my phone, I say, "We're cleaning up now, so I can be there as soon as I pack Britt up. Pizza? My treat."

"And cookies. Whatever he has leftover in the case. I need chocolate if you're peeing on a stick," Steph says as she pops the cork on another bottle of wine and I tap out the message verbatim to Brian.

***

Forty-five long minutes later, Brian and Britt walk in with a bag full of cookies and two large pizza boxes.

"Breakfast," Brian says as I eye the boxes. "Don't tell me you don't like pizza for breakfast? We can't date if you don't like it. Sorry, babe."

"Whatever. Give those to me," I say taking the pizzas and setting them on the counter next to the plates. Leaning into his muscular frame, I plant a kiss on Brian's lips. "I invented pizza for breakfast."

Steph helps Britt load a slice on his plate, then grabs two for herself and the bag of cookies before ushering him into the dining room to eat. It's shortly before seven at night, so a little late for dinner, but everyone needs to eat and I'm grateful for Steph taking time to be with Britt.

Once they've cleared the room, Brian touches my face, massaging his thumbs into the crease in my furrowed brow.

"She wants to be here when I test. She's my baby sister. I can't tell her no," I say in a whispered tone, my eyes closing as I revel in the way his fingers ease the tension from my face and I feel the muscles in my shoulders finally start to relax as well. "I'd be lying if I said I wasn't nervous."

"Whatever the outcome, we'll be fine. We'll work through it together. I'm not going anywhere Stella," he says softly, gripping my neck with his fingers and palms as his thumbs draw lazy circles over my cheekbones. "Are you ready to do this?"

My eyes still closed, I nod. The words won't come.

I'm scared to death of two pink lines.

Part of me is even more afraid of it being only one.

Brian

Chapter Twenty-One

We snuck upstairs through an old servant's entrance I didn't even know existed in Stella's house. I can only imagine the fun Britt could have playing hide and seek here if he knew about the hidden stairwell.

I'm trying to ignore my nerves, the butterflies in my stomach fluttering about, while I wait for the bathroom door to open again. The loosely made plan on the way upstairs was she would pee on it, not look, come in the hall, and then when that few minutes passed we'd look together.

She's been in there a long time.

It feels like a long time.

What if she looked without me? The thought crosses my mind just as the door opens and she turns to lean on the doorframe, a mask of unease on her face again.

We stand there, across the hall from one another, as we wait.

A few minutes pass and she says, "Are you ready?"

"As much as I can be," and I step toward her.

Like cowards, we peek around the corner. The test, as harmless as it is, is lying on the counter. I don't know if we're waiting for it to jump up and dance and sing a song telling us we're having a baby or not, but it doesn't do any of that. They apparently haven't created animated pregnancy tests yet. They should. It would take the fear of waiting out of the equation.

Stella grabs my arm, linking hers through it, and we shuffle into the bathroom so we can peer down at the very unanimated piece of plastic. And we just stare.

Mostly in disbelief, I think, and I don't want to be the first to speak. I don't want her to know my feelings. I don't want her to think I'm not happy about the result.

I am happy. But ... perplexed.

She's still looking at it when I lift my head to see her eyebrows pull together and the tension gather above her nose, so I do the only thing I know I can do that will hopefully make everything okay again — I pull her into my arms, kissing the top of her head as her arms come around me and hold on for dear life.

"Why does that hurt?" she asks.

"I don't know, Stell. But let's go have a glass of wine and think about it tomorrow."

***

I grab a couple slices of lukewarm pizza from the boxes in the kitchen and watch Stella as she pours us each a glass of wine. Hers is just slightly below the rim.

She takes a large swallow from the glass and tops it off.

That's the kind of thing a woman does when she didn't get something she wanted really badly. I've seen my mom do it after an argument with my brother when Tommy has proven her wrong — usually a result of some asinine discussion like the color of a shirt he wore for picture day in junior high.

But this is different. This isn't Stella not getting something she wanted really badly; this result is something she had prepared for and expected. The outcome, though, was the exact opposite of what she wanted.

I don't know how to fix this hurt. I don't know if I can fix it.

"Greg's handling the house alone tomorrow. I was thinking if Steph or your parents didn't mind, maybe Britt could stay with them and we could go out for lunch, maybe do some early Christmas shopping."

I need to think about something other than what just happened. Plans are already kind of set for Thanksgiving, so getting ready for Christmas is the next step. I know Britton wants Legos and a bike, so I've got to be sure I shop without him in order to keep them hidden and those opportunities are few and far between. Or, rather, they were before the Barbieri family came back into my life.

"Yeah, let's do that. I don't have anything going on tomorrow. I kind of figured I'd do the sweats and cold pizza and movie thing, but lunch out and shopping sounds like fun," Stella says, her voice tinged with sorrow for a moment before she clears her throat. "Were you thinking of going into Rochester or somewhere local?"

"Doesn't matter as long as I'm with you," I say, as I grab the plates and walk past her to the doorway leading to the dining room. I stop and turn around to look at her as she wipes a tear away. "Is this too much?"

"What?" she looks at me, a stunned expression on her face. "Is what too much?"

"Me? Britt? What we're doing?" I ask, motioning to the expanse between us.

I don't know where the questions come from, but I feel like I've let her down somehow. I don't want to be the reason she cries.

The sunshine in her smile breaks through the grey storm clouds in her eyes, and I want to be content. I want to be, but I'm so afraid we're moving too fast and she's going to push me away.

Her smile draws me back into the kitchen. Stepping away from the door I set the plates down and reach for her. I watch as more tears spill and run in rivulets down her cheeks.

"I don't—"she gasps and stops to collect herself. "I don't know what's wrong. I don't know why I'm not happy. I don't know why I'm crying."

She clutches my shirt and I pull her into me and let her hang on.

"You're not too much. You're perfect and everything you say is perfect, Brian," she says looking up at me, trying to catch her breath as tears slip from the corners of her eyes once more. "And I'm so afraid you're going to see how not perfect I am and you'll regret coming back."

"Stell, I don't want perfect." I look at her. Really look at her — the creases at the corners of her eyes, the shadows beneath them that tell me she hasn't been sleeping well again and it's probably all my fault, I see the stud earrings she wears and wonder why I never noticed them before; I take in everything about her. "I want you. You need to tell me if this is too much right now, though."

"It's not too much. God, Brian, I don't think there could ever be too much of you, of Britt. I feel like you belong with me."

I'm blown away by the honesty in her remark and want to spend the rest of the night kissing her, loving her. She's going to change me, but only for the better because her imperfections are a perfect fit for me and I'm flooded with an indescribable need to find her the most perfect-for-her Christmas gift.

"So what you're saying is you want to own me? Like a toy? A belonging?" I ask her, teasing to break the seriousness because the last thing Stella needs right now is serious. We can deal with serious tomorrow.

The laughter that trickles out of her makes my spine tingle.

"I'm going to tie you up and keep you forever," she says, easing back into the comfort we've found with one another.

"Now that's something I could truly enjoy," I say, grabbing one of those stud earrings between my lips and flicking the flesh with my tongue.

I feel her sigh before I hear it and the movement of her body against mine makes me wish we had the house to ourselves. I'll make it up to her tomorrow. We can do serious and sexy all in one day.

Stella deserves a seriously sexy Sunday and I plan to make it happen.

"You're drinking wine," Steph says from the doorway. "You're drinking."

I notice her face fall; even in the short time it seems she knew we were possibly having a baby she built it up in her head.

"I'm drinking," Stella responds to her sister, tucking herself under my arm. "It's okay."

I wasn't the only one to notice Stephanie's reaction. It's one of those things I can't fix for them. I want to but I realize now that I can't even try to fix it. They're having a silent conversation and I'm not part of it, but I can make one suggestion that will get us through the evening and calm our nerves.

"Come on, ladies. We have a bottle of wine to enjoy," I say, grabbing the plates off the counter again as Stella tucks the bottle under her arm and picks up our glasses. Walking into the dining room, I notice Britt asleep on the couch in the living room. "Looks like it's a sleepover tonight."

***

"Bike? Check. Lego sets? Check. New clothes, more crayons, a new baseball bat and balls. What else should we get him?" Stella has gone all out helping me shop for Britt's Christmas gifts. She's picked up a few things for her sister and parents, but mostly the day has been about my boy.

I think she's almost as in love with him as I am and the feeling squeezes my heart just a little, making me short of breath. She's a natural. The night before comes back to hit me, like a punch straight to the solar plexus that leaves you flat on your back wondering what the fuck happened. We haven't talked about it, though we've skirted around the topic. I think it's a conversation that will come with time, but we'd both prefer that time come sooner rather than later.

"Bri? Did you hear me?" She pulls me out of my thoughts and back to the present. "I think we should get him a helmet to go with the bike. Make sure he's safe when he's riding, especially if he's going to ride on the sidewalks. They're not in the best condition ..."

I stop her voice with my lips — right there in the middle of the mall, I pull her to me mid-sentence and kiss the hell out of her, putting our love on display for anyone who walks by and all the people who have to change their course to get around us. I don't know why she thinks she isn't perfect.

"I love you," I say breaking away from the warmth of her mouth but holding her face still in my hands. "I love how much you love my son. I love how much you care about us. Let me love you in return for forever?"

"Is this," she starts and stops. She swallows. She opens her mouth to speak and closes it again. "Did you just ...?"

"I might have. It depends on what you say." I lean my forehead against hers, gently pushing my hands into her hair and saying a silent prayer she'll be mine, that she'll let me have her for eternity.

"And if I say 'slow down, cowboy, maybe we should take our time getting there'?" She asks. Her voice is soft, tender, and it scares me because there's a possibility I'm screwing this up. She might stop being hypothetical. She might actually say no.

"Then I'd have no other choice than to wait for you," I say, regretfully. "Just don't make me wait too long. Please?"

She's silent and we're still standing in the middle of the mall with my head against hers. I breathe in the scent of her perfume and collect myself before opening my eyes.

"You okay?" Stella smiles as she takes in the emotions playing out on my face. I nod, making her giggle because our foreheads are still mashed together. "Good. Because I want to help pick out any sort of jewelry you were thinking of buying me."

I couldn't have heard her right.

"I don't really like yellow gold, but white gold and I get along." I lift my head and stare at her. "Diamonds are pretty, but sapphire matches your eyes, especially right now. You've got your sexy eyes on, Brian. You're undressing me with your eyes. I see you doing it. Should we maybe come back to look at jewelry?"

The heat rises in her cheeks.

"If we don't go to the car now, we're going to have to find a very secluded bathroom, and you're way better than kinky sex in a mall bathroom." The deep tone of my voice catches her off guard and she stutters out something incoherent as I turn and begin ushering her to the exit closest to where we parked.

We're almost to the Tahoe when Stella pulls on my arm and brings me to a dead stop. I follow her gaze to a couple pulling an infant carrier out of a car and snapping it into a stroller. Her grip on my forearm is tight enough I cry out and try to release her grasp. It's like her hand is locked around my arm.

"Stell? What's the matter?" I ask as I try to gently pry her hand from around my arm before she bruises it.

"It's them." I have no idea who "them" is, but I don't feel this is the time to question it or why they matter. "I feel like I should go thank them for simultaneously ruining my life and giving me a chance at something real and amazing."

The ex? That can't be who that is, can it? I look at the couple again as the woman pulls a pink blanket over the carrier to keep the wind off the baby. The man sees me staring at them, then his eyes trail down. To the love of my life; to the former love of his.

"Stella?" he asks, surprise in his voice. He turns to the woman and says something we can't hear while adjusting the diaper bag slung over his shoulder. Then he takes a step in our direction and I feel every muscle in my body go tense.

I've never wanted to hit someone I just met, but there's a rage deep inside me that I can't explain. It's not a "defend her honor" kind of rage. This is more a "you broke her and hurt her and you don't deserve her forgiveness" rage. But she's Stella, and Stella, I know, has come to terms with the ending of that relationship.

She's hardwired to forgive.

"Hi, Keith. How are you? Congratulations on your new addition," she says, gesturing to the stroller with a smile. Then, not out of her character, she speaks to the woman as well. "Hello, Beth."

Beth looks nervous and starts fidgeting with the stroller handle after giving me and Stella a short wave. She looks timid and shy. The exact opposite of Stella.

"Good. We're doing well. The baby came a couple weeks early, so this is our first real adventure out before it gets too cold. You look good," Keith says to her, reaching behind him to scratch his head, like he has something he wants to say but not sure how to bring it up.

It's like I don't exist, so I clear my throat and eye him up. That rage is still burning deep in my stomach.

"I'm Keith," he says holding his hand out for me to shake.

I do. I shake it just long enough and hard enough to make sure he knows I already don't like him.

"Brian." That's all he needs to know. I can feel the vein in my temple starting to throb.

"Right. I saw the story about you that Caryn wrote," he says, eyeing me cautiously, then looking at Stella again, "I should go, get Beth and the princess out of the chill. It was nice to see you, Stell."

"You too, Keith," she says.

As we turn and finish walking to the car, she says quietly to me, "You were posturing. He's not competition, Brian. You've won me fair and square."

"I wasn't posturing. I know you're mine. I just don't like that he hurt you," I say curtly, swallowing hard as I try to settle the anger I still feel. It's anger like I haven't felt in years — not since Britt was deserted by his egg donor — and I'm not sure how to put into words what that feeling is like for me.

"Please, don't be short." She leans back against the passenger door, grabbing the front of my Carhartt and pulling me to her. "You might be mad at him for what he did, but I lived it. I survived that storm alone. I survived that, Brian, and now you have me, all of me."

I do. She's mine. Placing my hands at the top of the door, I lean into her, pressing my body fully against her frame.

"I like that you're mine. Let me show you how much I like it."

She lifts her chin as if her mouth is searching for me and I drop my head down, seeking out the sweetness of her tongue against mine, her teeth nipping gently at my lips. Stella knows what her teeth do to me and I retaliate in kind, grinding my pelvis into her slowly, seductively, pinning her to the side of the truck.

"We're wearing too many clothes," she says, breathing heavily and shoving her hands into my jacket, grabbing the T-shirt underneath.

"It's chilly out here," I say, pulling her against me and reaching for the handle to open the back door to my truck. "Maybe we should continue this conversation inside?"

"Uh huh," she says, nodding her head and turning around to climb up into the back of the Tahoe, panties peeking out from under the skirt she's wearing along with her knee-high boots.

The things this woman does to me, I think as I adjust my jeans and climb up behind her, closing the door after me.

I'm barely sitting down before she's straddling my lap, that skirt fanned out to cover us both, and she's reaching between her legs to find my zipper.

"Let me help you with that," I say, a lazy smile falling into place across my lips as I pop the button on my pants and lift my hips up to meet hers. I release the teeth on the zipper. My hand brushes against her bare skin and she lets out a soft appreciative moan. "You're naughty. Here I thought you were going to make me work a little harder."

"No way. I need you, Brian, I need you inside me and I need it fast and hard," she says, releasing a raspy breath as I lift my hips again to push my jeans and boxers out of the way.

"Jacket. Inside pocket." It's a command. I'm not usually demanding of her, but we haven't had a chance to talk and I don't want either of us to feel any guilt until we do. She reaches into my jacket while I make quick work of nibbling along her jaw until I hear the unmistakable sound of the foil wrapper being torn open. Leaning back, Stella lifts off me and slowly rolls the condom down my thick shaft, squeezing the base of it before stroking her hand back up and positioning herself above me.

I grab her behind, urging her gently down onto me. I know she said she wants fast and hard, but I always want everything with Stella to be slow and gentle and perfect. She has other plans.

Stella rests her hands on the seat I'm sitting in and starts rocking back and forth on me, lifting up on her knees and plunging back down in piston-like movements, the shock of the force bringing me to the edge quicker than I have since I looked through a copy of Hustler for the first time when I was thirteen.

I lift up to meet her and feel her muscles constrict around me, her head drops back and a low moan escapes her lips as her hands slide down my chest. I grab her hips as she steadies herself, gripping my knees behind her, and take over where she left off, the angle of her body engulfing mine bringing us closer.

"Come for me, Stella," I demand, beg. I feel how close we both are to jumping off that cliff. I need her orgasm. I want to feel her body rock and pulse around me. Slamming my hips into hers once more sets her off like fireworks on the Fourth of July. I pull her face to mine to swallow her cries and muffle my own as my cock erupts in spasms deep within her body.

Her tongue licks along my bottom lip, lazily trailing along the flesh and eliciting a low rumbling moan from my throat. I press up into her, despite the fact I'm coming down from my own orgasm, and she cries out from the contact, her skin sensitive from the tremors that wracked her body moments ago.

"That has to be a record for us," she says, still catching her breath. Her eyes close and a smile plays at the edges of her lips as she lays her head on my shoulder, nuzzling into my neck while I draw figure eights along her spine. I feel her chest start to shake, a laugh working its way out from between her lips. "Did you really try to command an orgasm from me?"

"Does that not do it for you? I've read some trashy romance novels and it works for them every time. I'm shocked you can't come on command. I thought everyone could do it." I can't hold back my laughter and we hold onto one other as our breathing returns to normal, our bodies still melded together beneath that flowy skirt of hers until it feels we need to pull ourselves apart and climb into the front seats for the drive home from Rochester.

"Thank you ... for today," Stella says as we come up to a stoplight on the edge of town. We've both been quiet since leaving the mall; she spending a majority of the trip worrying her bottom lip, me just worrying.

I reach for her hand and ask her what's on her mind because I know there's something going on in there.

"I know things are still new with us. It's been, what, five weeks since my divorce was finalized? So, yeah, this is still really new. But it doesn't feel that way. The minute you stepped back into my life it felt like that missing piece had been recovered, and I fell in love with you quickly and I fall in love with you more every day because I have you and Britt." She bites her lip. "But, it doesn't feel, I don't know. It doesn't feel totally complete."

I give myself a moment to wrap my head around what she said, forgetting we're sitting at a stoplight until I hear the horn blaring behind me. Shaking myself free of the fog, I ask her, "What would make it complete?"

"Everything about that pregnancy test last night felt right, except for the result. I want a family ... with you. I want to make Britt a big brother, Brian."

Thank God we live in the middle of nowhere. I pull the Tahoe onto the shoulder of the road and throw it into "Park." Twisting to look at Stella, my left arm resting on the steering wheel, the conversation hits home.

"You want to have babies with me? Are you telling me that everything I was feeling last night you felt, too?" She looks me in the eyes, searching them, for what I don't know. "I was scared to death if that test was positive you'd never forgive me, Stell. I think part of me was convinced it was the last thing you wanted, even though the rest of me watched your reaction. I could see how much it hurt to not be pregnant."

"I want to make babies with you, Brian. I want to go to sleep every night with you next to me. I want to be your wife and the mother of your children. All of your children."

I reach across the console separating us and pull her to me, locking my gaze on her.

"Really? You want to marry me and Britt?"

"More than I've wanted anything in my life."

Stella

Chapter Twenty-Two

We're keeping it all under wraps until Christmas.

The decision was quick and conversation brief before it turned into a make-out session while we were sitting on the side of the road for who even knows how long.

That came to a halt when we heard a tapping on the window and I peeked over Brian's shoulder to see a newly familiar face — Officer Max Wyatt. I just put his picture and the Chief's "welcome to the community" message about him in the paper last week.

This isn't how I figured we would meet.

"Officer Wyatt, how are you?"

He eyes me suspiciously, and I see his hands move to his hips, his mannerisms both professional and authoritative. Brian's already reaching past me for the vehicle registration as I continue talking so he maybe won't draw his weapon thinking ... well, I don't know what he would be thinking. I'm not usually in this situation. Cops don't pull their guns unless they feel they have to, right?

I let my mouth do the talking.

"I'm Stella, the editor at the local paper. I just ran an article about you and recognized you from the photo the chief sent me. Welcome to the community," I say, putting on my best "no, I wasn't almost fucking my boyfriend in this car ... again" smile.

He's still eyeing me, but takes Brian's license and registration, glancing at it with minimal interest.

"It's nice to meet you, too, Stella and," looking at the license again, "Brian. Everything okay? I was on my way back to the station and saw you on the shoulder. Wanted to make sure you weren't having any car trouble."

He clears his throat, a blush creeping up from his collar.

"No, no car trouble, officer," Brian says, smiling. "We were just having a really important conversation and felt it would be safer to pull off the road to finish it than risk anyone's safety."

"Well, I do appreciate that," Max responds, an accent I can't place tinting his words. It's not southern, that's for sure. "Just don't make out too much longer. Someone else is bound to come through here soon."

He hands a dumbfounded Brian back his papers, turning to walk back to his cruiser an d throwing a "have a nice night" back through the open window.

I lift my hand and wave as the car rolls past us before I'm caught up in a fit of giggles that leave me nearly breathless.

"Oh, you think that's funny, do you?"

"A little," I say pinching my thumb and forefinger together.

"Well, future Mrs. Stratford, I'll have you know ... okay, yeah, it's funny. I got nothin'," he shakes his head and puts the truck into gear, signaling as he pulls out on the deserted stretch of country highway. "Let's get home and see what the kid has been up to. I'm sure he's driving your sister crazy by now and we need to figure out plans for trick-or-treating tomorrow."

***

It's going to be a really long two months.

I thought worrying about possibly being pregnant would eat me alive, but this? We promised each other we wouldn't tell anyone — not Steph, or Greg, or Caryn and definitely not Britton, because he has trouble keeping secrets — and not telling anyone means I need to really watch my Internet searches and window shopping when anyone other than Brian is around.

I'm going to be a mom. I'm going to be a wife to a really amazing husband.

There's that surreal feeling again, but it feels so right.

A whirlwind romance, that's what my grandmother would call this. Or she would straight up ask me if I was pregnant if she couldn't get a read on me, because that's how she was. No mincing words. It simply wasn't how she handled things. If she needed an answer to a question, she'd get it one way or another.

And if she asked me about this relationship, I'd be nothing but honest with her.

This isn't whirlwind or shotgun. This is me and my childhood sweetheart holding onto something innocent for years until he and fate brought us back together.

This is what fairytales are made of, just like Steph described it.

I'm off in my own world when I open the front door of my house and walk through. I opened it and walked through, without using my key?

"Stephanie?" I call out. She's usually the only one to use their key even though our parents and Caryn have copies in case of an emergency. "Stephie? Are you here?"

I call out again, dropping my laptop case, purse, and the tote full of notebooks and my camera to the dining room table.

"Yeah, I'm here," she says from the kitchen door, her face blotchy. Steph lifts her arm, tissue in hand, to wipe at her eye and the makeup running down her cheek. First one, then the other. I just stare. What the fuck happened to my sister? She takes a deep, shuddering breath. "I let myself in so I could start getting the candy ready for tonight. I wasn't sure if you'd be home in time to do it before trick-or-treaters showed up and I know how much you love Halloween, so I let myself in."

"You already said you let yourself in. That's fine — what happened?" It all comes out so quickly, but I don't know if she heard it all before she's wiping more tears and eyeliner from her face. It's when she lifts her arm again and her shirtsleeve slides down past her wrist that I notice the bruise.

"I'm," she pauses, "I'm fine. I just had a bad day is all. It's almost time for kids to start showing up. Let's sit outside?"

"What happened to your arm?" I say it, not meaning to sound demanding, but damn it, I need to know what's going on with my sister.

Her back is turned to me, reaching for the large bowl filled with miniature candy bars and packages of fruit snacks. She reaches for it with her left hand, even though she's right handed and like a majority of right handed people she generally reaches or grabs things with her dominant side. She doesn't this time. Bruised and painful? I just stare at her arms, wondering.

"Nothing happened," she says quietly. "Please, can we go outside? Please, Stella, I don't want to talk about this."

"If nothing happened, then there wouldn't be anything to talk about, Steph." The accusation is gone from my voice, but the concern is still there. "You've been somewhere else for a while. Pulling away, and when you are here, it's like you're not. Your brain is off somewhere else. You haven't stayed the night in weeks and we haven't been hanging out as much."

"You're busy with work. You're spending time with Brian. We just haven't had time. It's busy. Everyone is busy, Stella. I'm fine." The words fly from her mouth with such vehemence that, if they had been personified, they would have punched me in the gut and laid me out on the floor.

"Steph, I'm home every night. Brian and I aren't sleeping over at each other's houses. I try to be home from work by ten at the latest most nights. Nothing about my work routine has changed," I say taking a step toward her. "What's going on? Please, talk to me."

She flinches as I rest my hand on her shoulder, then sighs. It's resignation, the sound of giving up, but what she's giving up I'm not sure.

"I'm fine, Stell. Let's go greet the neighborhood," her voice is so small, it reminds me of when she was a little girl, one who tried lying once about other kids picking on her on the playground. I've heard her tell me she's "fine" before. I didn't buy it then; it's a giant load of horseshit now.

"This conversation isn't over, Stephanie. When that front light gets turned off, you and I are talking. I don't know what's going on, or what it is you feel you can't talk to me about, but I'm not taking your stance on the phrase 'I'm fine' as gospel." Taking the bowl of candy from her, I head back out through the dining room.

"I'm an adult, you know! I don't have to tell you shit, Stella. I am not a little girl anymore." The anger fizzles out as quickly as it flared and I see my sister as a broken version of the woman she was just a few months ago. How have I missed this transformation? It didn't happen overnight, that's for sure. "I'm just ... I'm not a little girl anymore."

"No, you're not. But you're still my little sister. We stick together, Steph." I look up at the ceiling to center myself before continuing, hoping she'll give in and do as I ask. "Stay here tonight. We'll talk about whatever is going on, just us. I just ... I don't want you to go home."

***

"Steph, look how much candy people gave me," Britt yells running up the front walk to the porch where we've been all night. It's nearing bedtime, so I know we're Britt and Brian's last stop.

"That's great, buddy. You gonna share it with me?" They're the first words I've heard Steph say since the last "fine" she uttered after I told her I wanted her to stay tonight. At least she's talking to someone. "I like Butterfinger the best."

Steph stands, opens the door for Britt and follows him through. Not even a "hello" to Brian. I hit a nerve and whatever one it was, I'm hoping to bare it and get whatever her problem is out in the open tonight.

I release a sigh and stand, wiping the seat of my pants since I'm sure there was dirt or stones on the stoop, before stepping down to kiss Brian.

"What's up with Steph?" he asks as soon as our lips part. "She's acting like someone pushed her down and kicked her in the shin. Is she okay?"

"No." He gives me a look, a worried glance, and then peers over my shoulder through the storm door. "I'm going to get to the bottom of it. I've convinced her to stay here tonight. I came home and she was crying in the kitchen."

"Crying? Steph doesn't cry. She gets sarcastic and bitchy, but she doesn't cry."

"I know. She's been like that since forever, but she was crying and kept telling me she was 'fine' and that whatever is going on is nothing. I don't buy it. Brian, she's into something and I can't even imagine what it is." I glance over my shoulder, making sure she's still busy with Britt. "She reached up to wipe her eyes and I saw what looked like a bruise on her wrist. It was yellowish, so if it's a bruise it's a few days old at least."

"You think someone hurt her?" His tone of voice changed so quickly. From sarcastic to protective and friend to big brother before I could finish my sentence.

"I don't know." I shrug my shoulders. "She broke up with that guy from school a few weeks ago and has acted off since then. Maybe even before that. I wasn't doing a good job of paying attention."

Brian's eyes land on mine and I hear them telling me not to blame myself.

"Stell, if someone hurt her, you'd let me know, right? I've loved her like a sister since she was a baby. I'm not going to stand by if someone is using her as a punching bag."

I touch his face, trying to calm the wild anger I see brewing in his eyes, as the front door swings open again and Britt announces he and Steph traded candies – Butterfingers for fruit snacks. It's an even trade. He's happy and exhausted.

"Take him home so he can get some sleep. It's getting late and he's got school in the morning," I say to Brian as I lean in for a kiss and, so Steph can't hear me, I whisper, "I'll let you know what I find out. I love you."

"I love you, too. See you in the morning for coffee." One more quick kiss, and a squeeze and kiss for Britt and the boys are off.

It's just me and Steph.

"Glass of wine?" I ask her.

"Already opened a bottle."

I turn and wrap my arm around her waist, remembering how she flinched when I touched her shoulder earlier, and we walk back up the stairs and through the front door.

***

We've been sitting at the island counter in the kitchen staring into our wine glasses for a good twenty minutes. I'm watching her right arm. Her wrist playing peek-a-boo with the cuff of her shirt and I wish she'd start talking, but she just keeps running her middle finger around the rim of her glass. She's playing a single chord of a glass harp on repeat and she's the only one invited to the concert.

"Get out of your head," I say breaking the silence and shattering her resolve.

A single tear falls from her eye and lands amid the velvety red liquid in her glass, leaving ripples in its wake, lapping at the edges and I watch little legs as they climb back down the sides.

"I-," she starts and stops. "Stell, I tell you everything. I did. Until about four months ago." She swallows, wipes a tear from her cheek.

"I met a man and, you know, you were so consumed by the divorce I didn't want to tell you. I was afraid you'd be happy for me, but sad, too, because your romance was ending and I was finally finding one. I guess I didn't want you to be 'just because' happy for me. I wanted you to be 'for real' happy for me."

Steph swipes her finger along the rim of her glass again before reaching down to the stem and bringing it to her lips. The liquid rushes over her tongue and I hear the slurping sound as she pulls the wine across her palate, but her face has changed by the time she places the glass back on the marble countertop.

"What happened, Steph?" I don't want to know. That churning feeling in the pit of my stomach tells me I don't want to know.

I have to know.

"Things started out nice, normal. We'd go out for drinks, dinner, lunch, whatever a couple times a week. It was sweet. Then after a few weeks I realized he's been the longest relationship I've had ever. It was nice to have someone to look forward to seeing on a regular basis other than you and Caryn and Mom and Dad," she says, her voice trailing off. "I could see myself falling for him."

"You didn't want to kick him through the revolving door? No being weird and keeping where you live a secret?" The revolving door phenomenon at Steph's apartment is purely metaphorical. She's lived there for a few years and I don't think she's once let a man come over. She says she doesn't want the calm in her home disrupted by a guy. Truthfully? She's always had a sixth sense about people and she won't trust unless that nauseating feeling remains at bay.

"No. He came off as ... perfect. That should have been my first concern because no man is perfect. Not even Brian, but he's amazing and I love that he loves you. He's safe," she says, looking me square in the eyes, and I can see it there — she fully trusts Brian, but there's fear underneath. "He's safe, and I thought Darren was, too. I let my guard down. After a month or so I let him come pick me up for dinner instead of meeting him at the restaurant. Things seemed to start going downhill from there."

"The night you went on that super secret date and told me you were doing yoga with Mom? You were with him?"

She looks like a fish out of water, her mouth opening to speak and no words coming out, so she takes another sip of her wine — this one less reserved, less professional wine taster and more drunk college girl. I reach across the counter and touch her arm gently as she looks down again.

Someone broke my sister. Who is this girl? Where is my strong, resilient Stephanie?

Her eyes meet mine finally.

"That's the night I tried to break it off with him, I wasn't lying about that. He'd gone from sweet and kind to possessive, questioning. I'm an independent person, I don't take orders from men and, Stella, I know he didn't like that. He wanted someone to submit to him, be at his beck and call. His whipping boy."

I wait. I feel the churning in my abdomen change from unease to pure, unadulterated rage. Submit? Taking orders? Sure those things can be fun in the bedroom with two willing participants, but this doesn't sound like that kind of relationship.

"He'd started asking me where I was all the time. Call me out of the blue, and at first it was whimsical how he'd call and ask me where I was and what I was doing. Then it was more frequent." Pausing, Steph swallows what's left in her glass and pours another. "I'm going to get fucked up tonight, Stella. Please don't be mad if I puke later."

I laugh because we need to. Maybe I'm even laughing because I couldn't care less if she drinks until she vomits as long as she's talking to me.

At least there's something other than anger to break through this wall of hurt I'm feeling for my sister.

"What happened after that? I'm so sorry it took me this long to notice something was going on with you. I swear, I thought you were acting like yourself until a couple weeks ago, Steph. I'm so sorry," I can't stop apologizing like whatever she's about to tell me is my fault, like I'm the one who sent her spiraling down the proverbial staircase into what I believe has been a controlling, abusive relationship.

One more sip for courage, she starts again. "It escalated from calls asking where I was to calls saying shit like, 'Who is that guy you're with?' when I was studying with Colton at the coffeehouse and Darren was nowhere in sight. Eventually, when I started ignoring his calls while I was studying or in class or had turned my ringer off to sleep ... he started getting physical. He'd push me when asking me where I'd been and why I hadn't answered–"

Steph's voice gets lost in the murkiness of her sobs, her hands covering her face as she loudly cries out the anger and fear she's still feeling. I could see it on her face while letting her talk. She's reliving any time he touched her, anytime he called her.

I pull her up from her seat and we collapse on the kitchen floor in a heap, my baby sister on my lap as I rock her back and forth trying to figure out a way to make this better for her. How do I fix this? If I do it the right way, I'll be in prison for the rest of my life.

"Did he come after you recently, Steph?" I finally get the question out once the wailing sobs have been reduced to shuddering breaths. I brush the hair away from her eyes and stare into eyes that match mine, my father's and our grandmother's. They're knowing eyes. "Your wrist and back, on your shoulder blade, Steph, I saw a bruise and you winced when I touched your back earlier. Did he come after you again after you broke up with him?"

It's barely above a whisper, but it's there.

"I can't do anything without him knowing." The fear in her voice is so thick it wraps around me like a parka in the midst of a Russian winter. "I feel like he's always watching me. After I went home from keeping Britt for you and Brian last week, he was waiting inside my apartment. I didn't give him a key."

"Breaking and entering, assault, stalking ... do you have a photo of him?"

I can't help it. She knows I can't.

"Stell, I can't go to the police. Can you imagine what he'd do to me if I went to the cops about this? Look at my body when I hadn't even told you," she yells, wiggling off my lap and pulling her shirt off.

The yellowing bruise on her arm I thought was just around her wrist travels halfway up her forearm. An imprint of thumbs and fingers wrap around each bicep. Steph slowly turns her back to me and when I see it, I understand why she flinched — a straight line of bruised skin makes a path down the edge of her shoulder blade to the middle of her lower back and spreads out along her ribcage.

She doesn't even need to tell me. I can see it plain as day that he slammed my sister's body against a doorframe. She might not be ready to go to the police, but I can at least ask some questions for "work" and document her injuries.

I'm on my feet and reaching for my Nikon before she turns around. I fire it up and start snapping photo after photo of every single mark I know God didn't put on her flesh. I suck in a ragged breath when she drops her jeans and I see the remains of a bruise in the shape of a boot on the back of her right thigh.

"Help me, Stella. Please, help me," Steph begs, hanging her head as I take the last few photos, her body consumed by silent sobbing.

"You're staying here indefinitely. I'm calling your landlord tomorrow to break your lease. We'll tell Mom and Dad I need a roommate to help with the mortgage," I say, the lies tumbling from my lips like they'd been planned for weeks. "I'm going to nail this guy's ass to the wall, even if I have to do it myself."

***

I put Steph in the spare bedroom — her bedroom whenever she would stay with me after a fight with Mom and Dad when she was still living with them — and rubbed her back where it wasn't still painful. It's almost midnight; we'd talked for a few hours, she had a few more glasses of wine and finally felt okay enough to sleep after a while.

If I didn't want to talk to Brian, I would have just curled up next to her and fallen asleep right there. It would be easier to make sure she stays safe if she's within arm's reach.

I made sure she was resting as peacefully as possible before slipping out the door. Leaning against the wall in the hallway I wonder again how could I have not noticed something like this, the fear she had, for even the short amount of time she's endured it?

For something to escalate that quickly and me not even see the damage before now makes me ill, but falling apart right now simply isn't an option. I brush the tears from my cheeks and head down the hall to my bedroom to grab Brian's hoodie. He still hasn't asked for it back and I'm not willing to offer it to its rightful owner.

Throwing the sweatshirt over my head, I make my way downstairs to the kitchen.

To eat chocolate.

And call Brian.

Mostly it's to eat chocolate.

"I was just about to call you. Steph's finally asleep," I say into the mouthpiece instead of a "hello" when I answer. It's like he knew my fingers had been poised to dial his number and he beat me to it.

"Good. Is she okay?" Brian asks, his voice low and gravelly.

I tear open a Kit Kat and shove it into my mouth so I can use my hands to open a bottle of beer. I bite the candy, chew and wash it down, the cold brew hitting my stomach like a brick after hardly eating all day and then giving up my wine. I needed to be sober and able to drive if Steph changed her mind about going to the police tonight, that's my excuse.

Not a chance I was afraid I'd get drunk and hunt a fucker down. Nope. Not. One. Bit.

"Well, I've taken photos and she's come clean about everything, I think. I hope there isn't more," I say, breathing deeply and taking another swig of my beer.

"What do you mean you took pictures?" Brian's voice has hitched up a notch, the quiet rough-and-tumble tone turning into protective brother with a side of "I'll kill him." I remain quiet, because I'm afraid how he'll react despite the fact he's the most levelheaded man I know. He's logical. "Pictures of what, Stella?"

"Bri ..." I try to get the words out but my mouth is dry. I swallow to work the lump down in my throat because I have to be strong for Steph, and part of me being strong means having someone I can also lean on. So, clearing my throat, I begin again and let the words fall without thinking too much about the impact. "Bri, he hit her and left a lot of marks. She's afraid he'll do worse to her if she goes to the police, but I want to document while the bruises are fresh. Steph's scared. I'm scared."

It's already late when we start talking, but our conversation goes well into the early morning hours. I climb the stairs while we're still on the phone, and across town Brian does the same. We climb into our separate beds, our phones connected to the walls with chargers in our separate homes so we can work to calm each other down ... separately.

"I hate this, Brian. I really hate this."

"Me too, babe. We'll help Steph through it though. You're going to talk to the police chief this week, so maybe he'll be able to give you some insight into how she can handle this legally," he says quietly.

"No, not that. I mean, yes I hate that — I more than hate that — but I hate this, too. Going to bed alone, Brian, this is what I hate. I would rather have this conversation with you here or me there so when I stop talking you're just holding onto me," I whisper into the phone.

"Soon, Stell, soon."

M.L. Pennock

Brian

Chapter Twenty-Three

There's been way too much excitement this week already.

I'm going to get married. We're talking about growing our family. Steph's weirdness has been decoded and it's done nothing short of throwing me into a murderous rage. The coffeehouse is the busiest it's been since we opened.

Thank God it's almost the weekend.

We're into November — pumpkin spice season is well underway and with the chill in the air, more people are asking for cinnamon everything. And my mom's been asking me almost daily about my and Britt's plans for Thanksgiving. I think she's a little afraid we won't go south now that we've settled into routines in New York.

Opening a spreadsheet on the computer so I can see what's needed for supplies, I feel my phone vibrate on my belt and answer it without looking at the screen first.

"Brian, I just miss my little man. You have to understand. I need to get my hands on his cheeks," mom says into my ear.

"Mama, stop it. We're coming to Tennessee for Thanksgiving, I promise," I say, letting out a frustrated sigh. "I'm seriously trying to order everything Greg might possibly need while I'm away so he doesn't have to worry about inventory on top of the baking and running the front, too."

Laying my head down in the crook of my elbow, I take a deep breath. I don't mean for it to be heard all the way down past the Mason-Dixon Line, but there's no mistaking it traveled all the way to Tennessee.

"Sweetie, if you and Greg are doing that much business, maybe it's time to look into a little extra help. One additional set of hands could take a lot of pressure off you," she says, an almost sing-song sweetness to her voice.

Kathryn Stratford has something up her sleeve. I love my mother to the ends of the earth, but she cannot keep a secret or idea to herself for long. I think that's where Britt inherited it from.

"What's going on, Mama? I know your voice and you only sound like that when there's something nipping at your heels like a yappy little dog trying to get your attention, so spill it," I sound short-tempered, which is nothing like me but there's so much to get done that she just needs to come out with it already.

"Your brother," she states matter-of-factly. "He's been doing nothing but pissing me off and he needs a change of scenery. Put him to work. He's got a degree in marketing that he isn't using, but you know he can bake and brew coffee as well as you and me."

Bingo. That's why she's been pushing for me to come home for Thanksgiving.

"I'll talk to him, Ma. Before I come down in a few weeks I'll talk to him and see what he wants to do, but right now I really need to get back to work," I say ending the conversation with an "I love you" but hating myself for not taking more time to talk to her and find out what's really going on with my brother.

I have every intention of going to Tennessee to see my family — even more now knowing Tommy's getting on our mom's nerves — but with everything going on with Steph, I worry about leaving.

The decision to go was made before Stella found out about her sister's stalker ex-boyfriend, who hasn't gotten a clue he's no longer welcome in Stephanie's life. Deep down, I hope Stella is honest with the police chief when she meets with him. I want the cops to be aware of this guy. I want them to know who he is and that he's bad news before something else happens, especially now that Steph's living with her sister.

"What are you doing, Buttercup?" Greg says from the doorway. "You're doing that spaced-out lost-in-thought thing again. You do that a lot lately."

I turn my head to look at him, chewing on the inside of my bottom lip.

"I love it when you look at me that way. Gets me all hot and bothered," he says, winking at me. "But seriously, what's with the super serious mode this week?"

"How would you feel about hiring someone to help out around here, maybe do some in house marketing?" I skip over all the bad things stressing me out and before the afternoon rush hits I jump head first into convincing Greg that hiring my baby brother would be the greatest idea ever for our flourishing business.

***

I definitely need to get into Tommy's head and get him to agree to moving north. After talking to Greg yesterday and looking at the way business has changed in the short time we've been open, it's apparent we need the extra help.

And I could use some extra sleep.

It's not even seven in the morning and I've already been at the coffeehouse going on three hours. Greg and I have been baking for an hour, prepping muffins and scones and biscotti, but before he came in I was trying to figure out what to say to Dale — Mr. Barbieri — when I meet him for lunch. Lunch on a Friday should give him the weekend to think about my request if he needs time to consider it, right?

I've never done this before.

I have part of a speech prepared, but it sounds like I'm trying too hard.

Stella and I weren't even going to tell anyone our plans to get married until after Christmas, but I respect her father. I want him to know how much I love his daughter. I want Dale to know I'm here to take care of her, and that she's in turn promised to take care of me and Britt.

I just hope I can ask for his blessing without fucking it up.

My body is on autopilot all morning, my brain acting much the same, and I've just gone through the motions — pour coffee, pack up baked goods, ring up customers, wipe down tables.

When I look at the clock again I wonder to myself, "How the hell is it already almost noon?" My head starts throbbing and the sound of the coffee grinder being switched on makes it pound harder. I've never had an anxiety attack, but I feel like this whole situation could be the cause of my first one ever.

"Do you love her?" he asks from behind me as I switch the grinder off and the whirring blades come to a halt. I turn around to find the man I pray will be my father-in-law staring me down, like it's a competition who loves her more.

"Sir. You're early. I was ... yes?" Fuck. I close my eyes hoping I didn't just tell him I love his daughter like it was a question, but I'm pretty sure that's what it sounded like. I open my eyes and Dale's still staring at me, hands in his pockets, waiting for me to continue. I notice a few of our regular customers watching the entire scene like a reality television show.

"Let's sit," he says turning and walking to the table Stella usually sits at when she comes in and has time to relax with her coffee and a scone before running off again for work. "I was thinking about it and I said to Jenny the other night how I thought it was nice you wanted to get together, just us guys, but that lunch is weird. Lunch is weird because we—" he points to himself, to me and back to him, "we aren't dating. You're seeing my little girl."

I swallow hard at the protectiveness in his eyes. Stella's been hurt and he's out for blood if anyone hurts her again. He should feel that way. That's what father's do and how they feel.

"Yes sir."

"So," he continues, "Jenny says to me, 'Dale, don't you remember asking my dad to lunch once,' and I'll be a son of a bitch, Brian, you move fast."

"Yes sir ... I suppose I do."

"So, answer me. Do you love her? Are you going to protect her and care for her? Are you going to make sure she knows every single day why you chose to love her?"

"Sir, all due respect, but I didn't choose to love her." I watch a frown form on his lips. "I was born loving her. She makes me whole. She makes my son whole. Stella's everything to us, and I would love your blessing, because I need to make her my wife. There is no wanting to marry her. I need her."

My head drops, my chin resting on my chest as I try to get a handle on the situation because I didn't say any of the things I wanted or planned to. I breathe in the scent of coffee brewing, fresh pots filling for the lunch crowd, and realize it's quiet.

The coffeehouse is eerily silent.

I tip my head to the side, my eyes darting around the room where Greg and a handful of patrons have stopped everything they're doing to watch. They all seem absolutely captivated. It's a small town despite the college being here ... everyone who isn't a student knows Dale and has gotten to know me, and they've all figured out Stella and I are together.

I lift my head back up to face him. I'm not sure what I expected, but it wasn't what I found.

Dale lifts a cloth handkerchief to his eyes, wiping the moisture from them to hide his emotions.

"Welcome to the family, officially, Brian. I think Jenny's been praying for this since you asked her to help you find a house up here," he says holding his right hand out for me to shake. "Your mom and dad ... they raised a good man. I'd be honored to have you as my son-in-law."

"I know it's soon, but I just ..." and it sinks in that he just said yes. Holy shit, he said yes. "You said yes?"

"You must really love her hard to have to double check. Yeah, I said yes. That child wouldn't stop talking about you when your parents up and moved all those years ago," Dale reveals. "I know she's close with her mom now, but back then she shared everything with me. Even as a little girl she held a flame for you that no one else could blow out, Brian. Not even that tool, Keith."

He's not telling me anything Stella hasn't told me herself. It's refreshing to hear it from someone else who's so close to her, though. I think it makes her love for me a little more real to know she's held out for so long and that, of all people, her dad's the one to share it with me.

"It took me a long time to find my way back, but I think I got here at the right time," I say to him, worried once the words leave my mouth that we'll end up really talking about Stella's ex-husband. The last thing I want is to feel like I'm comparing myself to him.

Dale studies me for a moment and I can see he's wrestling with something behind eyes the same startling hazel green as Stell's and Steph's.

"You did. I think with everything that girl's been through you saved her from heading down a destructive path. If you hadn't come into her life she would have worked herself into an early grave," he says. "When that ex of hers was out of town or working late, that's all our girl did ... she worked. There was always an excuse to be at the office, or on her computer at home."

"I'm hoping to put the word 'vacation' in her vocabulary soon," I say tapping my fingers on the table. "I don't know when the wedding will be, or even if she wants to do anything big, but I'm hoping we can plan something and Britt and I can take her somewhere for a week or so."

I should be working, but instead Dale and I spend another hour talking about places Stella loved as a kid — Alexandria Bay up in the Thousand Islands, Little Torch Key in Florida and San Diego — to give me ideas for vacationing.

"Y'all want anything to drink?" Greg says coming up to the table. "We're starting to get busy so I figured I'd ask before too many more people come in."

Watching as a few more people stream through the door, Dale and I agree to get together again soon to talk and catch up more.

Standing up from the table, he claps me on the shoulder, getting my attention before I head back behind the counter.

"Before I go, Brian, I just want you to know how much I appreciate you talking to me before putting a ring on Stella's finger. Some guys, well, these days not everyone thinks it's important to do something like that," he says, offering a shy smile as he drops his arm back to his side and meanders toward the door.

I hear some of the patrons snickering as I dance my way back behind the counter and tackle putting orders together as Greg takes them down. We turn the music up in the coffeehouse and eventually the good mood I'm in finds its way to Greg.

I catch him moving to the beat, light on his feet and he, too, seems less stressed than he has in recent weeks.

And I know that's the work of a woman.

Stella

Chapter Twenty-Four

"Chief, I'm glad you could meet with me. I know you're busy," I say shyly walking into police Chief Davis Frank's office. I've never been nervous talking to him before, but today is different. Ulterior motives and all that.

Davis holds his right hand up for me to shake as he quickly shoves three grapes in his mouth with the other hand.

"Sorry, 'bout the food," he says around the fruit in his cheek. "We're short today so I was on patrol all morning to ease the load and just got around to eating lunch. Want some coffee?"

I shake my head no and he motions for me to take a seat. Though I'd love some, I've had the chief's coffee before. I'd rather lick the jailhouse floor, but I wouldn't ever tell him that.

"You've got your notepad and you look scared, Stella. What's this story about again?" He knows. He's just trying to figure me out. We've had years to get into each other's brains. I went to elementary school with his kids, we all grew up together.

Small towns. I wish it were easier to get away from this part of it — the part where my personal and professional lives overlap and the police chief knows I wasn't a good kid every single day of the week. He was the one to find me skinny dipping with Keith all those years ago in the community pool and let me off with a warning as long as I promised to volunteer at the pool instead of break into it at night.

Now I'm here and he knows there's something up my sleeve.

I clear my throat and push aside the memory of a less innocent time in my life.

"It's about abusive relationships," I say matter-of-factly. "Specifically what can be done legally to the abusive party."

Davis' eyes go wide.

"Uh, oh. Well ... there are a few courses of action. Do you have a certain scenario in mind to get an idea of what someone could be charged with?" he asks with a professional tone as he leans back in his office chair, drumming his fingers on the upholstered arm. "Or is this something personal and you need an advocate?"

"Not me chief. Not me." I say, my head held high as I think about the shit my sister has been through. I say it while trying not to feel at fault for how physically battered and emotionally bruised she is. I try not to think about how I've been running into her room every night since she moved in because she's screaming in her sleep ... and I can't make her nightmares stop.

I give him a scenario. I tell him about the stalking, the breaking and entering, the bruises.

It takes less time than I anticipated telling him all of it, but it's easier because I didn't say Steph's name.

I can compartmentalize this today.

Today I'm just doing my job.

"From that scenario, if the victim intended to press charges against his or her aggressor, that person could easily be charged with third-degree assault, stalking and, of course, the breaking and entering would be a criminal trespass charge. However, if someone not the aggressor is injured in the process of trespassing, it becomes burglary, either first- or second-degree," he says. "Menacing could be added to that list. The instance you've related sounds like whoever was the victim here was put into a position of feeling fearful for his or her safety."

I'm writing furiously because I want to be sure I have all this information for Steph.

"Stella?" I look up when I hear Davis say my name. "You okay? I said your name like three times."

"I didn't even hear you. I was trying to get down the information you gave me and must have gotten too focused. What can you tell me about statistics? Out of the number of people who press charges like this, how many people are actually sentenced to jail time?"

Another hour passes and what was left of my notepad is filled with my scratchy shorthand, every space lined with information.

I'm armed with it.

This was initially about Steph, but the "story" I came in to ask questions for will now see the light of day. Campus violence is a thing, domestic abuse happens, rape and assault are prevalent, we're living in a culture where we still try to blame the victim. I feel like I owe it to my sister to write something about these issues.

The conversation is coming to an end and I reach down to put my notes in my bag as I hear the chief clear his throat.

"You know, Stella, if there's anything you want to talk about with me off the record, I'm always here or at home. I've known you since you and Steph were babies and it would kill me if something was going on and I didn't take the chance to offer you my advice or help as a friend as well as a police officer," Davis says as I stand from my chair. "You have my cell number and the house phone hasn't changed. Call me if you need anything."

I wish I could tell him it's just a story, that public safety is just an interest.

"It's just a story," I try the words on for size knowing they don't fit.

"You've never been a very good liar, kiddo. You're an amazing reporter, but you can't lie to save your soul," he says, standing up behind his desk, towering over me. He reaches for his hat, setting it on his head to complete the police officer look, and comes around the desk. "Stell, I've been friends with your daddy since we played high school baseball together. I know you."

Davis reaches out and sets his hands on my shoulders. I'm tall, but the top of my head only comes to his shoulder. I look up at him, feeling fearful that the walls holding back my emotions are starting to crumble under his gaze. He's looking at me like my dad would.

"This is between us. I know you aren't asking questions for yourself and that it's more than just a story right now," he says confidently. "You tell Stephanie to come talk to me when she's ready. If that child is in some kind of trouble, she needs to tell me. I can't protect her if she tries to fix everything herself."

"How do you know it's Steph? It could be a friend of mine ..." I quietly remark.

"Your eyes tell me it's not a friend you're worried about. Not to mention the amount of detail you gave me in that scenario. Did you get pictures of any injuries?"

I stare incredulously, my mouth dropping open.

"She's your baby sister, Stella. You're protective of her." He's right. There is no denying that.

"I did. But she doesn't want to come to you, I asked her to. She's afraid he'll come after her again. That's why I wanted to do a story on what legal ramifications there could be if an assailant had charges brought against them," I spill. The words fall from my mouth before my brain figures out I'm telling him the only part I kept secret through our entire conversation. "If she doesn't know for sure he'll be locked up and she'll be protected, she's not going to come to you, Chief."

"Photos. Get them printed and bring me a copy. Talk to Steph and, if nothing else, we can get together for coffee — the three of us. If she wants to talk to me, she can. It has to be her decision. I can go after this guy, but unless she's willing to press charges, I might not have a leg to stand on."

"Okay. I'll talk to her and let you know," I say, trying to keep myself strong when I just want to fall apart for my sister. "Thank you."

I want to say more, but there isn't any more I can say without feeling depleted and needing a mental health day. I'd have to go home early and Steph would find me curled up on the couch being sad.

I can't be sad when I need to be strong.

Brian

Chapter Twenty-Five

The last few weeks have come and gone way too fast.

Dale and I have gotten together a few times since our talk at the Jumping Bean. We have way more in common than just the girl we love.

He's been helping me in the woodshop behind the house making Britt the ultimate toybox for Christmas. It's a monstrous thing with bookshelves on the ends. We're trying to figure out how to incorporate a coat or hat rack into the design and I think we're close to figuring out the best way to do it.

When Britt and I take off for Tennessee tomorrow, Dale's coming over to stain and polyurethane it so it'll be done when I get back.

Then I can get working on Stella's gift.

I'm hoping another project will keep my mind from drifting down the dangerous path to mercilessly beating Steph's ex-boyfriend to death. It's been hard keeping what I know to myself while working beside her dad, but I promised Stella I wouldn't mention it. Dale would go nuts if he knew what had happened.

So, Stella and I talk about it when no one is around. Just like how we talk about the wedding when we lack an audience. Talks about babies and which house we're going to settle in are just as much a secret as everything else.

Christmas cannot come soon enough.

First we need to get through Thanksgiving.

"Stella! Do you know where my Orange hoodie is?" I yell from my bedroom. I'm packing and have been so busy with the coffeehouse I have hardly had time to put laundry away, or wash it, and I know I caught Stella scrubbing the bathtub the other day. She's usually busier than I am, but somehow found time to bleach the grout in the shower.

I don't know how she does it all.

I don't know how I got this lucky.

"Stell?" I call out again. Nothing.

Sticking my head out the bedroom door, I can hear her in Britt's room.

Walking into his room I see her, wearing my hoodie and sorting through clothes in his dresser to pack. She's so good at this.

"You know," I say, leaning against the doorframe to watch her, "if you want an SU sweatshirt, I could just get you your own."

Without missing a beat or looking up from the dresser, she says, "Why? I have this one."

"I love you, Stella."

"I love you, too, Bri. What's the matter?" she asks, stopping her hunt for matching socks to look at me. "You look sad."

"Just worried. About Steph, about bringing Tommy home with me, about us, the business, Greg and Caryn ... I feel like all I do is worry these last couple of weeks."

And she comes to me, wrapping me up in her arms, and she holds me in the doorway of our son's room. I breathe her in.

"Steph will be okay. She promised me she'd talk to Davis, but wants to get through the holiday. She says she hasn't seen Darren since the night he attacked her at the apartment, but I know he's tried contacting her," she says.

She won't answer when he calls, I know, but the fact he's still trying to talk to her pisses me off. Maybe it'll just be more evidence against him when she talks to the police. I hope.

"As for Tommy," Stella continues, "the sooner he's here, the more time we can have together and with Britt. I think Tom's the solution to your worries about us, Greg and Caryn, and the business."

"You really think so?"

"Yes. Once he's here and knows what he's doing with the business — the baking and brewing and basking in college girl glory — and figures out what he might want to do as far as marketing for you and Greg, you won't have to always be focused on the coffeehouse. We might even get a real date again soon," she says, smiling up at me.

I brush the hair from her forehead and kiss her there. There's still so much to do to get ready for the drive south, but I just want to get wrapped up in her body and never let go.

"I think we need to have that date as soon as I get back from seeing my parents," I say leaning down to capture her bottom lip between my teeth. She responds, sighing into my kiss, her body relaxing into mine. "Maybe sooner."

"If we do sooner, you'll never get packed in time to leave in the morning," she says turning back to the dresser. "You'll only be there until Sunday and then you'll be coming home. It's not that long apart. Even still,

I'm packing enough clothes to get him through a full week so your mom doesn't have to do laundry. Why are you looking at me like that?"

Spellbound by how amazing she is, Stella caught me staring at her again. It happens a lot. It's because she's more than I ever felt I deserved. She's. More.

"I don't know what you're talking about, crazy girl." I flash a wicked grin in her direction and turn, walking back down the hall to find myself a different sweatshirt to pack for my trip.

***

"Here's the last bag," she says handing me Britt's backpack filled with coloring books, crayons and snacks for the drive. "And one for you, too."

I open the bag and see crackers, a bottle of water and what looks like homemade cookies. I do the math in my head and figure if it's four in the morning on Wednesday now ... these will last until I make it to Buffalo.

"I hid extra cookies in the cooler in back for when you stop," she says, reading my mind and laughing. "Don't need you in a food coma while on the highway, cowboy."

Shaking her head, she wanders back into the house.

I take time to arrange everything in the back of the Tahoe. If I don't do it now, I won't know if I have room for Tommy's stuff on the trip back. It's still hard to believe my baby brother is going to move up to New York with me. It's even harder to believe we're going to be living together, but it'll be good for us. It'll be better for Mama to have him out of her hair.

My phone rings in my back pocket.

"Mama, why are you even awake right now?" I say as soon as the call connects.

"Because I wanted to tell you to drive careful and I love you before you hit the road," she responds. I hear a mug clunk the top of the wooden table in her kitchen. "I had to get up anyway, so I figured I would call now before it got too late."

I tuck the phone between my shoulder and ear, talking and organizing. She's happy Tom's coming home with me, but still hasn't let on what the problem was that started the ball rolling. Mama's keeping those cards close to her vest.

Stella opens the front door and walks out carrying a still sleeping Britt as I'm closing the back of the Tahoe.

"Hey, Mama, I'm going to let you go. I'm going to get Britt in the truck and we'll be on the road soon. I should be to your house by early evening," I say as Stella walks up to the car. Britt might be small, but when he's sleeping it's like carrying wet sandbags and I can tell he's already feeling too heavy for her. "Tell Tommy to chill some of his homemade apple pie moonshine. I'll have a drink with him tonight so we can talk."

Hanging up, Stella eyes me.

"Moonshine, huh? Better bring some of that home for me to try." She hands Britt over and I lift him the rest of the way into his seat, strapping him in for the ride. Someday this child might be big enough to not need the five-point harness.

"It's good stuff, but drinking too much of it can make your clothes fall off," I joke climbing out of the truck.

"And here I thought only tequila did that," she jests in kind. God, I love this woman.

I pull her to me and hold on for dear life.

It's only a few days.

It's less than a week and then we'll be back home with her.

The sky is still dark above us, but starting to lighten up. I'll be driving away from the sun for a little while.

Stella climbs up to give Britt a kiss before closing his door. I hear her whisper to him, "I love you. Be good for Daddy."

My heart catches in my throat.

I want to cry.

I swallow it down, put on a smile and walk around to the driver's side.

"The house is all locked up. I've got to get back to the other house so I can shower and get some stuff done around there," Stella says coming around the back of the truck. "I figured I'd stop down to the coffeehouse early and see if there's anything Greg needs before going to the office."

"I know you. You have a motive and your motive is free coffee in exchange for helping him." I kiss her forehead. "Make sure you take a couple extra baked whatevers for your stash at the office."

"I think I can handle that." She smiles up at me, her tired eyes staring into mine. "Call me when you get to your parent's?"

"Absolutely. Probably even while on the road. You have a meeting tonight?"

"No doubt. Starts at seven."

"I'll call well before then. We should hit Nashville by dinner."

To Have

I wrap her up one more time, my body at home against hers, and I have to force myself to let go. One more long kiss and I'm in the truck, me and my boy heading toward the only other real home we've ever known.

M.L. Pennock

Stella

Chapter Twenty-Six

I throw my purse and laptop on the dining room table on my way through the house.

Food. I need food, I think making a bee-line for the kitchen.

The meeting I covered tonight ran late and the story I wrote sounds like shit. Caryn was just leaving as I walked into the newsroom and our conversation consisted of nearly indistinguishable grunts that would have made our boyfriends proud.

Meetings the night before Thanksgiving should be outlawed. I didn't get back in the truck to come home until close to midnight and I haven't eaten a meal since ... I just won't think about when the last actual meal was.

My head is in the fridge when I hear the back door open.

"Mom? What are you doing here at," I glance at the clock, "midnight-thirty?"

I take a bite off the brick of cheese in my hand and stare at my mother, chewing but not really tasting.

"Steph called my cell and when I answered she wasn't there. I tried calling her back and no answer. I've been trying to call her for the last half hour," she says, pausing to breathe. She looks half frantic. My mom's not the frantic type. She's calm. She's the eye of the storm. "Finally I figured I'd just come here and see what she needed. She's not home from campus yet?"

Weird. Mom's acting weird.

"I just walked in, literally five minutes before you did, Mom. I haven't seen Steph since this morning." I tell her how I saw Brian and Britt off when they left for Tennessee and then came home. "We went down to the coffee shop together this morning and helped Greg since Bri's gone, but the last I saw her she was headed to campus and I was on my way to the office. Haven't even talked to her since noonish."

Mom takes a seat at the counter and sets her phone down. She looks tired. When did my mom start looking this tired?

"I've been worried about her. Davis stopped by last week and said you'd been in to talk to him for a story," she says, and I know he slipped.

"Mom ..."

"Don't say a thing, Stella. I know she's your sister and you love her, but you should have come to me if she was in trouble," she says holding her hand up so I don't interrupt.

I feel like a little girl. I'm in my thirties and getting scolded by my mom. This is the least awesome moment of my life.

"Davis didn't go into detail, but I've known him a long time, so I know something is up. He asked how Steph was and mentioned he'd visited with the two of you after that interview you did," she says pointedly.

She opens her mouth to say more, probably figuratively tear me a new asshole some more, when I feel the cold chill creep up my spine. And my phone starts ringing in my purse.

"No. No, no, no. Mom, don't," I say to her, watching the color drain from her face as I back toward to doorway separating the kitchen and dining room. "It's Steph's number, give me a sec."

I answer with a half breathless, "Hey!" when I hear a siren rip through the phone line.

My blood runs cold.

"Steph?"

"Stella Barbieri? This is Officer Max Wyatt."

I can't breathe.

"Max? Where's Stephanie? What's happened?" I ask, but I know. I already know. I look toward the kitchen and see my mother's outline in the doorway, her hand up to her mouth as she creeps into the dining room. I hear the radio in Max's cruiser, the dispatcher's voice, and I know something is irrevocably wrong.

I watch Mom as she crosses to me and see her tough exterior break more.

"Ms. Barbieri, your sister was attacked on campus this evening. I'm following the ambulance —"

"I'll meet you there. Call your chief," I say grabbing my coat. "Mom, get in the truck. Call Daddy. Max, if you get there before me, you don't leave my sister's side. Do you hear me?"

I feel like I'm yelling at him. I don't care. I'll yell all I want.

"Yes, ma'am," he responds and then is quiet, but I know he's still on the line. I can still hear the crackle of the radio. "Stella, I got there in time. I just want you to know, she was beaten pretty badly. I want you to be prepared."

I don't know why he sounds like he owes me something, owes me these words and kindness. I don't know anything right now other than to keep moving.

Out the front door.

Into the truck.

Onto the road.

And into the night.

***

"Jenny? Jenny?" I hear my dad yelling for her as he runs through the emergency room doors seconds before he sees us. "Where is she? What happened?"

He looks like a wild animal, caged and scared, as he looks around the room. He'd been sound asleep when Mom called from the truck and it took the entire drive here to get him to stop asking questions. We didn't have the answers to give.

"Dale, she's okay, but she's hurt," Davis says, walking up to my dad as he takes in the scene — Mom and I sit unmoving, staring at the doors they took Steph through as the shock starts to hit and reality comes crashing down around my mom. I can't let it get me, too.

I hear Davis' voice. It's low and rumbly as he tells Daddy what we know so far.

Steph was working late in the library on campus. She says she left when the library closed and started walking back across campus to her car.

In the shadows from one of the buildings, she heard someone say her name and stopped.

He left her lying on the ground.

Colton found her covered in blood and unconscious.

"She has a broken leg and we suspect a couple fractured ribs, Dale, but they just got her back there not too long before you got here," Davis says, his hand on Dad's shoulder as they stand eye-to-eye, friend-to-friend. "If it weren't for the Chauncey boy, we may not have even gotten a call yet. That campus is deserted for break."

Davis doesn't tell Daddy the worst part. The part about how the physical wounds will heal, but the emotional wreckage that's been left behind may never go away, not completely.

"I have an officer back there with her. He was the first to respond to the call and will stay with her until they get her stable," he says, moving easily from friend to police chief mode. "Let's go grab a coffee for you and Jenny. It's going to be a long night."

He doesn't tell him that Steph's panties were torn from her body. He doesn't give those details.

Davis doesn't even know those details yet.

Max told me. Max found her lying on the ground, her head in Colt's lap as he talked to her, trying to get her to respond to him, to give him a name or a description.

Mom is sitting on my left. I reach out my right hand and pull Colton to me as he starts weeping into his hands again, the blood still drying on his jeans where Steph's head lay while they waited for the ambulance.

My sister's best friend, her other confidant, the only boy who's never been a love interest for her, now has to prepare for a war on the emotional battlefield right beside her.

"If I'd known that guy was violent with her ..." Colton starts saying again. "Stella, I didn't know. I would never have let her walk alone if I thought she was in danger."

"Don't think about the 'what ifs,' Colt. Just don't. They'll chew you up and spit you out," I say rubbing his back. "I knew, we'd talked to the chief, she wasn't ready to press charges. Now she doesn't get a choice because it's been taken out of her control. Darren Judson's going to find himself in prison if he knows what's good for him."

I'm thankful Colton was there; I feel blessed Max Wyatt was the first to respond.

The "what ifs," the same ones I don't want Colt to think about, those are going to consume me.

What if I'd forced her to press charges, pulled the Big Sister card like I did when we were kids?

Would he have come after her anyway? Would he have found a way to hurt her? Or would he have already been sitting in a cell?

We know next to nothing about this person.

But I do know one thing for certain. I want him to pay for this with his life.

Dad walks up and hands Mom a paper cup filled with hospital grade coffee. He sits down in the hard, uncomfortable chair next to her, taking her hand in his as he does. These two people, my parents, they are a sign of strength and I hope that strength is enough to get us through whatever will come at our family now.

I watch for a moment as Mom lays her head on my dad's shoulder, closing her eyes and letting some of that strength seep out around the edges. He gently kisses her hair, whispering something for her ears only while massaging his thumb across her hand. And despite it all, she smiles.

He makes her smile in the face of fear and the unknown.

I'd be envious of their love if I didn't know I had that kind of connection with Brian. I let my mind wander, thinking about how I need to call him, but know I'll wait until I've seen Steph and know the details.

I'm absentmindedly rubbing Colt's back, thinking of all the ways I would torture and dismember my sister's stalker, when Max comes walking out with the ER doctor, a woman I'm not familiar with. The only thing that matters to me is if she's been able to fix my sister.

We've been here for hours, the minutes ticking by so slowly, and now we'll get some answers.

"Stephanie's stable, but understandably shaken. The break in her leg was fairly clean so we were able to set and cast it without surgery. She had some deep lacerations that we've stitched up and," she stops, looking at my parents, one standing on either side of me, before continuing, "we're running a rape kit."

"Rape?" My dad's voice waivers. "He ... someone forced himself on my baby girl?"

I watch his hands clench, rage flashing in his eyes as the doctor continues telling us the extent to Steph's injuries.

I try not to hear the word "trauma." I wish I could ignore the phrase "sexual assault."

I can't, so I slip away without notice, allowing my parents room to hold one another — Dad's fury barely contained, Mom's anger bubbling over.

"Max? How is she, really?" I ask, daring to glance in my parent's direction as Davis joins them, carrying himself like the cop he is instead of the family friend he's always been.

I don't want a medical answer. I need the truth and for some reason I feel Max will give me that.

"She's hysterical. They sedated her a while ago so they could check her over and do what they needed to. We're going to have to get an official statement from her once she's awake," he says, removing his cap and rubbing the back of his head with the same hand. His other hand rests at his hip and for the first time since I met him, the day he caught Brian and I on that back road, I see how much of a baby he still is.

"I'm sorry I called you on her phone, but it felt like this one was personal once I found out who she was. If the boy she was with hadn't said her last name, I wouldn't have known until we were here that she's your sister," he says apologetically.

"You're right, it is personal," I say, not even knowing what I mean by that. I clear my throat, trying to remain firmly beneath the cloud of ambiguity — show no emotion, not yet — and ask him if I can go see her. "I need to see for myself she's okay, Max."

Placing the cap back on his head, he takes my elbow and without another word leads me toward the double doors and my sister. I see Davis watching us, but instead of stopping me, he nods his head and continues listening as the doctor talks to my parents.

***

Max and I are silent as he leads me back to where Steph is. They plan to admit her at least for the night and move her to a room until they can be sure the extent of her injuries aren't more than what they appear to be and there isn't swelling where swelling shouldn't be.

It's medical terminology I can't even fathom right now.

Max holds a curtain back for me and I walk through, seeing my baby sister for the first time since yesterday morning ... but this is a horrible nightmarish version of my Stephie, and the strength I've exuded from the moment I answered the phone shatters.

"Oh God, oh Stephanie," I whisper, but it feels like I'm screaming.

I look at Max, and he turns his head as the first tears fall from his eyes, matching mine drop for drop. Placing my hand on his shoulder, I step further into the room as he lets the curtain fall, remaining outside — my sister's guardian on what feels like the coldest night of the year.

And suddenly I'm alone, with the beeping of a heart monitor and the steady rise and fall of Stephanie's chest as she sleeps.

Somewhere beneath the purple bruises lies my sister. Hidden under the sutures on her cheek and blood caked in her hair is the beautiful girl I grew up with side-by-side.

Pulling up a chair, I sit next to the gurney she's on and look her over. I make a mental note of every visible section of skin while going over the "what ifs" in my head again.

Steph's hand is laying on top of the thin sheet covering her good leg, and I touch it tenderly, afraid everything on her hurts and I don't want to add to her pain.

It doesn't matter that she's sedated.

All I want is to take her hurt away.

"You can't catch me! You can't catch me!" I yell running circles around Steph.

I'm eight; she's four.

We're in our grandmother's backyard playing. It's spring and almost all of the snow has melted except a few piles left over from the snowmen we built after the last good storm.

I keep running faster and faster until she's spinning instead of chasing me. Giggling, I taunt her again.

"You can't keep up because you're a baby still and I'm super fast," I call out.

Steph stops spinning and regains her balance while I keep circling her. Once she has her bearings back, she runs full force toward me like she's going to tackle me.

She's going to take me down. We roughhouse even though Mommy doesn't like us to, and I get ready for Steph to barrel into me.

Neither of us sees the pile of ice and snow until Steph's foot catches on it and she tumbles face first into the hard ground, scraping her chin and splitting her bottom lip.

We don't see the big kids in the neighbor's yard laughing at us instead of helping.

But I see her hurt.

And I never want to be the reason my Stephie is hurt again.

"Stella?" I hear Max's voice on the other side of the curtain, beyond the veil to my childhood memories. Wiping the tears from my cheeks, I respond enough so he knows I heard him. "I'm going to go out and talk to my chief. Will you be okay in here until I get back?"

"Yeah, we'll be fine. I'm just ... you go ahead. Let my parents know I'm back here, though? Please?" I ask, though it's not part of Max's job to be my personal messenger.

I hear him walk away and allow myself to truly look at Steph.

Holding her hand, I can't help but feel responsible. I should have pushed harder to keep her safe. I should have tried harder to make sure someone was with her if she was going to be on campus late.

"I'm not a baby, Stell, you don't have to watch me sleep," her voice cracks through the beeping.

Her eyes are still closed, but I smile.

"How about you not be a smartass and let me love you for a few minutes," I say, emotion thick in my throat, before letting the quiet settle back over us. "We're going to make sure he gets what he deserves, Steph."

"I know, Stella. I know."

Steph tries to sigh. She tries. But it hurts.

"What time is it?" she asks, finally opening her eyes a little against the dim light. "I know they knocked me out. How long have I been sleeping?"

"Just a few hours. How's the pain?"

She tries to scoot up in the bed. I try to help her.

"Everything hurts, Stell," and she looks at me with tears in her eyes. "Everything."

I crawl up on the gurney or bed or whatever the hell this thing is my sister is lying on and I pull her carefully into my arms.

"Everything. He's on me everywhere," she sobs into my chest and I don't care so much if I hurt her already wounded body because the one part of her I wish I could heal can't be hugged.

Brian

Chapter Twenty-Seven

Tommy and I stayed up way too late drinking.

It feels like someone kicked me in the head with a steel toed boot.

"Tommy, turn off the sun," I grunt, throwing my arm over my face. I grab for the covers with my other hand but come up empty handed.

"T, stop blowing on my face," I mumble feeling a warm breeze lift the short hairs lying across my forehead. I swat at him only for a cold nose to get shoved in my ear.

Sitting up faster than I should have, I scoot across the bed. Not a bed. This is not a bed.

The fuck happened last night? I wonder, grabbing my head as I feel my stomach roll and twist, the first waves of nausea hitting me.

I'm still clutching my head when I see two small brown paws stop between my legs. My bare legs. I have no pants on. Why do I have no pants on?

That tiny cold nose sniffs at my face, then plants a puppy kiss on my lips and I don't know if I want to treasure the puppy breath smell or vomit all over it. I reach up and push the pup away, petting him — her? No, that's a penis — as I move him to my side.

"You're up," Tommy yells reaching the top of the stairs and I glare at him as he starts laughing at me. "Just like old times, eh, brother? Next time you challenge me, make sure you haven't left your tolerance up north."

"Why am I naked in the loft? And whose dog is that?" I ask, swallowing. Correction, trying to swallow. Someone just put me out of my misery.

"Well, since you asked, you got crazy drunk on that apple pie moonshine and insisted your jeans were killing your manhood. Not sure what that's about. Then there was some ranting about how Stella was going to be really ticked that you were running around in just your boots and boxers," Tommy says, barely containing his laughter. "And then you decided you wanted to get Britt a puppy. So we went and bought a puppy from the farm up the road."

"I got hammered and bought my kid a dog? Who does that?" My headache suddenly seems like the least of my worries.

Tommy covers his mouth in an attempt to hide his shit-eating grin. "Apparently you do, dumbass. You named him Whiskey Sour," he says tossing my jeans to me. "Get dressed. Mama's got bacon on."

***

We got here in time for dinner last night. Britt was in all his glory running around the garage with my dad and helping Mama with Thanksgiving dinner prep after we cleaned up. Something tells me his specialty is going to be apple pies instead of muffins and biscotti, but I could be wrong.

Tommy and I walk through the mudroom to the kitchen, the smell of bacon grease and coffee making their way to my brain.

"Found your glasses by the fire pit. You really need to be more careful, Brian," Mama says handing them to me with a look of disdain. "You boys. You never learn with that homemade stuff do you? You're lucky Britton was asleep when you really tied into it. He doesn't need to be around that."

"Yes, Mama," Tommy and I say simultaneously.

"Now that we've had our morning after verbal lashing, may we please have coffee and food? Mama, I need food so bad."

I sound like a petulant child begging for a handout, but if I don't get something into my stomach soon to soak up whatever is left of the alcohol I'll be wrecked for the rest of the day.

"Mama, I need food," Tommy says mocking me. Some things just don't change.

So, I slap him in the back of the head and pull on my big boy pants.

"Never mind, Ma, I can get it," I say walking over and opening the cupboard for a coffee mug. "I'm fully capable of getting my own coffee, like a man. Here, T, let me get you one, too."

Rubbing the back of his head, I hear Tommy call me an asshole under his breath and the sound of Mama's hand upside his head right after. I smile to myself as I pour two mugs of coffee.

Just like old times, indeed.

"Watch your mouth, Thomas, you're still in my house."

"Yes, ma'am."

I'm starting to see why Tommy's moving north with me.

"And Brian, watch yourself, too. I can just as soon reach out and smack you, as well. Don't think I won't," she says, grabbing a laundry basket filled with folded clothes from the table and leaving the room.

I hand Tommy his coffee and lean back against the counter, staring at him while I sip from my mug and eat slices of bacon from the plate next to the stove. No point dirtying dishes.

"Spill. Why's Mama so pissed at you?" I have no idea if we talked about this last night. I don't remember.

"According to everyone in town, and all their friends, I'm not living up to my potential, whatever the hell that means," he says looking into his cup like it'll have all the answers to the universe within its murky contents. "I don't even know where to start."

"The beginning works," I say reaching for another piece of bacon as I wait for him to gather his thoughts.

It takes a few beats, but he finally shrugs and gives in.

"I've always been in your shadow or riding on your coattails," he says not looking at me. "The girls loved me in high school because I was your baby brother. The teachers loved me because I got good grades because you helped me. But, college was hard because you weren't there with me."

I watch him mull over everything he's just said and wonder if Tommy has ever said this to our parents. If he did, Mama wouldn't be so apt to call me for help.

"Since college it's just been hard finding things to do with my degree. It should be easy. Marketing. I just don't want to live in a corporate world. I went to school with uptight assholes who were interested in one thing — money — and that's not why I wanted to get my degree in it," he says, rubbing his hand across his stubbled cheek. "I don't know, Bri. I want to help the little guy."

I study him closely.

My brother's a man now and I've been blind to that for a while.

But he's a lost man.

"So, you don't want corporate America. You're coming to New York with me, that's been decided, and you know Greg and I could use some help with the marketing end of the business," I say, watching him nod his head in silent agreement. "So you start out with us, helping us, and once you get the word out you start your own business doing marketing for other businesses in the area. You have to start small, but with your background and mine and Greg's in entrepreneurship you'll be fine."

"You sure this'll work?" He questions me with fear in his eyes. He's such a homebody, more of a mama's boy than me, but he can do this.

"All you have to do is believe in yourself. Having a beautiful woman to bounce ideas off of helps, too. We'll find you one of those when we get to college town," I say, clapping him on the shoulder and walking out of the room to wake Britt up for breakfast.

I'm heading up the stairs when I hear the back door open again and Tommy whistle.

Whiskey comes barreling into the house and the sound of puppy nails sliding across the kitchen floor as he tries to gain traction makes me cringe. I try not to let my mind wander to what that dog just did to the hardwood floors I helped Dad refinish before I left for college.

Flattening myself against the railing so I don't spill my coffee, Whiskey runs as quickly as he can up the stairs. Or hops. It's more like he's hopping because he's still small.

Shaking my head I follow him up to Britt's room at the top of the stairs and find him licking Britton's face as the boy squirms underneath the covers trying to get away.

"Okay, okay, that's enough, pup. Get down," I say picking him up, cradling him like a football that's sprouted a head, tail, and legs that seem to keep running though there's nowhere to go.

"Dad." He says it with a lilt in his voice and I'm not too sure what's coming next, so I just set the puppy back on the bed.

"Right. Consider this an early Christmas present. Uncle Tommy and I got him last night ... uh, his name's Whiskey Sour," I say shyly, because there is no other way to tell your kid his dog is named after a chick drink. "Time to get up and start the day, so get dressed and I'll meet you two downstairs."

Someday my son's going to grow up and ask me about this exchange and I know for a fact I'm going to blame Tommy. I walk out of the room taking another sip of my coffee and try to figure out how the hell I'm going to explain this one to Stella.

Mama's standing over the sink when I get back downstairs.

Sidling up next to her, I set my mug down and reach into the sink to grab a potato. We stand beside one another silently scrubbing until the silence hurts more than one of her smacks to the skull.

"You know, that boy did nothing but talk about Stella and Stephanie last night when he was helping me with pies," she says to alleviate the quiet. "I was worried about you leaving, about him not being near family, but I have to admit I was wrong to fret over it. When's the wedding?"

"What wed— okay, I know I didn't tell you, but," I say looking at the grin on Mama's face. "I just wanted to talk to Dale first. It was important, you know?"

"Oh, I know, sweetie. I know. Jenny told me you'd asked Dale to lunch and we had a good laugh over it," she says, giggling.

My mom is giggling.

At my expense.

My head starts throbbing again. Must have more coffee.

Pouring another mug, I tell her no one knows yet that we're planning to get married, at least no one outside of Dale, Jenny and, apparently, my mom. And she breaks into hysterics.

"You're serious, baby? You think no one knows?" She's looking at me in all seriousness, trying desperately to hide the smile though her eyes are shimmering with glee. "Let me tell you a little something I've known since you were just a little boy, about your Britt's age. That child up north?"

Mama looks at me as she scrubs another potato while I lean on the counter drinking my coffee. I wait. I know she isn't done.

"She's your soul mate, Brian. You should've heard the way her Nana would go on about the two of you. I think it broke her heart as much as yours and Stella's when we left," she says, a sadness in her eyes I can't place. A flicker of grief and it's gone. "How long have y'all officially been seeing one another?"

It's only been a couple months. It doesn't feel like I should be this consumed by Stella, but I am. I tell Mama the whole story — from the day I sat down across from her to the night she showed up in the rain to the conversation on the side of the road.

Never once does her expression change. She doesn't interrupt me. She lets me talk.

It feels good to share this with her.

"The thing is, she doesn't just love me, Ma. She's as much in love with Britt as she is with me. I'm thinking about asking her if she'd be willing to adopt him when we get married," I say, swallowing the last of my coffee. "Emily gave up her rights. I don't think I'd even need to get her involved."

"You, my boy, do whatever you need to do to make your family whole," Mama says as she gets up on her tip-toes and plants a kiss on my cheek. "And don't hesitate to start working on giving me and Jenny more grandbabies. We aren't getting any younger and want plenty of time to spoil them rotten."

I feel my cheeks heat and nod at Mama with a simple "Yes ma'am" but nothing more as I feel my phone vibrate in my back pocket.

"Tell your bride-to-be I said hello and we'll be up for Christmas," Mama says as I answer the phone and she waves me away from the counter.

***

The call connects as I step into the living room.

"Hey beautiful, I was just talking about you," I say, hearing the smile in my words. "What are you up to this morning?"

I hear the silence from Stella and the oven door open behind me as Mama slides the turkey in.

In the quiet, something comes to life on her end of the phone, something that sounds like a doctor being paged over a loudspeaker.

"Stell, what's the matter?" I ask as my heart starts pounding in my chest.

"It's Steph," she says, drawing in a deep breath I can hear from more than seven hundred miles away. "She was attacked on campus last night. We've been at the hospital since a little after midnight."

"I'm coming home," I say as I start for the stairs so I can grab our bags. "I'll start driving now."

"Brian, slow down. She's okay, I promise. Mom, Dad, and I have been with her since Max was able to sneak me in while she was still sedated," she says, rambling like the information can't help but get out of her head.

"Who's Max?" I ask, stopping mid-stride across the room on my way to the stairs. "Stella. Who is Max?"

"The police officer who was the first on the scene, the same one who stopped when we were on that back road," she spits out. "He's been with us since the ambulance brought her in."

Mama comes around the corner, concern drawn on her brow and I know all she heard was my end of the conversation — me asking my fiancée about another man — so I quickly try to explain.

"Mama, Steph's in the hospital. Max is the cop. I'll explain everything before I leave," I say to her before turning my attention back to Stella. "How bad? What did he do to her?"

I try to control my temper as Stella tells me the details she knows, the only thing that keeps me from punching the wall is when she says Steph's underwear were torn off but the guy didn't have a chance to touch her much after that. It's the "much" I worry about. It's the "much" that keeps my anger on a hair-trigger.

"Tell me he didn't rape her, Stella." I need to hear her say it.

"Not that we are aware of. She was unconscious when Colt found her, and just coming to when Max got there." Pause. "The doctor who examined her ran some tests and said there wasn't evidence of trauma there. ... But does it even matter? She's traumatized everywhere else."

Letting her strength falter and fall, she allows herself to cry. I imagine her sitting in the hospital, holding her phone to her ear ... weeping. And I'm not there.

I can't handle this.

"Stella, I'll fly home and be there in a few hours. Tommy can bring Britt home in the truck," I say moving toward the stairs again.

I hear her sniffle and pull in a ragged breath.

"Baby, I can't ask you to do that. They're going to release her later today after she talks to Davis and Max again. I can't ask you to ruin your time with your parents when there's literally nothing you can do here where this is concerned," she says, putting up those walls again.

"I can take the time to hunt him down and kill him. I can make sure he never touches her again. I could do that," I say, the words seething and venomous. "Can't I come home and at least do that?"

She snickers. Stella's laugh cuts through the line straight to my heart.

"I love you. And yes, you could, but I wouldn't advise it," she says softly. "Davis told my parents they had a lead on him and the state police are involved now. I don't think he's going to get too far."

"Was Steph able to identify him?"

Stella's confidence takes over as she gives me more details from the nightmare her sister's been though today. "He apparently tried talking to her before he attacked her. She knows it was him, and has given the police all his information."

I take a deep breath, noticing Mama standing at the doorway again, as I hear puppy paws start down the stairs and Britt's footsteps right after.

"He wasn't using his real name when he started seeing her and he's wanted for a lot of the same charges in another state, Ohio I think," Stella continues. "Only thing is, the last woman he did this to didn't survive."

She says the last part so quietly I hope I heard her wrong until she continues, saying, "Steph's guardian angel got a real workout with this one. We could have been planning a funeral, instead we just need to help her with a cast and bruises and a broken spirit."

"Stell." I say her name like she's the air I need to breathe. "Please, don't tell me not to come home. I need to see you and Steph and your parents. I need to see for myself she's okay."

Standing in my parents' dining room, I let the tears begin to fall while my son runs through with his new puppy to play outside and my mom catches me in her arms, taking the phone from me on my way down.

"Stella, honey, he'll be home tomorrow. I'm going to feed him and put him to bed," I hear Mama say and then pause. "It doesn't matter if she's okay or not, he's not going to believe until he sees. You know how he is. Is your mama close by? Put her on and you go get yourself something to eat."

Ma leaves me sitting in the middle of the room. She takes my phone and I hear her saying soothing words to Jenny as she goes back into the kitchen.

Just like that, Mama makes everything okay and puts things in motion.

Burying my face in my hands, I let everything out. The fear for Stephanie's safety I've been holding in. The anger that anyone would hurt her in the first place. The devastation knowing I wasn't able to do anything to prevent this from happening.

I'm grateful she wasn't more seriously injured.

I hate that we couldn't protect her.

I cry it all out, the release working through my body like a serum.

Taking a deep breath, feeling the calm wash over me, I sit back on my heels and open my eyes.

Whiskey.

Sitting obediently in front of me, head cocked to one side, the pup stares back at me before bending his little body down and nudging my hand.

"Maybe ... maybe you'll be able to help her survive this," I say, picking his little body up to nuzzle under his chin and hoping Britt thinks sharing his Whiskey with Steph is as good an idea as I do. He nips at my nose and licks my face. "I think she'd love the hell out of you."

***

After getting the phone back from Mama, I sent Stella a text letting her know Tommy and I would head out first thing in the morning and be home for a late dinner if she was up for eating with us.

I didn't tell her about the puppy.

I didn't mention the nearly naked moonshine escapade.

I did remember to tell her I love her.

Twice.

Despite the absolutely shitty terms Tommy, Britt, and I are leaving Tennessee on, we make our way through dinner and dessert thankful we've been able to share the holiday together.

"So when is the wedding?" Dad asks as he pulls a second piece of pumpkin pie onto his plate.

I just stare at him. Tommy starts laughing at me and Mr. and Mrs. Blumenthal from the ranch down the road wait for my answer.

Mama really wasn't joking when she asked me if I seriously thought no one knew.

"Damn it, you guys all know?"

"Dude, you've been head over heels over that girl since we were kids. Yeah. We know." Tommy's such a jackass.

I look at Britton sitting next to me as he sneaks Whiskey a piece of pie crust under the table.

"Don't feed him scraps, Britt. We don't want him thinking he can beg at the table," I say, watching as he sneaks another piece of crust to the dog. "So, did you know, too?"

"Know what?" he looks up at me and asks innocently. "That Stella's going to be my mommy? I knew that."

And he goes right back to feeding the puppy his crust like all of this is totally normal while every adult at the table but me bursts into laughter.

"Yeah, that." Well, shit.

"Are we going to live at her house or our house? Uncle T should live at our house. I like Stella's better. It has a secret stairway where we could have epic lightsaber battles. When can I start calling her mom? What does epic mean?"

My eyes go wide because he hasn't talked this much all at once since we got to Nashville. It throws everyone into another fit of laughter.

"I have no idea. You have to talk to her about calling her mom. Epic means something is impressive, but a long time ago before the word was ruined by people calling everything from kick-flips to buildings 'epic' it was used in reference to long poems," I rattle off, answering all of his questions. "Like, really long poems. About real epic battles."

This kid.

I take another bite of apple pie.

"We haven't set a date for the wedding. I don't know if she wants to do anything big. We only started talking about it a few weeks ago and I really don't know who all up there knows about it yet, even though it seems the entire Volunteer State is aware of my pending nuptials," I say, shooting my mom a withering stare.

"You can't blame me for this one, Brian. Your Daddy gets on that computer and emails back and forth with Dale darn near every day," Mama points at Dad. "It's his fault."

The evening continues on with much of the same until I force Britt to get a bath, and wreck his entire night by not allowing Whiskey in the tub with him.

A sadness overwhelms him when I tuck him into bed and as much as I would love for him to have more time with my parents, I don't want to make that drive home without him.

I try to ease the pain, the homesick feeling he's grappling with before we even leave. "Grandma and Gramps are coming to New York for Christmas. I don't know how long they'll be there, but it's only a few weeks away, Bud."

I rub my thumb over his forehead. It's been a busy day and harder than I hope he ever has to know. It was hard enough trying to tell him we're heading back to New York early, but then I lied to him to protect him from the truth of Steph's situation.

"I know," he says through a yawn as Whiskey curls up on the pillow beside him. "Can I see Stephie when we get home?"

He knew something was wrong when he came in from playing in the yard and was looking for the puppy. He saw me in the dining room, half fallen apart and trying to put my pieces back together so I could function until we leave.

Britt's going to see her and think she was in an accident. That's what we told him. Steph had an accident. He's five. He may just assume a car accident. I won't correct him. It was easier to explain to him this way than trying to put into kid terms what really happened.

"Yeah, kiddo, we'll go see her when we get home. Stella said she'd be home tonight. Maybe we can get her some flowers," I suggest.

He contemplates it, mulling it over like the decision would change the course of history. "No. Not flowers, Dad. Steph needs chocolate."

"You got it, little man. Chocolate it is. Get some sleep."

I kiss his forehead, make sure his blankets are secure, give Whiskey a pat on the head and text Greg on my way back downstairs.

Me: I need you to save me at least a half-dozen chocolate chip chocolate muffins tomorrow. They're for Stephanie.

Greg: You got it man. I'll drop them at your house so you don't have to come to the shop. How's she feeling? Caryn told me.

Me: Stella said she's acting tough. Waiting for it to really hit. Thanks for the muffins. Should be back tomorrow around dinner.

Greg: Give your Ma my love. I know she must miss me.

Me: Absolutely. You're her favorite non-son.

Slipping my phone back into my pocket, I step into the kitchen ready to wash dishes and talk business with Tommy. Anything to get my mind off New York and the fallout that waits for me up north.

Stella

Chapter Twenty-Eight

Thanksgiving

"Daddy, she can come home with me," I tell him, trying desperately to put my foot down.

Instead it feels like I'm throwing a tantrum. I'm a five-year-old all over again not getting the toy I wanted at the store.

"And what if he shows up to finish what he started? What then?" He's obstinate. He's hardheaded.

He's like his mother.

And I'm just like both of them.

"You're going to fight with me and you aren't going to win. Dad, she's a grown woman. I had to threaten to barricade her in my house when she wouldn't just come out and tell me this asshole had hit her before this happened. Do you really think she's going to want to listen to you and Mom when you tell her you're taking her home ... to your house?"

I catch his eye; the look he gives me is all too familiar. I've seen it before where Steph is concerned.

"You couldn't have prevented it, Dad. Look at me," I say touching his face in a gesture that tells him without words to show me his eyes. "This wasn't preventable. I've gone over it in my head a hundred times since we got here."

Up until the night before Thanksgiving, Steph had always had someone with her after she moved in with me — I was there in the morning, we'd go to the coffeehouse together, she'd study there until she had to go to class or work, she'd study or hang out at my house with Colton until I was home in the evening. She didn't go anywhere alone until that night.

The best I can figure is he'd been watching her, waiting until she was alone. He wasn't counting on Colt leaving the library after Steph. If he had, we could have been dealing with abduction instead of a broken limb, bruised ribs, and some stitches.

There are a lot of different ways this could have ended. If Colt hadn't showed up when he did, it's more likely we would have been planning a funeral. Like the family in Ohio had to do for their daughter, a girl Davis said was described as quiet and reserved.

But Steph got lucky. She might only need some physical therapy, and that's a big maybe. The break in her leg was clean, nothing shattered or splintered that they found, so there was no operating to repair the damage.

She was really lucky. Or maybe luck didn't even play into it.

"He preys on his victims, Dad, but that doesn't mean Stephanie is going to admit she wants to go back to her childhood bedroom and Mom doing her laundry," I say shaking my head. It sounds harsh. I don't mean for it to come across that way. "She's been through a lot. Let her come home with me where she's become comfortable. She needs something normal."

Stephanie was a challenge for Darren.

She's a spitfire.

"We'll do dinner tonight, at your house. We missed Thanksgiving yesterday, but today we have a lot to be grateful for," Dad says matter-of-factly, clutching the baseball cap behind his back in one hand as he scratches at the back of his neck with the other.

He looks up at the same time I hear her mouth running.

"I still can't believe they made me stay the night. Mom, this is horseshit. I'm fine. Why do I need to be in a wheelchair?"

God, I love my sister. So. Much.

Looking at Dad, I see unshed tears in his eyes and know he's thinking the same.

"I know, Stephanie," Mom says in her "I give up talking to this child" tone, shakes her head and mouths, "She's all yours" to me before walking over to the waiting area chairs to get her jacket and purse.

"Stella, please tell this brute of a nurse I don't need to be in a mother—," she stops before letting loose a string of inflammatory curse words. "Hi, Daddy, I didn't see you there … standing right there in plain view while I almost cursed like a truck driver."

She sighs, the oblivious child.

The bruises on her face are darker, but the swelling looks better than it did when I first saw her a little more than twenty-four hours ago. I can't help but think it's a good thing Halloween has passed. Knowing Steph, she'd try to make light of her wounds and dress up as the Bride of Frankenstein.

As beautiful as she is, she's morbid and a little bit scary when dealing with her own tough situations. I've been through them with her before and I know climbing into her head after this will be the worst of all.

"Are you all discharged and ready to go?" I ask before the staring contest between her and Dad gets any more weird than it already is.

He reaches out and touches her chin, lifting Steph's face so he can get a better look. The regret on his face hurts me before his words register.

"I should have taught you girls to fight instead of treating you like … girls."

It's been a long time since I saw my dad cry. To watch him cry in public? It's been even longer than that.

Steph reaches up and touches his wrist while he still has her chin in his hand.

"You did teach us to fight, Daddy," she says as he places a kiss on her temple. I hear her whisper, "You should see the other guy. I think his testicles might be sharing a room with his Adam's apple."

Dad's tears turn to laughter and I turn away.

***

The dishes are done and put away. Mom and Dad have finally left and though it's still early, all the excitement from the last two days is enough to make me want to sleep from now until Monday when I'll have to force myself to get up for work.

Sitting at the dining room table, I lay my head down. For just a minute, I tell myself. But there's pie in front of my face.

Like, literally in front of my face.

And then a fork being thrust between me and that pie.

Pie.

"Eat, bitch."

"Stephie, I have no more room," I whine as she gives me a pitiful look. "Okay. A bite."

"Have wine, too."

"Wine's going to make me say things I could regret. It makes me ask questions."

She knows me, but I feel I need to forewarn her and it's a warning that falls on deaf ears as she waves me off.

"You can ask me anything you want. I should have been more careful," she says, blaming herself. "It was dark. I knew Darren had been watching and I was careless, tired."

The silence falls around us.

"I should have made sure Colt was with me, you know? I was stupid."

"Stop that right now," I say, getting up from the table and leaving the room. I come back in with a bottle of chilled white wine and two goblets.

Regular size wine glasses are just too small for this conversation and I don't think either of us is worrying about the pain medication she might have in her system. Maybe the mixture will help her sleep through the night without a nightmare. "I want you to talk to someone, Steph."

"I am talking to someone. I'm talking to you," she quips back, sticking a forkful of pumpkin pie in her mouth.

I don't like how she's not dealing with what happened, like she's the reason he hit her. She acts like she did something to deserve it.

She behaved that way when she first showed me the bruises a month ago.

When she breaks, she'll shatter.

"Just promise me you'll talk to me about everything. Promise you'll talk to a professional if it's more than I can help you with," I say, holding my little finger out. "Pinkie swear, Steph."

"Pinkie swear? Are we twelve?" she looks at me and under the strength I see the fear.

Hooking her finger around mine, she promises anyway.

***

I'm blissfully buzzed from the wine, teetering on the edge of drunk.

I could fall right over if I let myself.

"Stella." The sing-song voice creeps into my brain, weaving its way through the grapey haze left behind by the vino before bringing me back from the edge.

The weight of Steph's cast on my lap brings reality crashing back down as I try to move her leg off me before opening my eyes.

We must have fallen asleep talking on the couch after we finished the pie.

I open my eyes and am staring straight down at Sharpie marker stars in every color of the rainbow. The hot pink marker is still in my hand, poised above the plaster cast encasing the length of my sister's leg from knee to ankle like I was prepared to add just one more shining star.

Or we fell asleep doodling in her cast, I think as I rub my face and squint to make out the time on the digital clock across the room while capping the marker. *It's not even nine o'clock? My body feels old. That clock is a liar.*

The room is empty except for me and Steph, and she's passed out snoring quietly. I scoot to the end of the couch and lay her leg on the cushion, taking one more look at her sleeping form before hoisting my pie and wine filled body from the davenport.

Someone said my name. I know they did.

I yawn ... and then I smell it. The blessed aroma of coffee just being brewed wafts through the dining room as I let the scent draw me to it.

He's standing at the island counter, hunched over reading something when I walk into the kitchen.

Brian's home. Finally.

My hands need to touch him, my body craves the feel of his skin against mine.

Without a word I step up behind him and wrap my arms around his waist, laying my cheek on the T-shirt covering his back and I breathe him in. His body feels harder beneath my hands. I push my fingers up his chest as I snuggle closer to him, relishing the warmth he brought back from Tennessee.

The back door opens and the vibrations from his voice hit my ear as I press it into him more.

"Looks like your girl's loving on the wrong brother," says a voice. Not Brian's voice.

My eyes pop open wide as Not Brian turns with my arms still firm around his midsection.

"Tommy?" He nods as his smile breaks through the sleep fogging my brain. "Holy shit, you're here, too? Brian said you might be coming home at some point to help out at the coffeehouse, but I didn't know he meant this soon. How have you been?"

Out of the corner of my eye, I watch Brian pour three mugs of coffee. I pull Tommy in for a hug and quietly apologize for feeling him up, which pulls a hearty laugh from deep in his chest and a sideways glance from Brian.

Tommy winks at me. "It's all good. It's been a long time since someone groped me."

I reach out, taking the coffee mug Brian offers me. The heat and caffeine and just him being close make the chill that's permeated every moment of the last two days fall away, even if only for a beat, and I lean back into Brian.

"So if you boys are here, where's my little man?" I look up at him expectantly.

"Oh, we left him on the back stoop at home. We figure he'll figure out how to get in and put himself to bed. He's totally capable of taking care of himself, right?"

"Of course. I mean, he's a super smart kid, Stella. He's got a key and everything," Tommy adds as the back door opens again and a ball of brown fur runs full bore through the kitchen followed by my favorite towheaded boy.

The brothers Stratford burst out laughing while I'm left staring after Britton.

Son of a bitch.

"You got him a puppy? And you didn't tell me?" I ask, flabbergasted, as the smiles fall from Brian and Tommy's faces and Tommy mumbles an excuse to leave the room. "Brian. Are you kidding me?"

I'm mad.

"You didn't mention this when I talked to you yesterday. Nothing today before you got home." I feel the flush of anger rush up my neck. "Christmas is a month away, we want to plan a wedding, my sister is broken and beaten and you ... you show up back home with a dog. Damn it, Bri."

He's just staring at me as he walks back over to the coffee maker. He barely takes his eyes off me as he tops off his cup, places the pot back on the burner and takes a tentative sip. "Are you done?"

"No. I'm not done," I snarl angrily. "This is something we should have talked about and decided on together. I want to have a say in some things, Brian. I want to be part of the decision making process in our relationship."

I know I went one step too far, one step backward. Brian's eyes flare as he watches me finish my rant from across the room and I know I've fucked up. If not a lot, at the very least a little. A whole lot of little.

"I'm not him Stella. Don't put me in the same category as him." The anger rolls off him in waves as the full impact of my words hits home.

"I'm not. I never would do that, not on purpose. But a dog, Brian? That should have at least been a conversation at some point." I try to make my case. It's useless. Setting my coffee down, I don't give up. "You've never once mentioned getting a dog. You don't just impulse buy an animal. You're methodical and genuine and don't pull shit like that. I'm a little pissed."

Tension whips and swirls through the room, the warmth of his homecoming gone as quickly as it arrived and my skin prickles. My haven, my culinary sanctuary, is teeming with an energy that crackles and fizzes as Brian crosses the room. We stand toe-to-toe, me pissed off about a puppy, him angry because I compared the action to everything that was wrong with my first marriage.

His hands are in my hair, his lips crashing into mine as I cling helplessly to his jacket while he backs me up to the counter. Brian's kisses are commanding and demanding — they want from me and give to me without ever asking or telling — as he takes control of me. His tongue grazes my bottom lip as he tastes me like he's starved.

"Are. You. Done?" He punctuates each word, driving it home and making me feel more needy than even the first time I felt him against me, within me. Nipping my lip, he waits for my answer as I will my breathing to go back to normal.

"Will you kiss me like that again if I say no?"

"No. Because we have an audience," he says tipping his head down to look at the floor, "but maybe tomorrow if you're good."

Following his gaze, I'm met with chocolate brown fur and eyes that match, and paws that scream "I'm going to be huge and ruin your house." I sigh.

"I won't bitch about him, but you need to explain," I say sliding between Brian's body and the counter until I'm sitting on the floor next to the dog. "If you eat my furniture or ruin my quilts, I'm packing you up and sending you back to Tennessee. Got it?" I say to the puppy, who cocks his head and yips at me. I feel like we've come to an understanding.

***

Midnight is right around the corner again as I head to the kitchen to take care of coffee mugs and put leftovers away after feeding Brian and Tommy.

A chill creeps through the kitchen, a draft from somewhere in this old house makes me shiver as the temperature continues to drop and we prepare for the first real snowfall of the season. The thin shirt I have on won't do, and I go quietly from the kitchen to the second floor using the hidden servant's stairwell in search of the coveted SU hoodie.

I hear him as I walk back out of my bedroom, the subtle cry combined with covers being kicked off the bed in the spare room across from Steph's.

Then another cry and I'm there, sitting on the edge of the bed as the dream twists his features and makes him lash out.

"Britt, it's okay, I'm right here," I whisper softly, reaching out to touch his forehead and brush the sweat soaked hair from his skin.

Whiskey creeps down from the pillow to nudge Britton's hand until he lifts it enough to squeeze under. Britt's eyes lazily open and meet mine as I'm touching his forehead and a yawn sneaks out before he speaks.

"Daddy told me I have to talk to you about it," he says.

"Talk to me about what, sweetie?"

"When you marry us and you're my mom I don't want to call you Stella anymore." Shyness I'm not used to seeing in Britt takes hold of him in his sleepy state.

I crawl up onto the bed with him and wrap him up in my arms, breathing into his hair and kissing his head as he settles into me, laying his head on the swell of my breast, laying his little arm across my belly.

"If you don't want to call me Stella anymore, what will you call me?" He's already given me the answer, but I'm so selfish I need to hear this little person in my life say it. I don't want to read into the whim of a five-year-old.

He yawns again and wiggles to get more comfortable before answering, "I'm going to call you 'mom' because you're the only mom I'll ever have and I love you."

I don't get to ask him anything else. The words silence me as he and his puppy fall back to sleep, one curled up in my arms as the other lays his head on my leg.

Sleep takes me over and I'm falling into that darkness, the one that comes when you're mildly aware you're drifting off but can do nothing to stop it from consuming you.

It pulls me down, drowning out the laughter climbing the stairs from the living room.

It wraps me up, like a blanket on the coldest New York winter night.

It replays the scene I just lived and even in that semi-conscious state, I feel like my home is finally full.

And I sleep beside one of the boys who have stolen my heart.

***

I'm falling. I'm on the edge of a cliff, staring down at a jagged outcropping of rocks that will split me open and leave me bleeding until I'm empty.

Nothing can stop my body as it hurtles through the air and begins that plunge downward.

Destiny.

It's bound to happen.

Until I fly.

Until I defy gravity.

"I'm flying, Brian. Look, I'm flying." The sound of my voice brings me back to now and he's staring down at me. "I flew."

"I bet you did. Let's go to bed," he says as he lifts me the rest of the way off the bed and turns to walk out of Britt's room and into ours.

Looping my arms around his neck, I place a tender kiss on the underside of his jaw while my fingers play lazily with the longer hairs at the back of his head. He smells like Old Spice and cinnamon.

I love Old Spice and cinnamon.

I love him.

"I flew and you caught me," I whisper sleepily as he makes his way quietly down the hall. "And you didn't let me fall."

The meaning of my words isn't lost on him. Our argument, my crumbled marriage, my childhood, my everything.

Somehow, Brian has always been here to catch me.

Destiny.

It's bound to happen.

"I love you," I say against his silence.

"I'll never not find you, Stella." He sets me down on my side of the bed and slowly begins peeling my socks off before crawling up my body. "I'll never let you fall."

And his lips are against mine, consuming me hungrily, gently, needing and savoring every moment of contact as we work to shed piece after piece of clothing. The feverish burn building within me is enough to light our way to eternity and back. It burns so hot I wait for the searing pain that never comes, because perfection created from two imperfect people doesn't hurt. It grows and winds its way around them like morning glory vines in springtime.

His lips touch my neck, my shoulder, my breasts as he works down my body quietly finding places I've forgotten in his absence. His fingers press insistently into my hips as I open for him, feeling the warmth of his breath at the tops of my thighs just before he leans in, placing a kiss on my hip and methodically kissing, worshiping, his way toward my core to bring me to the edge of that cliff and back down again.

Moaning into my pillow, I feel him climb back up my body and I'm ready. I'm needy. I'm in need of him.

"Please, Brian," I say breathlessly, hoping that's all it will take for him to slide into my waiting body.

And it is.

We move together in solidarity, not caring who reaches the stars first. He's gentle but commanding while I'm insistent and vulnerable as we climb higher and higher.

Until I feel like I'm falling all over again, only this time he falls with me.

Brian

Chapter Twenty-Nine

I pull her closer to me in my sleep and feel her curve her body into mine. A perfect fit. It pulls me the rest of the way out of my slumber.

Placing a kiss at the nape of Stella's neck, the night before floods my memory and a smile creeps onto my face.

My imperfect girl.

"What are you smiling about back there, cowboy?" she asks, sleep still coating her voice. "If I didn't know better I'd think you were thinking naughty things."

"Maybe I was. Is that a bad thing?" I laugh into her hair and feel her body tremble as a shiver works its way down her spine.

She turns toward me, throwing her leg over my hip and pulling me into her. "No, it's not."

My body is responding before her teeth even graze my lip and I thrust my hips up to meet hers, nothing barring my entrance.

A low moan escapes her throat and I muffle the sound with my mouth, slowly licking along the seam of her lips as she opens up for me.

The heat of her body envelops me, wrapping around me as she moves to straddle my lap. A look of pure ecstasy graces her features and she presses herself completely onto me.

"I missed you," she says leaning down on top of me, steadying herself with her hands on my shoulders, her taut nipples drawing lazy lines on my chest. I lift my hips in response and hear the slightest gasp escape her lips.

Her body is a livewire.

Our lovemaking is slow, sensuous and perfect. The longing in her voice replaced by the insistence of her body as she paces herself, building us both up to the moment when there is no turning back and wave after wave pulls us under.

Her body pulses around mine as a silent cry tries desperately to escape her throat, her eyes shut tightly against the rising sun streaming through the window as an orgasm wracks her body, pulling me the rest of the way under. My back arches, my hips pressed firmly against hers, and I shudder, biting back a pure unadulterated groan as I find my release.

Stella pulls her legs up, sitting on my hips even as my body begins to go limp within her, and rocks forward to place a kiss to my chest. Laying her head against my heart, Stella sighs. I push her hair off her face and watch her — all her beauty, no make-up skewing the real her, her hair a tangled mess spread across my body — as she holds onto me, our hearts racing to slow down.

I speak first. "Are you okay, Stell?"

Lifting her head and crossing her arms on my chest, she rests her chin on the backs of her hands and watches me watching her.

"I will be," she replies, the slightest hint of a smile creasing the corners of her mouth. "Getting there."

And she closes her eyes before speaking again.

"We should get up before Britt comes in and finds us like this," she says, sliding her body off mine to lay her head in the crook of my arm. Pulling the covers up over us, she places another kiss to my jaw, nipping at three days' worth of stubble. "I'm glad you're home."

"I kind of got the impression you'd missed me. I mean ... twice in less than twelve hours is a lot even for us." Her laughter hits all the soft spots in my soul. I want to wrap her up and keep her in this room the rest of the day. I kiss the top of her head before rolling over onto her still flushed body and I capture her bottom lip between my teeth, pulling it gently. "But you're right. We need to get up. I need food. Waffles? Bacon? Not crappy coffee from a truck stop? Yes?"

She laughs again and pushes me away from her to scoot off the other side of the bed in a rush to find sweatpants and a hoodie. I should probably start referring to it as "her hoodie" because heaven knows I'm never getting it back.

"I'll race you to the kitchen," she says with the enthusiasm of a child and walks out of the room while piling her hair high up on her head and securing it with a band.

I watch her leave from the middle of the bed where she's left me. I give her a head start knowing she'll take the long way before I pull myself from beneath the covers, find my boxers and jeans and head out the door.

***

Coffee is brewing and Stella's already got the waffle iron warming when I walk into the kitchen. The entire scene looks like something out of a movie — the well-oiled inner workings of a Saturday morning. Tommy hands eggs to Stella and Steph sits reading at the counter, her broken leg up on a chair across from her as she reaches down to gingerly scratch the puppy behind his ears. Britt's standing on a chair with measuring cups and a mixing bowl in front of him on the counter ready to make breakfast.

"Did we get up late?" I ask walking across the room to kiss Britt on the top of the head. "Good morning, little man. Need help with that?"

"Nope, I can handle it, Daddy. Mom and I are making waffles," he says excitedly, dumping flour into the bowl. I look at Stella waiting to see her reaction to Britt's claim on her, but she's busy going on about her business.

"Stell?"

Without looking my way she says, "Apparently we did, because I got down here and everyone else was in the kitchen starving. If it weren't for me, we'd be eating cold turkey and mashed potatoes for breakfast."

"There's nothing wrong with cold turkey sandwiches for breakfast, Stella," Stephanie pipes up without looking up from her book. "It was Tommy's idea, anyway. I wanted the frozen peanut butter pie, but he told me no and I'm kind of in no condition to fight him to the death for peanut butter pie."

I catch Steph shooting a glare in Tommy's direction as he sticks his tongue out at her.

"Once you're all healed up, then you can fight me, Princess."

She huffs out a laugh and goes back to reading. I catch Stella's eye and give her a look of my own as I walk over to her.

"And the other thing?" I say quietly, hoping she understands the question so I don't have to make a big deal out of it.

Leaning into me, she whispers, "Our son," she glances in Britt's direction, "told me you told him he had to talk to me about that. We talked. It's settled. Maybe we should also set a date soon since everyone knows."

She says the last part with a questioning tone.

"My dad, your dad, our moms ... they all talk. They all have big mouths," I respond, shrugging my shoulders.

She laughs.

"They never could keep secrets between the four of them," she says pouring mugs of fresh coffee. "I still don't know how it is we didn't keep in touch all those years if they've been talking since you guys moved. How does that happen?"

Quiet falls on the room, save for the scraping of a spoon against the mixing bowl, and it seems we're all wondering the same thing.

"Sometimes, shit happens and we don't have an answer for it." Tommy's words break the silence. "But, isn't it better this way?"

Stella and I look at each other, smile, and respond simultaneously, "Yeah, it is."

"They even say things at the same time," Steph mumbles to no one in particular. "It's so cute I almost want to vomit."

We all turn to look at her and then fill the kitchen with laughter the moment she realizes she spoke out loud. Covering her face, Steph starts apologizing but Stella walks over and gives her a hug.

"Oh, poor Stephie, I'm so sorry we're too adorable for you to handle. Just remember, you and I finish each other's sentences. I mean, ew, how gross that we'd do that," Stella teases, winking at her sister.

"Ugh, okay I get it. Get off me. You're such a jerk." Steph pushes at Stella's arm and buries her nose in her book again.

Stella goes back to helping Britt with the waffles while Tommy and I talk a little more about the coffee shop, picking up a conversation we left off last night when I realized Stella had been missing for a while.

A knock sounds on the front door and is just barely audible above the conversations and cooking. Steph's the first to hear it and maneuvers herself out of her chair and up onto crutches before the rest of us realize what she's doing.

Tommy tries to tell her to sit back down and he'll get the door, but Steph's obstinate attitude is firmly in place, so he backs off with his hands up.

"Please, southern charmer, slow your roll. I can handle answering the door," she bites out before swinging her way through the dining room.

"Who pissed in her Cheerios?" Tommy says, baffled at Steph's sour mood toward him, as he returns to the counter.

"She's just really independent. Since getting home yesterday she's hardly let me do anything for her other than help her off the couch." Stella's voice is confident, but her eyes are sad. Despite our bedroom antics, the weight of worry about her sister is resting fully on her shoulders, pushing down more and more as the morning progresses. "She'll come around."

A muffled yell rips through the kitchen and Stella calls out to Steph as she bolts from the room.

Stephanie is standing with the door wide open when Stella and I get to the front of the house, a uniformed police officer I vaguely recognize and Chief Davis Frank standing just inside.

"Stephanie, look at me," Davis is saying when we approach them. He reaches out to touch her shoulders and she grabs him around the waist pulling him to her.

Confused, Stella and I watch as it all unfolds, as tears stream down Steph's cheeks and the other officer fidgets with his jacket zipper.

"Are you sure? Please, Davis, please tell me this is real?" Steph's frantic yelling reaches into my heart and squeezes tight as she pleads and begs for information. "Please? Max? Is he telling me the truth?"

Her wild eyes pin him in his place and Max blanches, the color draining from his face.

"Yeah." He clears his throat. "Yes, ma'am. Chief wouldn't lie about something like that. We will need you to identify him though, but just through photos, if you're able to. I'm so sorry we have to do this to you after all you've already been though. It's a formality so we can proceed and close the case."

His brown eyes are wide, waiting for a response from Steph. She nods, quickly and silently, giving Max the confirmation he needs for him to complete his job.

"What the hell happened?" Looking from Steph to Max and back again, Stella finally reacts. "Davis, does this have to do with Darren?"

The chief's been quiet, more father than police officer, but it's a hiccup in his demeanor. Turning to face Stella, he nods.

"He's dead," Davis says, glancing at Max. "State Police tracked him down in a cottage by the lake and when they went in, he opened fire on them. No one else was hurt, but it looked like he'd been prepared to hide out for a while."

Stephanie looks like she's ready to pass out, so I nudge Stella and tell her quietly to get her sister to the living room.

"Why don't you gentlemen come on in," I say. "We've got a fresh pot of coffee on and it's cold out there."

Max and Davis follow me to the kitchen where Tommy's taken over the waffle making and Britt's disappeared with Whiskey Sour in tow, I'm sure.

"T, this is Chief of Police Davis Frank and Officer Max ... sorry, man, I don't know your last name. How do you gentlemen take your coffee?"

Everyone shakes hands and conversation starts to flow, the usual "how you doing?" moves into questions about how long Tommy's staying in New York, how we knew the girls, and talk of the girls leads to talk of Steph's injuries.

"You and Stella knew she was in danger and didn't do anything?" Tommy's incensed tone catches me off-guard.

"We didn't do 'nothing,' Tom. Stella and Chief had talked, we'd all been keeping tabs on Steph, she was letting us know where she was and what she was up to if not with Stell. The poor girl practically had herself on house arrest." I feel like I need to lay it all out for him, like we should have had a damn schedule and clocked in and out. "Steph's stubborn, Tommy. She's not stupid. This guy was waiting for an opportunity."

Max nods his head in agreement, a solemn look on his face like he understands the situation completely, but not from a cop perspective.

"The point is, though, his body is in the county coroner's refrigerator and he can't hurt her or anyone else again," Davis says, shooting a look in Max's direction that makes me feel like we don't know the entire story. Somehow all the pieces haven't fallen into place.

We all lift our coffee mugs simultaneously, sip, and place them back on the counter as though we've all just come to some misguided understanding that the world is a much better place without Darren Judson here to harm another woman.

Stella

Chapter Thirty

I get Steph settled on the couch and kneel on the floor in front of her.

Watching her face, I wait for her to get her bearings before asking, "You okay?"

Her eyes flit up to meet mine and there's an irrevocable sadness in them.

"I think so? At least this way he can't make bail and come after me again, right? He can't kill me now instead of just breaking my leg?"

Swallowing hard, she starts fidgeting with the hem of her sweater.

"I don't know how I'm supposed to feel. It was like he was so many people all in one body, one brain, that I want to cry over the death of the nice guy who bought me flowers ... but I want to spit on the corpse of the one who did this," she says motioning to her bruised face and broken limb.

"I think that's normal, Stephie. Want me to call Mom and Dad so they can come over?"

Strength in numbers, right? I can't walk this road with her alone, I say to myself.

She nods and I pull my phone from the pocket in my sweatshirt to call Mom as the front door opens and she walks in unannounced, Dad trailing right behind her.

"Stella? Steph?" Mom calls out as she wanders into the living room, dropping to the floor beside me and gathering us up like little children. We're huddled together, our mother kissing our heads, trying still after more than thirty years of parenting to heal wounds with affection, because that's what parents do. They kiss away the hurt.

Breaking free from her embrace, I glance at Dad and nod. "Brian, Tommy, Davis, and Max are in the kitchen, Dad. Go get coffee. You look like you need it."

He walks over and kisses Steph and I each on the top of the head, tears in his eyes, and then quietly walks to the kitchen where I hear a cacophony of male voices.

The rumbling of baritones in the other room, the sedate breathing beside me as my mom curls up on the couch beside my sister to soothe the ache ... they mingle and breathe more life into this home, more life than lasagna night and Thanksgiving together.

"Shit happens, Steph. Shit just happens," Mom says to her. So much truth in one simple statement.

"Darren was shit. Now he's dead," Steph says and swallows a sob. Lowering her voice and closing her eyes, she adds, "Is it wrong for me to be happy he's dead?"

Mom and I look at one another, a thousand conversations passing between us in the silence, and we know this is the beginning. The hurt and harm has only just begun and it goes way beyond the physical — the bruises, scars, and broken bones — to a place where Steph can bury it away, allowing it to fester.

"I don't think it's wrong to feel that way at all, not after what he did to you physically," I say breaking eye contact with Mom. "Definitely not after the emotional and psychological upheaval he's put you through. Hopefully, his end is your new beginning. It's closure. I'll go with you when you're ready to spit on his grave."

"Stella!" My mother sits forward on the sofa and scolds me, but it's the tone of her voice that tells me it's okay. I know that tone. It's the one that says "don't let your father hear you talk like that, but I agree with you a hundred percent and call shotgun."

Mom curls back up onto the couch, clutching a pillow to her chest as my sister tries her best to crawl up to her. Laying her head in Mom's lap, Steph grasps for a sliver of normalcy.

Anything that makes everything okay again.

"Promise?" Steph says to me as tears flood her eyes. She holds out her pinkie finger, and I wrap mine around it.

"Promise."

I've been a rock and I feel like I'm starting to crumble. Steph is safe now in Mom's arms. I can leave her for a bit. Just a little bit.

Whiskey walks into the room and jumps up on the couch, seeking a warm spot to snuggle behind Steph's good leg.

"Brian. Moonshine. Now we own a dog," I say when I see the look on my mom's face.

A burst of laughter from her lips lights up the melancholy that's settled over the room and she reaches over to scratch the puppy's belly. Pulling myself up from the floor, I ruffle his ears and make an excuse to leave this space and find comfort somewhere else.

I'm drawn to the low voices in the kitchen.

***

"How's she doing?"

Max's voice startles me out of my single-minded goal of getting more coffee. Getting away from the living room for a bit and searching for Britt were also part of the plan until now.

Sitting in one of the dining room chairs, he has his phone out looking intently at the screen, a forlorn expression in his eyes as he locks the device and puts it back in his jacket.

"She's shaken, understandably. Were you there?"

I ask because I'm curious and because I'm a reporter.

I ask because there's something creeping up the back of my neck telling me Max knows more than he and Davis have let on.

That cold chill reaches my hairline and I shiver visibly despite my baggy sweatshirt.

Max taps the tabletop with his index finger, absentmindedly grabbing his top lip between his teeth.

"I was." He stops tapping and looks through me. "It was my bullet."

I suck my next breath through my clenched teeth. *Oh, Max*, I think, *you poor soul.*

"Don't. You have that look in your eyes that people get when they hear you did your job. That 'I'm so sorry it was you' look and I hate that look," he says standing up from the table, his full height causing me to look up more than I have to when looking at Brian. He's looking right back down at me. "After what I've seen that degenerate do to women, to your sister ... I was happy to kill him. That's off the record."

He starts for the kitchen until I speak up, work past his words.

"I may have been thinking 'oh poor you' but I owe you." I speak deliberately and quietly. "You've done me a favor, Max. I have a question, though. If it was State Police who tracked him down, why were you there when they went after him? Is it because it was a joint effort?"

Enough has happened over the last seventy-two hours that I feel completely clueless about everything, but this is one thing that doesn't sit well. Departments work together a lot, but this is more than just a combined effort to catch a guy who beat up his girlfriend. I feel a little queasy when I watch Max scratch the back of his head before shoving his hands in his jacket pockets.

"I was close to the original case," he says, his eyes downcast.

I know when people don't want to give me a whole story.

"You know I'm good at getting answers, right, Max? I'm a journalist and while this isn't a story — not for me — I'm going to get to the bottom of this. What original case? Who was Darren Judson?"

"That's a good question, Ms. Barbieri. A really good question," he says in a compartmentalized official tone, detached from my reality of the situation but firmly situated in his. I've heard Davis use it a hundred times. He's said it's what keeps him sane and sober. "He was a predator. He sought out women he thought were weak, ones he could control. Stephanie isn't his first victim. But, she's the first to fight hard enough to live."

Nine words. Those words — *she's the first to fight hard enough to live* — make the room spin.

I absorb them. All nine of them. I repeat them in my head.

I close my eyes.

"How many didn't fight hard enough?" I let the words escape my mouth without hesitation. "How many?"

"At least two others in a different state."

I open my eyes and reach for him, pulling him into a thankful embrace, thinking first with my heart instead of my head.

"Thank you. Thank you for saving my sister," I whisper into the fold of his jacket as he wraps his arms tight around me, enveloping me in an embrace I swear he needs almost as much as I do. Maybe he needs it more.

I silently say a prayer for the others who couldn't fight back against this monster. I pray for their families. And I say one for Max because this wasn't just him doing his job; it was personal.

A throat clears behind Max and we drop our arms and step back from one another as though we've been caught doing something we shouldn't be.

"Wyatt, we need to get back. Paperwork, coffee, and then you need to head out for some time off," Davis says, as though walking into my dining room and seeing me hugging one of his officers is totally within the norm.

"I'll meet you in the car, Chief. Thank you for the coffee, ma'am." I watch him walk away quietly, peeking into the living room — at Steph — with a longing glance and he's out the door.

"You okay, Stell?"

Davis brings me back to the here and now.

Taking a deep breath I turn back to face him. "Yeah, I think I will be. It's going to be a long road for Steph, a few months of recovery, but we'll get there."

"I didn't ask about Steph. I heard part of what Max told you," he says. "When you told me Steph was in a bad relationship, I had no idea it was with this guy. Then when I talked to your sister a week ago and she told me his name ... we were already investigating him."

"You feel guilty?"

"Of course I do. You and Stephanie are like my own kids. I should have had someone escorting her on campus. I should have made sure she was safe."

"Careful, Chief, you're going to start sounding like the rest of us," Mom says from the living room doorway. "If you'd put someone on Stephanie duty, you know as well as I do, someone in this town would have been beating on your office door wanting to know why you were giving preferential treatment."

"But still, Jenny! I should have—" I watch as my mom holds her hand up against his rant.

"Stop, Davis. Stop. Some people are just plain evil. This man was pure evil as far as I'm concerned. He would have found a way. This way ... at least this way we're fortunate enough to have brought her home from the hospital with us in a car rather than a hearse. So, please, don't jeopardize your sanity for the sake of her safety. It was in God's hands. The girl has forever had a guardian angel and they were obviously there, so stop," she says. "Shit. Happens. She's safe now."

Davis is quiet. Contemplative.

"She's safe," he repeats, "I know. It's just so hard to think I could have done more. But you're right. He would have found her alone eventually."

Quiet nestles into the nooks and crannies of the room, the clock on the wall ticks through the seconds, I hear the puppy barking upstairs and Britt running down the hall laughing.

She's safe.

We're all okay.

"Bring your bride over tonight for drinks, Davis. You need a night filled with some down time. Dale and I could use the company," Mom says in the silence. I see the look — she's giving the Chief of Police the "mom look" — and let out a laugh as she walks over and hooks her arm through mine.

"Yes, ma'am," he says as Mom and I plant kisses on each of his cheeks. "We could use time with friends."

Mom releases my arm as she gracefully steps from dining room to kitchen and I wrap both of my arms around Davis' neck, a whispered "thank you" passes from my lips to his ear, and he squeezes me firmly and releases me.

"You call me if you need anything, you hear me?" he says sternly, then follows Max's previous path out the door.

Brian

Chapter Thirty-One

Christmas

The last few weeks haven't been easy.

They've been damn hard.

Almost as hard as the stone I've been carrying around in my pocket.

It's not too small, but not big. Definitely not gaudy.

It's perfect.

It's delicate and beautiful, a ribbon of silver — because she doesn't like yellow gold — dotted with tiny diamonds surrounding a pale blue gem nestled in the center. Her birthstone.

Standing in my office at the Jumping Bean, my back to the door, I pull the box from my jeans. I hold my breath as I push the top back and hear the creak of the tiny hinge, and say a little prayer she'll love it.

I had every intention of letting Stella help me pick out her ring, but when I saw this I couldn't leave it at the jeweler's. It cried out to me from the display case, my eyes drawn to its simple beauty and I knew it belonged on Stella's left hand.

"Aw, you shouldn't have. Thanks, dude. How did you know I wanted one of these?" Greg says as he looks over my shoulder at the ring in my hand. "Seriously, that blue will totally complement my eyes, don't you think?"

"Bitch, please, it would never fit on your beer guzzling, skirt chasing man hands. Plus, it matches my eyes," I fire back before looking at the band again and getting serious. "You really think she'll like it? I don't know why I'm so nervous."

Greg leans against the filing cabinet, looking me up and down with his chin resting in one hand.

"I haven't known Stella very long, but her world revolves around you and Britton. It wouldn't matter if you'd gotten that ring out of the bottom of a Cracker Jack box or one of those quarter machines at the grocery store, Brian. That girl's heart belongs to you. Yours belongs to her. And Britt? Shit, man, he's the ribbon and bow on the package deal," he says, winking at me.

"Dudes don't wink at other dudes, Greg," I say and he slugs me in the shoulder. "But yeah. Yeah, I know what you mean. I'm just scared.

Everything moved so quickly, but every move we've made together has felt like it was meant to happen. I can't imagine my life without her, without being here and having this time with Stella."

Snapping the ring box shut, I take a deep breath in and breathe out all my worry.

Greg pushes off the cabinet and, clapping me on the shoulder as he walks past, says, "Man, I hope someday I find a girl who gets me all tangled up like that. It's a good look on you."

He's back out in the kitchen headed toward the doors to the counter before the sadness in his voice hits me and I don't have time to ask what he means.

***

There's a car in my driveway when we get home and, as soon as I park, Britt detaches from his seat and launches himself out of the truck to run full speed toward my mom.

"Come here and give me some love, child," she says holding her arms open for Britt as he flings himself into her embrace. "Oh sweet boy, I swear you've grown in the month since we've seen you."

My mom makes every homecoming worth coming home to, even if it's just me pulling into my own driveway and letting Britt out of the car. I watch from the driver's seat as Mama pulls him in for another hug and my dad ruffles his hair — he's convinced me and Stella we should let him grow it out to see how it looked; apparently it's the "in" thing up here — and I hear Whiskey barking in the house at the commotion.

Stepping out of the Tahoe, Dad clasps my hand in his like we didn't just see one another a few weeks ago.

"You found yourself a really nice place here, Bri."

"I wish I could take the credit, but Jenny's the one who found it," I say looking up at the front of the house I've turned into a home for my son. "We've really done quite a bit to make it ours, though."

"What's going to happen to it when you and Stella get married?"

No beating around the bush with this man. I take a minute to think about it because we haven't even discussed where we'll live or if we'll sell one house or the other. What if she wants to sell both and buy one together?

Dad's watching me carefully and a smile breaks his still tanned face.

"It's okay, Brian. One thing at a time," he says like he's read my mind.

"I don't know if I can handle one thing at a time. Lately I feel like I'm juggling a hundred different things and failing at it. Horribly." Britt leads Mama into the house, talking her ear off the entire way, while I help Dad with their bags and have a little one-on-one. We may not have this chance again while they're here. "Between the coffeehouse, getting Tommy settled into the business and all the wedding talk, it's just been a lot. Not to mention trying to be there for Stella and Steph while Stephanie tries to heal after all she's been through."

I'm gasping for breath by the time I'm done and Dad's grabbing either side of my neck, urging me to look at him.

"Brian. You need a break." But I'm still panicking inside. "You need a break. Take Stella for a long weekend while we're here and get out of here. If the weather stays mild, go stay in a cabin in the woods for a weekend and keep each other warm. I'm sure Dale's still got his old hunting lodge in the Southern Tier. Pack a bag, get your girl, and get gone for seventy or so hours."

"But-"

"Don't talk back, boy."

My dad never calls me "boy" anymore. He used to do it when I was a teenager because I was being argumentative, which I am being now, but with good reason. I don't feel right just dropping everything and leaving Greg and Tommy with the shop.

"Time with just Stella would be nice, but I can't expect Tom and Greg to be okay with me taking off for the weekend at the drop of a hat. I'll think about it, though, and talk to the guys to see if they'd be set for a few days without me." I'm making excuses and I don't know why.

Dad looks at me out of the corner of his eye and makes a disapproving tsking sound with his tongue and teeth.

"Sometimes I think we did too good a job with you, Brian. Such a good head on your shoulders and good work ethic you don't know when to give yourself time to recharge," he says taking his ball cap off just to put it back on. "That's how burnout happens, kid. Don't burn out."

He walks off toward the house, leaving me dumbfounded and standing in the driveway holding my mom's purple paisley suitcase wondering why I can't just let work go for one weekend.

***

"Want to go to the woods with me?"

"Are you feverish? Did you get bit by a tick and are suffering from a Lyme related illness? The woods?"

Stella stops folding towels and stares at me from across the table.

My parents have taken Britt out to visit something called the Shoe Tree and left us at the house. Dad's reasoning was that we needed "down time." It's more like he didn't want Mama smothering Stella and forced her out of the house under the guise of showing the little man all their old haunts.

Stella's still watching me, waiting for an answer.

"Not, like, the woods, but a cabin in the woods. I was thinking a few days away to talk about things, our future, you know." I set the towel I just folded into the laundry basket and step around the end of the table and deliberately toward her, wrapping my arms around her shoulders. "Things have just been crazy for the last month or so. I want to get away and spend time with just you for a while. Preferably naked, but we can find some middle ground if twenty-four seven nudity is an issue for you."

She lets a low laugh rise from her belly. I feel it vibrate through my ribs as she pulls me closer to her and lay her head as high up on my shoulder as she can without standing on her tiptoes.

"Nudity I don't have an issue with, provided we bring all the food we'll need so we don't have to leave," she says, the smile on her face pulling at my shirt. "When can we go? I need a break from reality."

I lift my head away so I can look down at her eyes, shining bright with an urgency — a need — for an adventure, even if it's just us in a cabin exploring one another.

"As soon as I clear it with the guys. When do you want to go?"

"Next weekend. We'll get through Christmas with the family and leave the next morning. Britt can stay here and hang out with your parents ... right?" She adds the question a little late and I can't help but grin.

"Dad got to you first, didn't he?"

"Maybe." She laughs again, holding her thumb and index finger together. "Just a little."

Stella puts her thumb nail between her teeth, biting gently and giving me puppy dog eyes, and it's nothing I ever thought I would see her do.

It makes my body come alive.

Every time I watch her bite down on that thumb, pulling the digit into her mouth a little further, I feel my boxers get a little tighter.

"You're trouble," I say gruffly, reaching up to pull her hand from her mouth and kissing her thumb as I move my other hand up to her neck, urging her mouth closer to mine. "You're in trouble. How long do you think we have until they get back?"

"Probably not enough time …" she says and lets out a squeal as I bend down, grabbing her by the waist to hold her in place on my shoulder before standing back to my full height. "Brian! Let me down!"

But she's laughing like I haven't heard her laugh in weeks. I love that sound.

I also love the sound of my palm connecting with her backside. I rub gently over the soft denim covering her and I hear a moan escape her lips.

Reaching the bedroom, I toss her onto the bed and crawl to her, settling myself between her legs.

"You're the most beautiful girl I've ever met. I want to spend the rest of my life with you, Stella." I swoop down and capture her lips with mine, deepening the kiss as our bodies meld together and sink to the mattress.

Breaking the kiss, her eyes closed and a graceful smile on that precious mouth, she says, "I thought we'd already settled that."

"We did. But I want to make it official. I wanted to wait until Christmas, but I want this moment to be for just us instead," I say rising up off her to crawl to the head of the bed. Reaching into the nightstand I pull out the little box I've carried with me everywhere since the day I bought it.

Dropping onto the floor in front of her, I rise up on one knee and it's like the rest of the world falls away — the worry and wonder and what ifs are gone. It's just us.

Opening the box, I take the ring from within and hold it up, staring at the stones as the sun glints off them, casting light onto my fingers.

"I promised you I would let you help me pick out your ring. But then I went shopping alone and decided to browse. It isn't too small, and it isn't too big, but if you look, the band splits and forms the infinity symbol. There is no limit to our love, Stella, and I wanted you to wear that always and know it forever to be true. You're my everything. Be my wife."

I haven't looked up at her once since I started talking, but when I lift my eyes to hers, there's no denying the answer is a clear and present "yes."

She holds her left hand out to me and I slide the band into place. It shocks us both a little that the fit is perfect.

"It's like it was made for me, Brian." She covers her mouth, shutting her smile away from me as the tears stream down her face. "Yes. A thousand times, yes."

I stand up and lean into her, forehead to forehead, and ask, "Are you sure? I don't want to push you or rush you into making a decision you're not—"

She cuts me off wrapping her legs around my waist, quieting the butterflies in my chest as she shoves her fingers into my hair and kisses me like I'm the last breath she'll ever take.

I say a little prayer my parents keep Britt out for at least another hour.

We shed our clothes quickly, silently, and never stop touching. My hand on her face; her lips against my chest. My mouth on her neck; her hands sliding down my legs.

We lose ourselves in one another and fall beyond the edges of bliss.

Stella's curled up in my arms, trailing her fingers along the center of my chest, when she whispers, "We never finished folding the towels."

"Forget the towels. They're just going to get dirty again later. Five people in this house full-time for the next two weeks? I should just color code them and refuse to wash anything for at least a week. We can just reuse them. They're not really dirty if you're just drying off, right? Not if you actually washed."

And she laughs like it's the funniest thing she's heard in a long time while we go to work untangling ourselves from one another.

I stand on my side of the bed, yanking my boxer briefs into place and jumping into my jeans but stop short of buttoning them when I see her, really see her, on the other side of the bed.

I watch as she pulls on her red lace panties and straps the matching bra in place over her swollen breasts. Stepping into her jeans, she pulls them slowly up over her hips and leaves them undone while grabbing the tank top she hid beneath a pink and black flannel button down shirt. She pulls the tank into place and starts pushing her arms into the flannel, shaking her hair out of the way as she adjusts the fabric on her shoulders.

"Fuck, Stella," I growl, my jaw going slack while my body is anything but. Again.

"What? What's the matter?" Concern etches in her features. She really has no idea.

"You're stunning," I say breathily, because it's the truth. She's practically glowing. "You look good in love."

"Yeah? Well, cowboy, you're to blame for that," she says walking around the end of the bed to kiss me chastely and walk out of the room. She calls back over her shoulder, "You don't look too bad yourself."

Stella

Chapter Thirty-Two

I've never had to set out milk and cookies before, but they say there's a first time for everything and I plan to embrace every second of this first.

The holiday isn't even about me — it used to be only about me before Keith walked out, but now it's so much more. There's this little boy who stole my heart and I don't ever want to think about what this time of year would be like without his enthusiasm.

I don't know who's more excited for Christmas morning, me or Britt, but I never want another holiday without him and Brian.

Christmas Eve is just a few days away, so Brian and I have been sneaking off to the woodshop every night when I get done at the paper to wrap presents we've gotten for Britt, my parents, his parents, Tommy, and Steph. We've finally found a few little things for Caryn and Greg, too, since they plan to join us Christmas morning for my family's traditional brunch that's being held at Brian's this year.

The second floor of the shop is bathed in white twinkle lights — the extra single strands of holiday lights we had after decorating the tree and front porch and bannisters — and it casts a warm glow throughout the storage area, giving off enough light to wrap by. I imagine if Santa's elves worked by candlelight there would be a similar situation happening at the North Pole.

"Ready to work your magic, beautiful?"

I hadn't even heard him walk up the stairs and turn at the sound of his voice.

"I suppose someone has to," I reply as he hands me a glass of wine and a roll of clear tape. "Let's do this."

We start pulling out jeans, T-shirts, board games, books, a new hat to go with his new baseball glove, more books. Lord, this child loves books. If I didn't know better I would swear he was biologically mine.

Honestly, I don't think I could love him more if he was.

I'm lost in thought, working away quietly at the pile of gifts in front of me, and never realized Brian got up from his spot on the floor until I'm finishing up.

Placing the last piece of tape on the last gift of the night, I listen for him and hear the soft sound of smooth sandpaper working away at a piece of wood in the shop below me.

Sand. Silence. Sand. Silence.

I listen as he blows on the spot he's working on to remove the dust.

Sand ... silence. He makes another pass with the paper.

I inch my way to the edge of the loft area and look down into his workspace to find Brian concentrating on a project I haven't seen before. It's simple but gorgeous in its simplicity — a storage bench — and Brian swiftly and gently sands it in sections, one stroke at a time in preparation for what I guess is a second coat of polyurethane. Even in the dim light, I can see the wood is lightly stained, the grain popping out in a perfect harmony of brown hues.

The little girl in me remembers what it was like watching my dad work away on projects in the garage, and I let out a barely-there sigh as I lay down on my stomach to watch Brian work.

The muscles in his back flex against the fabric of his T-shirt, the sleeves pulled up his forearms straining against his biceps with each pass of the sanding block. He moves around the bench with ease, gracefully wiping his hand along the top of the box as a satisfied look passes across his face.

This is where he's most content. This is where he comes to get rid of the things he cannot control.

I watch until my eyes draw heavy and think his must be getting that way, too, as I hear a cloth being pulled over the top of his secret project and he makes his way back up the stairs, nearly catching me laying on the floor of the loft.

My long hours at the office are catching up to me and I let out a yawn as he reaches the top step.

"You look exhausted, Stell," he says.

"Thanks for that, Captain, because it's not obvious enough." I laugh as he grabs my hand and pulls me up off the floor and into his arms.

Pushing my hair off my forehead and tucking it behind my ear, he whispers, "Stay the night so I don't have to be alone."

And I feel my body shiver down to my toes, this time not from the cold December wind howling outside the woodshop.

"But you're not alone," I whisper back. "You have a full house. And you didn't pick a color for my towel selection. That's imperative."

"You can just use mine." The lights twinkling above reflect in his hopeful eyes and I can't stop myself from agreeing to a sleep over.

"And that's ... I'll just shower at home in the morning."

The smell of Old Spice and cinnamon mingles with the sweet scent of pine from the sawdust splashed across his shirt, and I breathe in the fragrance that's intimately male. It's Brian. I don't see a reason to ask questions about the beautiful box he's working on below us.

It doesn't matter.

He looks like whatever weight has been on his shoulders has momentarily lifted just from that little bit of time working on a project and I'm thankful once again for finding a man who has an outlet for his frustration that still includes me somehow.

Brian turns and wraps his arm around my shoulder, I hook mine around his waist, and we step toward the stairs.

We reach at the same time for the light switch on the way down, his larger hand cradled above mine to shut down the night, and together we descend into the darkness of December.

***

The smell of freshly baked Christmas coffeecake reaches my nose. The sun is just starting to peek through the windows in Brian's bedroom and despite the few hours of sleep I've gotten, I'm too excited to stay in bed. It's time to start the day.

I pull one of Brian's sweatshirts on over my leggings and push my hair back into a messy knot as I walk down the stairs, allowing my nose to lead me to the goods like a foxhound finds deer.

The strands of blue bulbs wrapped around the tree are the only lights on in the front of the house and glow in stark contrast to the orange fire crackling in the fireplace. The combination of baked cinnamon, sugar, and butter wafting through the rooms and a roaring fire tells me Brian's been up for a while, no doubt living on his baker's hours even on his day off.

I peek under the tree, adjust Britt's stocking one more time and, turning to view the entire scene, smile before making my way lazily to the kitchen doorway. Brian's busying himself with breakfast foods, giving me just a few minutes to watch him work his magic before I hear the stairs creak. Brian looks to me in the doorway as I look at the stairs as Tommy pulls in a breath, stopping midway to the first floor.

"Sorry," he whispers to me before leaping from the fifth step up and landing gracefully next to me in the doorway. "I don't know this place like I know Mama and Dad's."

I shrug and turn my attention back to Brian as the two of us meander into the kitchen and prop ourselves on opposing counter tops.

"Whatever, T, as long as that boy sleeps long enough to really enjoy today," Brian says without looking up from the bundt pan he's turning over onto a platter.

I watch as the syrupy cinnamon and sugar concoction melt down the edges of the coffeecake and feel my stomach turn.

Shaking it off, I move to grab mugs from the cupboard and get the coffee brewing.

"What time do you think he'll get up?" I ask, knowing with school on break he's bound to sleep in a little.

"Probably not too late," Brian says walking past me and placing a kiss at my temple while holding his sticky fingers away from me. "He's more ready for Christmas this year than I've ever seen him."

The words are barely out of his mouth when the three of us hear a little voice call out from the front of the house, "He came! Santa found me in New York!"

Brian smirks at me. "See, I told you so."

Sticking my tongue out, I pour a cup of coffee and head out to see the first of many Christmas mornings with Britt.

By the time I reach the living room, he's pulled his stocking away from the tree where it was laid after being filled to the brim and too heavy to hang on the mantle. I watch him as he sits down in the middle of the room, slowly turning his head to survey the magic of Christmas.

"This is the biggest Christmas ever," he whispers before his eyes fall on me. "I musta been real good this year, huh?"

This moment is what today is all about and, my God, how have I gone this long without a child to share it with?

I smile and wipe a tear from my eye before it can escape and roll down my cheek.

Brian and Tommy walk up on either side of me, each wrapping an arm around me and it feels like we're kids again.

"Is it time?" Tommy says conspiratorially.

"Oh yeah, it's time," Brian answers with a nod of his head.

"Time for what?" I say, the question falling flat as I watch two grown men race up the stairs.

I hear a door fly open and a bed squeak to life —

"Mama! Daddy! Santa came!" they yell and I hear more jumping. Brian exclaims, "Get up, get up, it's time for Christmas," and I burst out into a fit of giggles.

Moments later Kathryn and Ben descend the stairs. Making eye contact with Ben, he just shakes his head and turns into the kitchen.

"Good morning, Stella. Merry Christmas, sweetie," Kathryn says, giving me a kiss on the cheek. "Any chance you can train those boys once we leave?"

I bark out a laugh and look at her from the corner of my eye.

"I tried my best when I was a kid. I don't know if they'll listen to me now. Did they really jump on the bed?"

"Nah, just gave it a good shaking," she says with a wink. "Now, what have you got there, Sir Britton?"

She walks over and sits down beside Britt. He looks up at me expectantly.

"Can I open my stocking?" His voice is laced with anticipation, his body humming with kept enthusiasm.

"Dig in, baby, today's for you," I say and watch his eyes light up as he starts pulling trinkets and little wrapped presents hidden within the fabric.

I watch as he pulls out one thing at a time, admiring it and genuinely pleased with things like new socks and crayons.

I've never been so content watching someone move at the speed of molasses, but I've never been openly happy with my adult life. I think this is what happiness feels like. It's watching your son smile because of a new pair of socks. It's witnessing untainted joy on the face of a child and knowing you're the one who helped put that look in his eyes.

This is one time of the year when I feel like I can put the rest of life on hold and absorb everything the holidays are supposed to be, what they're supposed to feel like — food, family, laughter and love.

The back door opened when Britt was halfway through his stocking and my parents walked in with their arms loaded down with gifts and food.

I watch as Stephanie swings through on her crutches and sits down in the rocking chair next to Britt, ruffling his hair and bending to kiss his top-knot.

"How ... did we get so lucky?" Brian whispers in my ear, the scent of cinnamon, sugar, and coffee rolling off his tongue, and I smile wondering how long I've been standing here unaware of him behind me. "I mean, look at how happy he is with just his stocking? I don't think that's ever happened before."

"Maybe it's not the stocking," I say casually, leaning back into his warmth. "Maybe it's the extra love that it was filled with. I wonder if it was missing that last year."

Wrapping his arms around my waist, I wait for him to respond. It's possible that this year is just better because it's our first year together. It could be because Kathryn and Ben and Tommy are here. It could be anything and nothing related to me being here.

"You're a pretty smart lady, Mrs. Stratford," Brian says interrupting my thoughts. I glance back at him. "He's never had a mom to spend Christmas with, Stell. You can't tell me this year is already better than the first four because of anything but you, because you made this happen."

I look around the room — the lights on the tree, the ivy on the mantle, little snowman figurines in the bay window — and it shines.

And I shine, too.

***

"Let me see your ring," Steph demands after everyone's left the table.

She lets out a low whistle.

"It's not very big, but that is gorgeous." Steph's holding my hand, admiring the simple band, and I see the whisper of a smile appear at the corner of her sullen eyes.

Then it's gone.

"It's not the size that matters Stephie, hasn't anyone ever told you that?" I say laughing a little louder than I should, trying to bring her out of her darkness. "We were both a little surprised it fit perfectly when he put it on my finger, like it was designed for me. I'm so glad he didn't wait for today. I don't think any of the parents would have appreciated how I thanked him."

She lets loose a hearty laugh and I feel the warmth creep into my cheeks when I realize what I just told her.

"So when's the big day?"

Such a good question and I wish I had the answer. "Spring would be nice, but I just want to do it — have something small, just us and, well, everyone here. I want you and Caryn to stand up with me, Brian will probably have Greg and Britt."

Steph watches me contemplatively. I see her remembering something and she tugs the corner of her bottom lip between her teeth right before biting the bullet and making her confession.

"Your first wedding was such a big show. It wasn't even for your benefit," she says casting her eyes down to the table and watching her hands as she mindlessly picks at the skin edging her fingernails. "Keith wanted this big elaborate thing. You're a country girl, Stella. You want simple, small and all homemade. He made every decision about him, just like he made your marriage about him and only him."

I wish I had seen that then, then maybe ...

"Not that I would have been able to fix anything by seeing that then, but I definitely wouldn't have enjoyed myself as much if I knew he was going to turn out to be a lying, cheating prick," she continues.

"Who's a prick?"

Steph's face blanches when she hears Dad's voice behind her. I just let her talk on because she needed to get it out and flash a smile up at my dad.

"Keith, Daddy. He's a prick," I offer sweetly.

"Yeah, he is. What he put you through, he's lucky I haven't gotten my hands on him. He's laid low all these months," Dad says, curling his fist and shaking it in the air, sending me and Steph into a fit of giggles. "I'm just waiting for my chance to have words with him."

I take a deep breath to regain my composure, wiping a tear from my eye.

"Really, Dad, that's not necessary. If he hadn't screwed me over like he did," I say cautiously as Brian walks into the dining room. "Well, if that hadn't happened, do you think fate would have handed him back to me?" I ask pointing at the blonde-haired blue-eyed baker in question.

Mulling it over, I see his eyes soften.

"You've always been smarter than your old man, Stell, but you don't have to show off." Winking, he turns, clasps Brian's shoulder in his protective grasp and stage whispers, "I'm really glad he broke her heart so you could come fix her properly again," before moving back into the kitchen to visit.

Confusion clouds Brian's eyes. There's concern there, too.

"What was that all about?" he says pointing over his shoulder in the direction Dad went.

"Revenge. Mostly, Dad hoping he'll get a go at Keith someday." Steph says it nonchalantly, but I see the fire in her eyes that tells me she'd still like to have a piece of him herself.

"Eh, he's not worth it. He already lost. I got the girl," Brian says, leaning down to place a kiss on my lips.

"Okay, lover boy, get out. We were trying to talk about wedding things and we keep getting interrupted," she says.

Brian pulls out a dining room chair, turns it backward and straddles the seat. "Well, if it's a wedding I'm going to be heavily involved with, can't I be part of the conversation, too?"

"No," Steph and I say at the same time.

"But ... I bake for you. For both of you. Let me at least help pick out flowers."

"Flowers? I'm going to take your man card away, Bri. You know you know nothing about flowers. Now, me, on the other hand, well, ladies, I know the difference between a daffodil and a daisy," Tommy says settling himself into a chair next to Stephanie and handing her a bottle of beer while sipping from his own.

"Thanks, Tommy, how domestic of you to bring me a beverage," she quips, twisting the top from her beer and chucking it at him.

"I try to get girls to think I'm housebroke every now and again," he retorts.

I lock gazes with Brian, silently asking him what's up with our siblings, but all he does is shrug so I turn my attention back to the original conversation. "So, weddings. Steph and I were discussing how my first one was too showy and it's not me. I want something small, simple, with a very small guest list. Thoughts?"

Brian's demeanor transforms from lighthearted to serious, brooding almost, and I'm expecting him to give me a reason why our wedding should be a huge event.

"Can we do dessert trays instead of cake?"

"That's it? That's your biggest concern?" I ask, astounded that he thought about food instead of people from college or friends in Tennessee he'd absolutely want to invite.

"Yeah. As long as you and I are there, and someone to actually perform the ceremony, the next most important thing is the cake," he says reaching across the table to grab Tommy's beer from his hand and takes a swig. "Oh, and we need to make sure the beer stays cold."

"I swear to God you were made just for me," I say staring at his profile as he hands the beer back. "Where do you want to have the ceremony?"

"If we move my tools and projects around in the wood shop we could have it in there. Put up more of those white Christmas lights to set the mood. We could have dinner upstairs — I'm sure between my house and yours and your mom's we have at least ten slow cookers — and then have a little dancing downstairs." He finishes talking. The only sounds are the low rumblings of our parents visiting in the kitchen around a bottle of wine and Britt and Whiskey playing up in his bedroom. "What?"

I swing my head around slowly and see Steph and Tommy staring, open-mouthed, at Brian until Tom reaches over and closes Steph's jaw for her.

"Did you read her diary or something? Jesus, Brian." Only Steph knows how badly I always wanted a wedding in a barn. She's the only one I ever confided in that I wanted homemade everything from decorations to food.

"When do you want to do it?" I ask without waiting for Brian to respond to my sister.

"Beginning of April."

"Why then?" I'm intrigued. Steph's at a loss for words. Tommy ... well, he looks really confused by all of this.

"The trees are starting to bud and even though the nights are cold, the days are usually warm. It's when everything comes to life up here," he responds, not even stopping to think about what he's saying. "Everyone's twitterpated."

"There it is. This is about sex. I knew my brother was in there somewhere," Tommy shouts like he just discovered the cure for cancer. "Right, man, this is a sex thing?"

"No, it's not a sex thing, Tommy," I say, my eyes never leaving Brian's face. "This is about rebirth. Spring. Second chances. Isn't it?"

Brian turns to look at me and I feel like we're the only two people in the room.

"Do you remember when we were, I don't know, we were maybe seven and we watched that wedding in the park? You and I met up over there on our bikes and we sat on the swings for the longest time. It was the oddest thing because we didn't talk much and then a few people started showing up. We watched some random couple get married in the gazebo and it was magical," he says as I nod my head, the memory flooding back and filling my senses. He reaches over and tucks a piece of my hair behind my ear, the gesture sweet and kind just like the memory. "You sighed. I remember the sound of that sigh all these years later. That little wedding with just a few guests was your dream wedding. I want to make all your dreams come true."

"I can't believe you remember that," I whisper.

"I remember everything about my time with you," he responds quietly.

The sound of a throat clearing brings us out of our memories. It was more than memories though; it felt like we were there all over again.

"So, April in the wood shop. We should start working on a menu, Stell, don't you think?" Steph's eyes are barely holding back tears as she takes another swig of her beer. "Meatballs, lasagna, a salad or two. Flowers, you'll probably want stargazer lilies and daisies, right? I'm going to go get some paper and a pen so I can start writing this down."

She slowly rises to her good foot, places the crutches beneath her, and hobbles out to the living room.

Brian

Chapter Thirty-Three

I watch Stephanie try to leave the room as gracefully as she can, which isn't graceful at all, and when she's a safe distance away I excuse myself from the table, leaving Tommy and Stella to discuss my use of the word "twitterpated" — she thinks it's adorable, he thinks I'm horny.

Walking into the living room behind her, I ask, "Are you okay with all of this, Steph?"

"Yeah, I'm fine. Why wouldn't I be?"

She responds but doesn't turn to look at me. Instead she stops and I see her head droop slightly as she reaches up to push a lock of hair behind her right ear.

"Steph, look at me when you lie to me," I joke. "I've known you a long time. I know it doesn't seem that way, but I have, and I can tell you're upset. Talk to me?"

Slowly she turns on her good foot and scrutinizes me while assessing her words before she's spoken them.

"Yeah, no, I'm not okay. Not in the traditional sense. I'm happy for you and Stell, please don't think it's anything other than that. I love you guys together. I'm just ... I just thought maybe at some point it would happen to me. I thought it was happening to me."

Reaching out, I take her gently by the shoulders.

"You thought he was the one?"

"For a while. It's stupid. He was so great in the beginning and —" she drops her head back staring at the ceiling "—I thought he'd change. Why are girls always so naïve? Why do we always think they'll change? Do you know what he said to me the night he attacked me?"

The hate in her eyes kicks me straight in the gut and I just shake my head in response. It's all I can do.

"He told me I would always be his. Always," she whips the words at me. "And I said I would never be a man's property. Then I spit in his face and he pushed me to the ground and did this."

"And you survived. You are surviving —"

"Barely, Brian. I'm barely surviving. I'm living in my sister's spare bedroom. I put a night light in the bathroom because the darkness scares the living shit out of me now. My best friend is afraid to talk to me because he might say something that hurts more than it should and I can't get him to understand it's not his fault. I'm still living in fear even though Max put a bullet in that fucker's head and literally killed my living nightmare. I'm still afraid," she finally admits. The strength drains from her, her shoulders slumping as the weight of the confession is lifted from her frail body.

"Stephie ... oh, Steph, it's okay to still be afraid. Just because his body is dead and cold doesn't mean the memories ever will be. You're allowed to be scared of the dark, just don't forget there are a whole lot of us waiting for you when you're ready to find the light," I say, placing my index and middle finger under her chin so she'll look at me. "We're all here for you."

"I know. I know, you guys are always here and I should be talking to you about all of this stuff, or to Stella, or someone, but I just don't want to be ... a burden." Her eyes glisten with unshed tears. "I want to be happy around all of you. I don't want to subject you to this."

"You mean you don't want us to be privy to the wit and charm you possess? You'd take that away from us? I'm shocked," I feign, clutching my chest like she physically wounded me, and catch a small smile at the corners of her mouth. "So, let's grab that paper and pen you pretended to come get in order to get away from us happy people and go start making some lists. It might make you feel a little better to do something with your brain. Let's go forget for a while why you're on crutches and instead eat rum cake and talk about flower arrangements."

"You don't think I'm a burden?" she questions warily.

"If I thought you were a burden, I wouldn't have followed you in here in the first place to make sure you were okay. If I thought you were a burden, I wouldn't have driven through the night from Tennessee to get home just to see for myself that you were still in one piece." I pause and collect myself while watching her reaction. "Steph, even when you were a baby and wanted to tag along with me and Stella, you were never ever a burden. You never will be."

"If you're just saying this because you're marrying my sister, I'm going to make your life miserable. You know that, right?"

Steph lets out a laugh, a real laugh, and I'm glad the gloom has left her eyes for the moment.

"Kid, I wouldn't have it any other way," I say grabbing one of Stella's notepads and a pen from the coffee table.

***

"Not bad for our first holiday together. We did food, presents, lots of visiting, planned a wedding, and ate more food. Is there anymore apple pie?"

Stella's practically climbing into the oven when I walk out of the bathroom with a towel draped over my shoulder. I don't hide the fact I was staring at her backside when she stands up and turns around with a pie plate in her hand and a fork hanging out of her mouth.

"You look yummy, too. But I want this pie. No way am I letting Tommy eat it for breakfast," she says pulling out a barstool and hunkering down at the counter.

"You looked like you wanted to run away at the sight of coffee cake this morning and now at midnight you're eating pie right from the dish. Are you feeling alright?" I ask only somewhat joking.

Stella finishes chewing the bite in her mouth and swallows, watching me suspiciously before popping another forkful of pie in her mouth.

"I feel fine. I just really love pie. Where did you get this recipe, anyway? It tastes really familiar," she says before taking another bite.

It should taste familiar to her — it's her grandmother's recipe. I'd never believed cayenne pepper belonged in pie until Jenny let me go through her recipes for the holiday and I came across a faded piece of paper with Nana Barbieri's handwriting on it.

A low moan jars my senses and I snap my attention back to Stella at the counter.

"I remember her making this pie when we were kids. Oh my God, Bri, I haven't had this in years. Mom never makes it like this."

She's going to eat the rest of that pie if I don't stop her. Another moan escapes her lips and I swallow hard against the reaction my body is having to her, to that fork in her mouth, to the fact my soon-to-be wife loves food as much as I do.

She's changed out of the clothes she wore all day. Sitting in front of me with one leg propped on the stool she's perched on, I watch her thoroughly enjoying her foodgasm while wearing a strappy top that accentuates the natural curve of her breasts. Her hair has grown long enough that she drapes it over her left shoulder and it falls to the channel between her breasts.

With each moan, I watch as they rise and fall; it's mesmerizing.

"You need to stop that," I say, my tone a gentle warning.

"This pie, though. Brian, please tell me you had some of it earlier," she says, closing her eyes as her full, soft lips wrap around the fork again. "This ... is worthy of an orgasm."

"Which is why you need to stop," I say, having moved to stand beside her. I take the fork from her hand, set it back in the pie plate and swiftly cover her shocked mouth with my own as she turns to me ready to protest.

She tastes damn near sinful.

Stella reaches up and pulls my mouth harder against hers, ravenous.

"Bathroom. Now."

She's commanding. Demanding. She's in charge.

Stella grabs my hips and pushes me backward until my shoulders are pressed against the frame of the bathroom door. She stands on her tiptoes to reach my neck, licking and nipping at the tender flesh. I drag my fingertips from her neck down her spine, feeling her shiver in their wake as she presses her body fully into mine and breathes out a moan so low it's barely audible.

"I need you naked and in me," she whispers.

I cup her face in my hands and capture her bottom lip with my teeth as I turn her back to the open door and walk her through, pushing the door closed with my foot once we're safely on the other side. My hands still on her face, I feel her begin pushing down my legs the grey sweatpants I threw on after my shower, my boxer briefs bulging from the barely restrained erection.

Reaching behind me, Stella turns the lock on the door despite the late hour.

"Brian," she breathes out my name. "I want you. This isn't about need. I want you and if you don't hurry it up, I'm just going to take what I want."

A smile forms on her lips knowing full well I'll give her what she wants.

"No need to take it." The words are hardly out of my mouth before I'm lifting her shirt above her head and the swell of her breasts fall from their confines like forbidden fruit. I lift one to my mouth as I wrap my other arm around her waist, cupping her firm ass in my hand. Flicking my tongue across the tip of her nipple, I feel her chest rise with the sharp intake of air.

Her hands are in my hair, her fingers threading through it and holding on as I continue my gentle assault on her breasts.

I lift her up, wrapping her legs around my waist, and pin her against the wall with my hips, grinding into her as I find her mouth with mine again.

Breaking the kiss and glaring at me, she says, "You're teasing me."

"Not on purpose. I've had to share you all day. Don't be mad because I want to take a little extra time with the foreplay."

"The pie wasn't foreplay enough?" Her smiles lights up my life and I move in to kiss her again, my cock twitching in my underwear when I feel her tongue slide along the seam of my lips.

I stand her back on the floor, sliding her yoga pants down her legs until she steps out of them and notice she's opted for no underwear.

"Commando, eh?" I ask, shaking my head. "It's like you planned for this to happen."

"The only thing I planned was for me to eat food and go to bed. This —" she laughs gesturing to the space between us and then the room "— is because of that damn pie and your dirty mind."

"It wouldn't have been so dirty if you weren't moaning and practically mouth fucking that fork," I say, and watch her pretty little mouth fall open, knowing I can't make her wait any longer.

I strip my boxer briefs off and pull her to me, the heat of our bodies colliding as a rush of cool air swirls around us.

Stella walks me backward until the backs of my legs touch the bathtub and she pushes on my shoulders making me sit on the edge. Resting my hands on her waist, I pull her body to me, kissing her belly, her hips, down to the apex of her thighs. She shudders, holding onto my shoulders, and pushes me back to climb on and straddle my lap.

She lets out a pent up sigh, her head falling back, as I enter her. I rock my body as best I can, feeling myself hit deep within her. Stella moans and begins moving her hips, pushing herself up off me while I'm left unable to move in this position.

Holding her hips, I push her back and forth on my cock, rubbing her clit into my pelvis, and watch her skin begin to blush. I love the way it creeps up her neck as an orgasm builds deep within her and I rock her faster.

She opens her eyes, staring directly into mine, and I'm done. I hold Stella close to me, her legs instinctively wrapping around my waist, and stand up. I replay the first time we made love, in this bathroom of all places, with her on this counter. I set her down, still deep inside her, and hold her close as we find that rhythm again quickly. Her grip on my shoulders tightens, her nails digging into my flesh, and she's biting her lip as I thrust into her.

She doesn't say a word as I feel her body grip mine and the first wave of her orgasm pulls a gasp from her and she cries out my name. I'm right there with her, tumbling toward oblivion, and thrust once, twice more, holding my body tight to hers as my orgasm wracks my body.

Pressing my forehead to Stella's, we hold each other waiting for our hearts to stop racing.

With her, though, mine will never slow down.

"Thank you ..." I say cautiously as I tilt her face toward me, tipping her lips into mine to taste her again. "Thank you for being absolutely perfect for me."

"I'm glad you're not thanking me for the sex. We really need to start doing this in a bed more often. I'm getting too old to be flung around like a ragdoll." She winks at me and smiles before pulling me in for another kiss.

"You sure you want to wait until April to make this legal?"

"No," she whispers against my lips, "but I think we need the next few months to figure out what we're doing with the houses and I'd like to have a plan before we get married."

"We're being responsible adults."

Stella chuckles, because since we first saw one another after all these years some might think we've acted like anything but responsible adults. We definitely have acting like horny teenagers in the back of my truck and love struck kids while holding hands in public down to a science, but it feels like responsibility has woven itself in and around all those moments, too.

"I think we have a nice even mix of acting our ages and acting like we would have if this had happened fifteen years ago," she says like she's reading my mind. "I hope it stays this way forever. I don't want to feel like our life is routine, Brian. We have been in love with one another since we were practically babies and even though our lives took us in different directions, we're right back here where it started."

"In my bathroom connected at the hip?" I cock my eyebrow and give her a crooked grin.

"That dimple. It drives me a little crazy." She touches my cheek and bites her bottom lip. "But no. I'm talking about fate and the fact we're right back here in this little town where I first found you."

"How do you know I didn't notice you first? You and your pigtails sitting on the swing out back, you looked like an angel." I swallow hard remembering the first time I saw Stella, all alone in her parents' backyard. I was supposed to be helping unpack boxes in the kitchen when I saw her through the window. "I couldn't wait to get to know the girl next door. If I thought I loved you then, I was crazy."

"I thought I loved you then, but I've never loved you more than in this moment," she says wrapping her legs around my waist and pressing her still naked body as close to mine as she can. "If you're lucky, I might even love you more than this tomorrow."

***

We finally made it from the bathroom to the bedroom an hour later, our biggest distraction being what to do about the double home situation. In the end, we left it up in the air because things seem to have a way of working themselves out in the end.

I figure one way or another we'll have somewhere to live, somewhere to love and somewhere to grow our family.

And maybe if we're lucky Tommy will want to buy the other house and make an effort to truly settle down instead of crashing in a spare bedroom or on Britt's floor.

I'm still pondering and mulling over the conversation from the night before when Tommy walks through the backdoor at the coffeehouse. He catches me leaning against the counter, my sleeves pulled halfway up my forearms and a cup of coffee in my right hand.

"You wanna buy a house?"

"Huh? I haven't had coffee yet. I'm doing this up at five in the morning thing to get down here and need caffeine before you pull shit like that," he says without stopping to look at me before going out into the coffeehouse. I hear him pull a mug off the shelf, pour a cup and put the pot back on the burner. "Shit!" And burn his mouth.

"You really need to let that cool down before taking a swig," I say as he walks back through the swinging café doors into the kitchen.

"Too early to remember hot liquid burns. Now, what about buying a house?"

A smile breaks the bleakness of the early morning and I explain the situation — eventually Stella and I are going to have to live together which means at least one house will be available.

"If you're interested in owning one of the houses, I think we'd prefer selling to family. Steph's not really in a position to own, but if you want a roommate to help with the bills I'm sure you could talk to her." I spell it all out for him. There's no point beating around the bush and hoping he understands what I'm implying. "I don't think she's going to be ready to go out on her own again yet, and knowing her she isn't going to want to live with newlyweds. She isn't the kind to swallow her pride and move back into the bedroom she had as a kid, either."

Tommy leans against the opposite counter, blowing across the top of his coffee before taking a tentative sip, and stares at me.

"You forget I've met Steph. I know she can't swallow her pride. She can be a super bitch, too, when her pride's at stake. Some things just never change." He takes another sip from his mug and I notice the wary look in his eyes. "It might not be the best idea, but I'll talk to her. You know she's going to accuse me of having some knight in scuffed up cowboy boots complex, right?"

I push off from the counter, slapping him on the shoulder as I walk past.

"Yeah, but she's nothing you can't handle."

Stella

Chapter Thirty-Four

"I need a longer headline for our lead story and a shorter head for the rail, Caryn. Help me out here. My brain is fried," I say without looking up from my desk. It's not even noon and I'm ready to fall over.

Brian's parents left a few weeks ago but it's like all the excitement of them being in town, all the family dinners so our parents could catch up, and the hours I normally put in at the office have totally wiped me out. I thought my energy would make a reappearance after the weekend away at my dad's hunting cabin, but I came back home more tired than when we left.

Caryn walks over to my desk, red pen in hand. She's a human thesaurus and within a few minutes has fixed the issue.

"There," she says with finality. "Let's get lunch."

Grabbing my jacket and wallet, I follow Caryn out of the newsroom door and into the brisk January air.

"You calling it an early night tonight? You look like hell." Caryn's never really been one to sugarcoat anything.

I try to answer, but instead a yawn sneaks out. "It's that obvious I'm exhausted?"

Keeping pace so we can get to the pizza shop quickly, she glances over at me. Hands in her pockets, blonde waves blowing back, and a navy peacoat hugging her slim waist, she looks like a head cheerleader instead of a rip your throat out watchdog reporter.

"I think you fell asleep at your computer yesterday afternoon. I'm pretty sure when I walked through the door after my last interview, your head was propped up in your hand like you'd been reading but your eyes were closed and you had a little drool right here —" she points to the corner of her mouth and starts laughing. "You're going to make yourself sick if you don't get some sleep."

"Brian keeps telling me the same thing. It's just been crazy between his parents being up here and now that the spring semester is in full swing, he's up before the sun to make sure they have all the display cases filled, so staying at his place means less sleep than normal. I don't sleep alone well at my place anymore ... it's strange. I never had trouble falling asleep when Keith wasn't home to go to bed with me." I divulge the information like it's a state secret, lowering my voice out of fear someone might hear me admit I slept just fine when my ex-husband wasn't home. "I know it's a completely different situation. I don't think I ever loved Keith like I'm in love with Brian. He's the one I settled for, not the one I longed for."

As we step through the door to the restaurant, Caryn says, "I think it's cute how you waited for him ... in a self-destructive married-the-wrong-guy kind of way. Almost makes me think love can be worth the pain it sometimes brings."

"Greg?"

"We hit a wall. It's me, though, not him. I don't even know how to talk about it with him because there are just too many things going on. I'm not even sure where the beginning is."

"You'll figure it out," I say stepping up to the counter to place my order. "Sometimes ... sometimes it just takes time."

We wait for our food in silence, each likely mulling over the conversation we had as we walked into the building. I'd like to believe I won't dwell on Caryn and Greg's relationship status, but I'm the dwelling type. They never officially said they were dating, but they acted like falling in love was certainly on their agenda and I have no idea what happened.

Our names are called, we grab our lunches and head back to the office, bowing our heads to the wind and snow.

***

"I thought you were leaving early?" Caryn says spinning her chair around and placing her elbows on my desk.

"It's not even three o'clock yet. No way can I leave now. I thought you meant a normal hour when you said 'early' earlier ... like six." She can't be serious about me going home now. "I feel fine. I just need a cup of coffee."

I turn to get up from my desk and barely make it to the trashcan in the back of the room before lunch reappears. Caryn's chair rolls across the newsroom and I hear the heels on her shoes clicking their way toward me. When my stomach stops revolting, my eyes sting and my throat is raw. I want to curl up in a ball and cry.

"Holy shit, Stella. Are you okay?" She's reaching to move my hair off my forehead as I try to get up off the floor. "You're so pale, Stell. Can you make it to the bathroom?"

I simply nod my head, fearful if I open my mouth to answer I'll vomit on her. Grabbing the trashcan, I hug it to my chest while I make my way down the hall to the restroom.

The cool water feels heavenly against my face until I feel another wave of nausea come over me and I'm shoving my head back into the trash. There's no way I would have made it into a stall.

"I think ... I think I'm okay now," I say to Caryn as she hands me a wad of damp paper towels.

"You look even worse now. You need to go home and get some sleep." Caryn sounds like my mom for a second. "It's flu season. We can't afford to have you out of the office when there's usually at least one other person sick every week during the winter. I'm serious, go get rest."

"I think it was the food. I was feeling fine before I ate."

"Excuses. Go home and sleep. I'll button up things here for the night. There isn't much going on anyway and the paper's pretty much laid out because, you know, it's a slow news day and people actually returned calls," she says, knowing what to say to ease my mind. "There's no point in you staying if you're going to be sick and worthless anyway."

I rub my hands over my face and reach back to pull my hair into a ponytail, praying I didn't throw up in it.

"Fine. I'll go. But I'll be here tomorrow unless I'm on my deathbed."

"I wouldn't expect anything less, my love," she says, leading me out of the ladies' room.

***

"So ... Caryn said you puked at work and blamed it on food," Steph says from the other side of the shower curtain. I pull the plastic back and glare at her as she slowly lifts her cell phone up for me to see. "She texted me. Wanted to make sure I made you park your ass on the couch with some chicken noodle soup and movies for the night since Brian's working late for that open mic night Tommy scheduled."

"Where's Britt?" I ask, worry replacing the fatigue.

"With mom. She's going to take him home after dinner to get him ready for bed and stay until Brian gets home since you aren't feeling well."

"Sounds like Caryn took care of everything," I say, sticking my head back under the spray.

"Actually, I called mom. I figured you could use the early night. Since you've been nursing me back to health for the last few months, I figure I'll repay the favor," she declares, playing with the drawstring on her sweatpants. Soon, the cast is going to come off and she's going to force me to go shop for new pants since most of hers are missing a leg now. "Besides, we haven't had much just us sister time."

"You're going to chance the flu to watch movies and eat soup with me?" I ask incredulously.

"Well, I'm not going to sit on the same couch as you. I don't need your cooties. Plus, most people with the flu can barely stand up to take a shower, let alone hold a conversation with this much fluidity. Last time you had the flu you communicated through a series of grunts and groans," Steph says, standing up from her perch on the edge of the closed toilet. "It was probably just the grease from that calzone, right? You rarely eat that shit anymore."

I think about what she said. The last time I was sick, it hit out of nowhere and I was down for a good four days.

"Probably was the food. This is nothing like when I get the flu. I'm just so exhausted." I shut off the water and reach for my towel, wrapping it around myself and stepping from the shower. "I seriously have never been this tired in my entire life. Well, not since college when I was pulling all-nighters, but I haven't had one of those since Brian and I got together."

Steph's watching me expectantly.

"What?" I ask, as I run my fingers through my hair, trying to get the tangles out of it.

"Nothing. I'm just thinking," she says curiously. "Anyway, since you're out of the shower, I'm going to go get some soup ready. Figure out what movie you want to watch and I'll meet you downstairs."

Then she's gone from the bathroom and I'm clueless about what just transpired.

But I'm starving and tired.

I yell out the door, "Make me a peanut butter and jelly sandwich, too, please!"

Wrapping another towel around my hair, I shuffle down the hall to my bedroom and find Brian's SU hoodie and a pair of sweatpants I also "borrowed" from him. He's never getting them back. It's part of the dating and marriage code.

I sneak down the hidden stairwell to the kitchen and watch Steph hobble around without her crutches making canned soups and tea.

When she notices me leaning against the doorframe, I smile. "It's nice to be taken care of once in a while. What can I help with?"

"Can you carry this stuff to the living room? I'm starting to hurt from not using the crutches. This stupid broken leg fucks up a lot of stuff," she spouts off as I grab the tray she put the soups and tea onto. She slowly follows me through the house until we're settled on the couch, me with my legs folded up under me and her with her good leg propped up on her cast.

"We're a couple of crazy chicks hanging out on a Thursday night in jammies with soup. If I knew this was how it was going to be getting older I really would have enjoyed college more," I laugh, grabbing the remotes and turning on Netflix. "Sixteen Candles? Pretty In Pink? I'm in a John Hughes-y mood. Or Breakfast Club?"

"All three, in chronological order."

"Game on," I say, holding my fist out for her to bump.

***

"I feel fine Caryn. I'm coming to work." She's still talking in the background but I stopped listening. "You need to let me go so I can put this eyeliner on without stabbing myself in the face. I feel a lot better today after soup and sleeping, so stop trying to mother me. I'll grab coffees from Brian on my way. You want your regular?"

Caryn huffs out a sigh on the other side of town. "Yeah. I appreciate you getting it. I just don't even want to go to the coffeehouse because there's never a day Greg isn't working. Can't deal with it right now."

"You're going to have to explain all of this to me someday soon, you know. Bri and I thought you two were on fire and then ... I don't know. It fizzled. It makes me worry a little," I admit.

"I know. I'll explain, just not now," she says and the line goes quiet. "I'll see you at the office in a bit. I have a few things to get done before I head in."

I hear the apprehension in her voice but drop it knowing any line of questioning would be for naught.

Eyeliner on, knee-high boots zipped and my hair done, I feel mostly human.

I yell to Steph as I open the back door, letting her know I'm leaving for work, and grab my laptop bag and purse as I walk out onto the porch.

The sub-zero temperature hits me in the face making my eyes water and I hear the red oak tree behind the house crackle angrily from the severe cold. I'm barely in the truck long enough for the heater to kick in before I'm pulling up to the coffeehouse and turning the engine off.

"Hey, Greg. I need my regular and Caryn's. Large, please," I say as I walk through the door. The seating area is half full of students on laptops getting their morning caffeine infusion but there's no line. "Can I grab one of the chocolate chip muffins, too? I'm starving."

He shakes his head and smiles at me before turning to the coffee selection along the back counter. "Sure thing. I mean, you're marrying the boss, so I think you could probably ask him to bake you a fresh batch of cookies and it would happen."

"Bleh. What fun would that be?" I say eyeballing the café doors that lead to the kitchen. "Is Bri busy? I didn't see him last night."

"I heard you made it an early night and weren't feeling well. He's in the office. Go on back," Greg says without turning back around.

I scoot around the end of the counter and through the doorway. The kitchen is still warm from the morning's baking session and the smell of peanut butter and cinnamon hits my nose as I reach the office doorway.

"Hey there handsome." I close the door behind me and sit down in the armchair behind his desk. "It's Friday night. Want to do anything amazing? Like order a pizza and wings and build with Britt's Lego set?"

He turns his office chair to face me, concern lacing his features.

"Are you sure you feel up to it? Your mom told me when she came to get Britt yesterday that you went home from work after getting sick at the office," he says, reaching out to touch my cheek. "I didn't want to call after I was done here in case you were sleeping."

His worry makes me wish I'd called him last night just to let him know I was okay. "I got busy into a John Hughes movie marathon with Steph and a cup of tea. I think it was the stuff I ate for lunch. Greasy calzone. It was delicious going down. But really, it's nothing. My stomach just couldn't handle it and I've been exhausted from late nights and early mornings."

"If you're sure. You want pizza after getting sick from something that's basically pizza in pocket form?" he says, squinting at me with confusion on his face.

"Yeah, that sounds kind of crazy. Burritos?"

Brian starts laughing and rolls his chair over to me so we're eye-to-eye. "I love you. Burritos it is. You pick Britt up after work and I'll grab food when I leave here around six. Greg and Tom are closing up tonight."

I stand up and stumble back, Brian's hand shooting out to grab my wrist and steady me as he stands up. The dizzy feeling subsides and I smile at him.

"I'm fine."

"You're pale. You don't feel warm though," he says, pressing his wrist to my forehead first, then my neck. "Dizzy?"

"A little when I stood up. I haven't eaten much since lunch yesterday, though."

"Grab a bottle of water from the cooler and have Greg put an extra muffin in your order," Brian says pulling me into a gentle hug. I breathe in his familiar scent only for it to knock me back, my stomach turning at the smell of his beloved Old Spice. Not even his beloved. Mine. I love that smell. He pulls away and looks at me. "You're going to be sick aren't you?"

"Nope," I say emphatically shaking my head from side to side as he reaches under the desk for his wastebasket. I grab it and fall back into the chair as he walks out of the office.

I take a deep breath in through my nose and close my eyes waiting for the nausea to pass. Brian and Greg walk back into the office, a bottle of water in Bri's hand and a damp cloth in Greg's.

"You two don't have time to nurse me back to health. I feel fine —" Brian cuts me off as I carefully stand up.

"You're not fine, Stella. You're pale, you're dizzy, you were sick yesterday and you —" he glances down into the trash bin "— almost got sick again a few minutes ago. You need to go home and sleep."

I fight him on it.

"My stomach is fine now. I'm not dizzy anymore. I'm probably dehydrated and starving. Give me my damn muffin, a bottle of water, and my coffees. I need to go to work," I say, loudly, using my own boss tone of voice. Remorse hits me when I see his face fall and watch Greg's eyes widen in surprise. "Please. I promise if I feel worse when I get to work I will go home. I'll call you and let you know if I leave the office or if I'm curled up in the ladies room hugging the toilet, but I need to at least go to the office."

Greg leans over to Brian and, in what couldn't even be considered anything in the realm of a whisper, says, "She really is a stubborn one. I wouldn't mess with her if I were you." He steps backward out of the office, retreating to the safety of the front counter.

Brian takes a step toward me, reaching out to hold my face between his hands. "Promise me you will call if you so much as think you're going to hurl. If you're sick, the guys will understand and I'll leave. Promise you won't overwork yourself today."

"I wouldn't think of it. I don't want to get you or Britt sick. I just, I really don't feel that bad. This was the first time today this happened," I say, hoping he isn't going to quarantine me and lock me in his office.

He walks me back to the front of the coffeehouse, insists on carrying my coffees out to the truck and kisses me on the forehead before letting me leave.

***

"Why are you here? Brian texted me asking I keep an eye on you." Fuck.

I sigh deeply, because it's all I can think to do, and rub my hands down my face.

"I'm fine. He worries worse than I do. Plus he's a dad, so it's natural for him to worry every time someone he loves feels yucky," I say, then regret saying it because she's giving me the evil eye. "I'll see how I feel at lunch. If I feel worse, I'll go home. I told him I wouldn't overwork myself so drop it."

She gives me a "mmhmm" under her breath as she unbuttons her coat and hangs it on the coat tree next to the newsroom door. Picking up her coffee, she takes a sip, looking at the ingredient checklist printed on the side of it before she sets it on her desk.

Caryn smiles at the cup.

"What was that?" I ask.

"What was what?"

"You smiled at your cup. That thing drove here with me and I carried it in and put it on your desk. Greg left you a message didn't he?"

"What? No. Nah, I'm just smiling because you had him put an extra shot of espresso in. I thought it was nice of you to think of my caffeine needs," she says, genuinely thanking me for the order.

"I didn't tell him to put anything extra in there. I ordered my regular and your regular," I say, turning back to my computer screen. "Boy's got it bad if he's trying to buy your heart with coffee. That's how Brian got mine."

"Yeah ... I know." That's it. Nothing else. Caryn sits down, starts her computer, goes through the mail from her inbox, checks her email, and drops all conversation about Greg.

We sit in silence, working on stories and answering emails, answering the phone and calling for interviews.

There's finally a break, so I jump up and rush to the bathroom knowing if I don't go now the likelihood of someone calling me when I do go later increases. It's newsroom law — call people, leave messages, wait all day and when you walk out for a cup of coffee or to pee, they always call you back.

"You were taking forever. Are you okay?" Caryn says when I walk out of the restroom.

"Jesus Christ on a cracker, Caryn, I am fine." I can't keep the irritation from my voice. "I know you're worried about me, thinking I'm sick or coming down with something but seriously, this is bordering on crazy stalker best friend status. What's the deal?"

"Honestly? I don't think it's the food from yesterday and I definitely don't think it's the flu." She looks down at the tile floor like it's the most interesting thing in the building. Quietly, Caryn says, "Stell, when was your last period?"

Brian

Chapter Thirty-Five

"Two café Americano and a chocolate chip scone. Good luck with your research," I say handing the order to a college age kid who looks like he has the fear of God in him. He's rattled off a ton of information about researching things for a graduate thesis topic I don't think I can even spell. "A lot of luck."

"Thanks. I really need it. You'll probably see me again later for a pick-me-up, though," he says, walking away.

I hear Greg laughing behind me and turn to see him, arms crossed in front of his chest, shaking his head back and forth.

"Remember when we were that kid? Seems like it wasn't that long ago we were trying to figure out what the hell we were doing with our lives. Now look at us," he says holding his arms wide.

That's what I do. I step forward and turn to lean on the counter next to my best friend and take a look at what we've created — a life, a thriving business, careers in an industry we didn't really expect to have, and family.

"It is pretty amazing how far we've come. When we first decided to jump and move up here, I really didn't expect this much ... success. That's what we've found though, you know? Success."

"And now you're getting married, adding to the family —"

"Huh?" I interrupt him. Stella and I haven't said anything to anyone about our plans to try for a baby right away. "What do you mean 'adding to'? We have Britt and that's all right now."

Wide-eyed, Greg stares at me with a crooked grin on his lips and starts laughing again. "You're joking right?"

"I have no idea what you're talking about," I respond in all seriousness.

"Hold on," he says and walks up to the counter, calling to Tommy who's washing off a table out front. "Come here. We need to have a chat with your big brother, dude."

I'm being accosted and feel claustrophobic as Tommy comes around behind the counter. We're between the morning and afternoon rush, so there are just a few stragglers sitting with their coffee and laptops enjoying the quiet.

"What's up?" Tommy asks, leaning to rest against the counter across from me and Greg.

"You notice anything weird about Stella lately?" Greg asks him.

I watch Tommy mull the question over, chewing on his thumbnail as he thinks, before talking.

"Where should I start? Anytime I see her lately she's either starving or looks like she's going to vomit in the nearest trashcan. At Christmas, she had like a glass of wine. Singular. That chick will usually down a bottle or more during family gatherings from what Steph has told me," he says, tapping his chin with his forefinger trying to think of something else that's stood out recently. "Bri, don't get pissed at me, but her shirts? The buttons have started straining."

I look back and forth between him and Greg.

"I don't think he understands," Greg says to my brother. "Brian ... we're no doctors, but we've all been around women who have been pregnant before, especially you. You can't tell me you didn't notice any of this."

"She's been busy with work, I've been busy here now that the college is back for the spring session. She's been exhausted, so when we do spend the night together she's out as soon as her head hits the pillow," I ramble trying to make sense of it. "There's no way. She would have told me. We had a scare back right after we started seeing each other, but we've been careful since then."

"Are you sure?" Greg asks.

How could she be pregnant and not tell me? Haven't we been careful?

"Oh shit." I say it more to myself than either of the guys, but they both turn to look at me. "Thanksgiving. When we came back from Tennessee after Steph was attacked."

I count in my head.

"That was what, two months or so ago?" Tommy says.

"Nine weeks." For nine weeks I've been stuck inside my own head and not seeing things going on right in front of me. "Christmas morning, when I took the coffee cake out of the pan, she looked like she was going to be sick, but I figured it was because we'd hardly slept. When Stell doesn't get a lot of sleep she gets queasy, you know, so I didn't think anything of it."

I didn't question the porn-worthy noises she was making while eating apple pie either, but I don't mention it to them.

"Why did you decide to bring this up now if you guys have been noticing all of these things for weeks? I've been oblivious to any of it and have no idea how. I see her every day, every night. I see her naked and I've missed all of this. Even the expanding bust line," I say angrily, glaring at Tommy.

He opens his mouth to say something and, like a fish out of water struggling to breathe, closes it again.

"Honestly, Bri, I thought you knew but you guys were just keeping it quiet. I mean, you've got the wedding coming up in a few months, we've got a ton of stuff going on here at the coffeehouse, Stella's always super busy at the paper," Greg says, breaking the tension between me and Tommy. "It wasn't until I saw how you acted this morning with her almost getting sick in your office that I figured out you have no fucking clue. Oddly enough, she doesn't seem to know either."

"She blamed it on food she ate yesterday. I figured she was coming down with a bug, the flu or something," I say looking at my boots and wrapping my hands around the back of my neck. "She's just stubborn enough to think it's not the obvious, too. Fuck."

Tommy steps across the small walkway between the counters and then the Three Amigos are standing together, Tom and Greg each with a hand on one of my shoulders. It's like when I found out Emily was pregnant with Britt, they were both there with me, only that wasn't a happy time — I wasn't in love with Emily and I wondered how I could have been so stupid. If this is true, if Stella's pregnant, I'm ecstatic, but still scared.

"Y'all are getting married. This should be a happy thing, Brian. You're a great dad and you love kids, so you can't for a second make me think you're not happy about this," my brother says quietly in my ear.

He doesn't get it.

"I am happy, T, but I'm more worried about my soon-to-be father-in-law," I say and watch as the fear registers on both their faces. "How's he going to take it when he finds out his baby girl got knocked up before her wedding? Dale can be scary when he's mad, guys. I never want to be on the receiving end of his anger."

I cover my face with both hands.

What is he going to think of me?

Maybe it's worse that, despite my profound respect for Dale, it really doesn't matter what he thinks.

"It'll be okay. I have to talk to Stella, though, and find out if she seriously thinks she's getting sick or that it's because of something she ate," I say more to myself than anyone else. "We both know how babies are made."

"Yeah, they come from the stork. Everyone knows that," a familiar voice says from the other side of the counter.

I uncover my face and watch a rare grin light up Max's features. He's usually the broody, miserable police officer type — a sight the guys and I have gotten used to since he's started coming in daily after Steph's attack — and the smile looks good on him.

"Hey man, what can I get you? Your regular?" Tommy asks, holding his hand out to shake Max's.

"Yeah, that'll be great. Make it a large, though. Rough morning with the cold temps. People forget how to drive in this weather," Max says making small talk. "So, Brian, what's the deal with the baby talk? You and Stella finally telling people?"

I stare at him. What the fuck?

If Greg, Tommy, and Max have noticed something is off with her ... "Seriously, how the hell did I miss all the signs?"

"Is he for real?" I hear Max ask Tommy.

"Yeah, afraid so. Seems our boy here hasn't noticed all the weird going on with my future sister-in-law, which is odd because, in his words, he sees her naked all the time. What have you noticed?" Tommy queries the officer while pouring his coffee.

"For starters, our hardened reporter came in for police reports last week and burst into tears when she was checking the board with all the missing person fliers on it. Not just a few tears, guys, like full on sobbing. Chief had to pull her into his office while she calmed down. It was bizarre. Plus, her shirts," he says and then chances a glance in my direction. "If looks could kill, I'd be a dead man."

I'm strangling him with my mind powers. What is it with my friends, my brother, checking out my almost-wife's breasts? Men are pigs. I can't even be that mad, though, can I? I used to do the same thing to every woman who walked past me.

No, I'm pretty sure I can be that mad.

The more important question is, how many fucks should I give about my brother and friends' comments? About them noticing things about Stella that I seem to have ignored?

"Don't even worry about it, Max. I said the same thing and got the same look," Tommy says laughing and pointing his thumb over his shoulder at me. "Good thing she's madly in love with that guy."

"No doubt. Tell the missus I said congratulations. That's going to be one good lookin' kid," he says dropping a couple bills in Tommy's hand and taking a step toward the door as his radio sounds. "That's my cue. Another one in a ditch, I'm sure. See you later, guys."

***

It's not often that I don't know how to tackle something — a project, an upset customer, Britt's homework, Whiskey chewing on something he shouldn't.

When it comes to Stella, it's the same. I'm almost always spot on when I jump in as a problem solver. Or I try to be.

This time, though, I'm at a loss for solutions.

I'm distracted.

No. That's an understatement.

I'm confused and distracted ... not sure how to handle this situation.

"How could she not know?" I say into the silence of my kitchen, dumping another cup of flour in my large stainless steel bowl.

I came home to bake after the afternoon caffeine rush. I needed to clear my head and that can only happen a few ways.

Since it's a little early to tie into a six-pack and try drinking my way through problem solving, woodworking or baking were the only options left when I walked through the house this afternoon. I could bake bread in my sleep, so it won out over the chance of cutting my arm off in the woodshop because my head is somewhere else.

Slowly, I sink my hands into the dough, pulling it from the bowl to the counter and I give myself fully to the moment. Pushing the dough into itself, I thrust aside the fears and uncertainties; I knead away the confusion and doubt.

"This isn't our first go 'round, Bri. There's no reason to be scared. You're not a kid anymore, you're not immature or unprepared for fatherhood," I say out loud.

I'm right.

I continue kneading the dough, clearing my mind, adding more flour to the countertop and working it in until the texture is perfect before placing the ball back in the bowl to let it rise.

"If this is happening, it's time to make serious decisions about the houses ..." The only answer in the quiet house is Whiskey yipping beside me. I meet his gaze as he continues looking up at me with a cocked head and sad brown eyes. "Where do you want to live? Here or at Stella's?"

No answer. "I didn't think you'd be much help. All you care about is food and getting attention, doesn't matter where we live."

I wash my hands, cover the dough to let it rise, scratch his ears and head to the shower, hoping the hot water on a cold day will help ease the tension in my shoulders and clear my head more.

* * *

I hear the back door open and close quietly, as though she's trying to sneak in unnoticed.

But I listen to her every move as I sit on the couch with my feet propped on the coffee table in front of me, a copy of Lois Lowry's *The Giver* nestled in my hands.

"Stell, can you check the oven?" I yell from the living room. "There are buns in there. For dinner. They should be about done."

She doesn't come right to the living room. Stella can't help but open the door to smell what's being cooked, so I'm surprised when I don't hear the oven door squeak open, but instead notice the sound of the bathroom door closing — and I imagine the nearly silent *click* as the latch falls into place because I can tell she held the knob to quiet the noise.

The clock on the wall ticks louder and it feels like forever before I hear the toilet flush, the water run, the door open, the squeak of the oven, and her footsteps making their way across the hardwood floor.

I lift my eyes from the book I'm reading and watch her walk out of the kitchen, through the dining room to the living room. And time seems to stand still as I notice for the first time what my brother and Max have noticed.

The buttons on her blouse strain against the fabric pulled taut against her chest.

There's a supple curve to her breasts that wasn't there a few months ago.

Before she notices, I drop my eyes back to Ms. Lowry's words and Jonas' story wondering how I'm going to begin this conversation instead of reading the words on the page, words I've read time and again.

"They have about six mon- minutes left on the timer," she says. I heard her slip.

"Six months, eh? Makes sense. I think I put them in there about three or so months ago," I say not looking up from my book, afraid that once I look at her I'll melt, and I try not to look for as long as possible.

She lets out a nervous laugh and settles herself on the coffee table in front of me. My heart pounds loudly in my chest, the sound of blood rushing in my ears nearly drowns out the sound of Stella clearing her throat.

"Brian, look at me." She's quietly demanding and I can't help but lift my eyes to finally meet hers.

Instead, I'm met with two pink lines.

Two pink lines.

I stare at them, because my life is about to change.

Again.

Before this moment it was just a "what if," now it's ...

"Holy shit."

"Yeah. So much for bad food and the flu, huh?"

I glance at her face and I see it there — the worry and the relief all mixed together.

"I feel like everyone knew before us," I blurt out. "I mean ... the guys, they kind of noticed things that I didn't even pick up on and thinking about it all hurt my head so I came home to bake. I bake when I get overwhelmed. I feel like you really need to know that because I don't think you've seen me overwhelmed since we were like seven years old."

Her eyes grow wide, almost terrified. "What did they notice?"

So I tell her.

"Tommy and I are going to have a talk about where his eyes shouldn't roam. Lord help me, that man is going to be my brother and the uncle of our children." Stella tries to say it in all seriousness, but her no nonsense demeanor cracks as she smiles widely, sending all the worry packing. "We're having a baby, Brian."

"We're having a baby," I say back, leaning forward to catch her face in my hands and kiss her forehead, then her cheeks and finally her lips. Leaning my forehead against hers, I say softly, "Your dad is going to kill me."

And she sighs. That's it. She just sighs, deeply, as though she's thought about it, too.

"We'll tell them at dinner on Sunday."

Stella

Chapter Thirty-Six

We have to tell Daddy and Mom. I can't keep this from them.

I pull the brush through my hair one last time and set it on the bathroom counter before grabbing my eyeliner out of the bag I carry with me in case I stay at Brian's instead of my house. I don't know why I don't just have two of everything at this point — one for each house. It would be easier.

Brian walks into the bathroom and stands behind me, watching in the mirror as I put my makeup on.

It's only a little after five in the morning, on a weekend ... and I'm awake, showered and touching my eyes with a pointy object. Shit is getting real.

He wraps his arms around my midsection and leans in to kiss me beneath my right ear. I groan and drop my head back onto his shoulder.

"So, we're telling them today, right? We agreed we would announce at Sunday dinner. Mom wanted to get all of us together to eat since it's the only day of the week you close at a normal hour." It's the best I can offer, it's the only way we'll be able to do this together. "Daddy can't get too mad if everyone is there. And it's not like we're teenagers or going to screw up our futures by having a baby. You're a successful business owner, I'm managing a newspaper, we're educated and we're already raising one child and Tommy."

Brian dips his head down to kiss me again.

"Take a deep breath. When did you get so smart?"

"Don't patronize me. I've always been this smart, you just like to ignore it because you're afraid I'll show you up in front of our friends."

"You're not wrong. So ... we should probably consider getting a doctor's appointment and all that scary 'we're going to be parents' stuff taken care of, huh?" Brian sits on the edge of the tub and picks nervously at a tear in the knee of his jeans. Looking at me over the tops of his glasses, he just got even more beautiful and I feel the fear and love radiating off him. "We're amazing parents, but we haven't done this together from the beginning."

I'm not sure what he's getting at, but I keep quiet, silently urging him to fill me in on what's going on in that head of his.

As though he heard my thoughts, Brian looks down at the spot he's picking at on his pants and softly says, "I'm basically convincing myself I'm going to screw it up. Talking to your parents, being a new dad again, all of it."

Kneeling down in front of him, I take his face in my hands and force him to look up at me instead of at the hole in his jeans, a hole I'm going to eventually have to fix now that he's making it worse. Taking a deep breath, I try to steady my heartbeat and swallow back my emotions. "Listen to me right now, Brian. You're not the same guy you were six or so years ago when Britt was conceived. You aren't the same man who was left to fend for himself with a newborn. You are, however, a fantastic father and an amazing husband and the perfect partner to do this with. We're both going to screw up. It's normal. We just need to make sure we don't screw up the important parts."

I make it sound easy. The crazy thing is it doesn't have to be difficult, so I need to believe the things I say and maybe he will, too. I can, at the very least, hope and pray we can believe the things I say enough to get us through.

Brian's eyes linger on my face. He seems to be soaking me up and I wonder what it is that's got his attention until he reaches to push the hair out of my eyes and tuck it behind my ear.

"You make everything make sense."

"It's my job."

***

We're standing on my parent's back porch. My hand is resting on the doorknob and I feel frozen in place. Brian reaches in front of me, placing his hand on mine, and turns the handle.

"I don't know if I'm ready for this." My nerves are getting the better of me. I've been alone with my thoughts all day and now ... I'm not sure I'm ready to go sit at the table I used to do homework at and tell my parents their recently divorced and newly engaged daughter is now also pregnant. Unwed and pregnant. "I know it's silly to think they aren't going to warm to the idea, but what if they aren't even a little excited? What if we should just wait a little longer, until after we see the doctor?"

Brian stares down into my eyes, his gaze reassuring and calm, and says, "When did we switch roles?" And then pushes the door open.

"You'll be fine. We'll be fine. They're going to fall in love with the idea of us giving them another grandbaby. I've already decided." His smile takes away some of the tension in my shoulders, but it isn't until I step through the door and little arms wrap around me that I relax.

"Have you been good?" I ask Britt. He's been with my mom since this morning helping with dinner and spending time together, giving me a break I didn't realize I needed. Now that he's back in my arms it hits me just how much I've missed him, despite it only being a handful of hours.

Instead of answering me, he nods his head excitedly and gives his dad a quick "hi" before running back into the dining room. I glance back at Brian, smile, and shake my head before stepping further into the kitchen and slipping my jacket off.

This is home. No matter where I live, coming back here will always be home.

"Oh my God, it smells like it did when we were kids," Brian says quietly from behind me. No matter how often we come here, he always says the same thing. "It doesn't matter how many times I've been in this house since moving back, this place always smells like our childhood."

My mom walks into the kitchen and gives us a look. It's one of those "I know what you're up to" looks that causes a deep laugh from Brian. Without saying a word, he leans forward placing his hands on my shoulders and pulls me back into his chest.

"I saw it, too. Go talk to your mom. I'm going to see what Britt's getting himself into," he says into my hair before placing a kiss on the crown of my head and gently pushing me forward, propelling me toward the truth.

***

"Here's the thing, you have to go back. You're almost done with your master's. We'll help you out, you know that, Steph. You can focus on your school work and live at the house for as long as you need to." This argument is new, but it's already going to get old real soon and I can't even drink wine while fighting with her about it. "Were you able to finish your papers for last semester?"

"Yeah, I got those done during the winter break, but I don't know if I can go back. It's more than I can handle right now." She eyes me suspiciously. "I don't want you bending over backwards for me right now. You guys have more than enough on your plates."

Mom's head snaps up; Dad looks at me and then Brian curiously. Shit.

"What do you mean we have more than enough on our plates? I don't think our loads at work are any more than normal for this time of year, Steph. It would be no different than what we're already doing. You've been living with me for a few months and I like having you at the house," I say, my tone biting, maybe a bit more forceful than I intended. "You're doing us a favor by being there. At least it's not sitting empty all the time when I'm working late or staying at Brian's."

"But what about when you guys get married? Aren't you going to sell one of the houses? I can't imagine you holding mortgages on both," she says, and then almost under her breath she adds, "It's not like you guys are going to have enough room, anyway."

Our parent's heads have been twisting and turning, watching our verbal volley with little interest — to them it's just another heated discussion between their daughters — until Steph mentions not having enough room.

I almost choke on my broccoli. Brian does choke on whatever is in his mouth. I recover in time to see my mom snap her mouth shut while Daddy props his elbows on the table.

Everyone here but Dad and Britt know what's happening in my uterus.

The conversation with Mom was quiet. I had pulled her into the bathroom earlier, climbing up on the counter to talk to her like I used to when I was a teenager. Regardless of my age, I felt like a child picking at my nails and staring at the diamond pattern in the tiles on the floor as I explained to my mom that we'd been careful ... mostly.

"How far along are you?" she asks, her eyes wide.

A smile plays at her lips, but she's trying to hide it and I'm trying to get a grip on reality because there's no way she can be happy about this.

"I'm not really sure. We think it likely happened when Brian came back early from Tennessee, at Thanksgiving. That's the only time we can recall not using anything." I look back down at the floor, counting the blue tiles that separate the white ones. Taking a deep breath, I realize I'm going to cry. "I'm so sorry, Mom. We didn't plan this. We wanted to get married first, but ..."

She doesn't let me finish. I find myself wrapped up in a hug, if you can call it that. It's more like a death grip.

"I'm going to be a grandma?" She asks as she pulls away from me, holding my face in her hands. "Really? Finally?"

"You're not mad?"

"Stella, oh Stella, why would I be mad? We love Brian, we love you, we adore Britt ... fill that house with babies already, would you?"

And the hugging continues, interspersed with laughter and tears.

"I have a problem, Mom." I watch as her smiles falls and her eyes turn serious, but I continue before the worry can climb in and cloud her vision. "How do you think Daddy is going to react?" I bite my lip to keep it from trembling as another peal of laughter sneaks out from between her lips.

"Oh, kiddo, I don't think you have to worry about that."

"Please don't get mad, please don't get mad," I silently plead. Or I think it's silent until Brian elbows me in the ribs. "Shit!"

I look at Britt, his mouth open and his eyes wide, and try to redeem myself. "Sorry, buddy. I didn't mean to cuss."

"Yes she did. It's her favorite language." A chuckle erupts from my dad's throat, deep and powerful. "She was about your age when she learned her first swear word, Britt, and I'll never forget how unaffected she was when we tried to scold her for saying it. Just don't repeat the words and you won't get in trouble."

"Got it," Britt says to him and then winks at my dad.

"I think you two might be spending too much time together." Mom is laughing so hard she can barely get the words out. "Lord, I can't wait for more of this."

"So, Stellie, do we need to have a heart-to-heart like you had with your mother earlier?" The twinkle in my dad's eyes is more than I can handle and I nudge Brian to get his attention.

"Britt, Steph, can you two help me take these dishes to the kitchen?" Brian stands and starts gathering plates and silverware.

As they walk out of the dining room I hear Brian's laughter when Stephanie whines, "But I wanted to watch!"

"Stella. You know you can't hide things from me." Dad runs his forefinger around the rim of his water glass as he stares at me, daring me to just blurt out what it is I'm keeping from him. "I realize I'm your dad. Growing up, your friends thought I was big and scary. That asshole ex-husband of yours didn't think he needed to give me the respect he should give his elders. I was strict, but there was always enough love to go around."

I swallow. I remember my childhood. We had everything growing up, including a protective dad, and why wouldn't he be? Two daughters in this town, one of them reserved and the other rebellious, both on the deeper end of beautiful; he needed to be strict.

"I see that look. Close your mouth and listen to me a minute," he says, looking at Mom before continuing. "You see, there's a point in every father's life, I think, where they see their children grow up, move out and become successful, but then something is missing. The house isn't baby proofed anymore, there aren't toys scattered everywhere, there aren't Legos to step on in the middle of the night. To be honest, Stell, it sucks."

"Daddy, I will be sure to buy you your own Legos for Christmas this year. I promise." I say it as a joke, to break apart the seriousness in his voice.

"You can buy me all the Legos you want, as long as you be sure I get to spend more time with that little boy," he says tapping his knuckle on the tabletop. "Judging by the way everyone was acting at dinner, I suppose I'm going to have to buy baby gates, too, huh?"

"Is that something you're okay with?" Hold my cards close to my chest, don't show him my hand. Yet.

"Young lady, don't make me take you over my knee. I've always been strict, not stupid ... and you aren't stupid either."

I've been staring at my hands and picking at my fingers, again, but my head snaps up when I hear his tone.

"How okay with this are you? I need to know Dad, because this —" I point to my belly "— wasn't planned. Like I told Mom, Bri and I planned to get married, or at the very least be a lot closer to the wedding, before trying for a baby. I feel like I'm fifteen again. There are all these emotions and feelings and shit and I don't know how to get a handle on any of them."

I take a deep breath and try to calm myself down. My heart is beating so fast I feel my pulse throbbing in my neck.

I feel Brian and Steph watching from the doorway as I watch my dad's face and whisper, "I was fine until I had to face you because I don't want to disappoint you."

Getting up from his seat, Dad picks up his water glass and walks around the end of the table to sit beside me.

"You see this cup, Stella?" I nod my head. "Now, let me show you something."

He sets the cup in front of me and picks up the pitcher of water in the center of the table.

"This was my heart before you got here this afternoon. It was there, kind of empty, but beating. But then, I got a good look at you, at your face, at your eyes, at the man you love, and this ... is what happened," he says as he begins pouring the water from the pitcher into the glass until it's almost full.

"And then I saw how your mother looked after the two of you had your powwow in the bathroom and this happened," he says as he continues pouring the water into the glass, and it overflows, water rushing down the sides and spilling across the table. "If you want to know how okay I am that you and Brian are giving me another grandchild, take a look at this. This is my heart, Stella, and it is overflowing."

M.L. Pennock

Stella

Chapter Thirty-Seven

Spring: The Wedding

It's my wedding day. Again.

The only difference is, this time, there is no fear — no worry that I'm making a mistake. Today is just another day that I get to celebrate with my best friend, the love of my life and the father of my children.

Today, I'll finally say "I do" to Brian, just like I did when we were little kids playing house. I'll kiss him in the barn and shove cake in his face and dance until the sun goes down, as close to him as my expanding belly will allow me.

"You almost ready?" Steph's voice at the bedroom door brings me out of my memories and away from the thoughts of what today means for me and Brian. The cast finally came off and, though she still has a little limp, she's walking better every day on the broken one with minimal physical therapy.

I make eye contact with her reflection before turning from the antique cheval mirror Brian bought for our bedroom as an early wedding gift. I take her in, all of her, and notice for the first time in a long time a lot about my baby sister, my Stephie. My sister is gorgeous, and after months of no fire in her eyes she's bubbling with life. Her cornflower blue dress hugs her figure and accentuates the curve of her waist. Her chestnut colored hair is pinned at the back of her head and falling in soft waves down her back. Her eyes sparkle.

"Almost," I say smiling, taking a step toward her. "Come here and turn around."

With her back to me, I drape my arms around Stephanie's neck and slide my fingers around her throat to secure the necklace in place. A small token of my appreciation for all she's done for me in the last year, the small butterfly that dangles precariously from the thin chain is a symbol of the changes we've drifted through — side by side, hand in hand —and how we came out on the other end of them. Beautiful and graceful.

She reaches up to touch the pendant before stepping around me to look in the mirror.

"You didn't have to get me anything," she says, locking eyes with me in the glass. "But I love it."

"I didn't have to, but it's customary that the bride purchase the jewelry for her attendants. That's not why I bought this piece, specifically, though," I say. "Remember what Nana used to tell us? That butterflies were the most beautiful of all God's creatures because they had to endure so much to get to that point, to be able to show who they truly were? I've been thinking about that a lot lately."

Steph turns from the mirror and takes my hand in hers, pulling me over to the bed where we both try gracefully to sit among the mounds of silky fabric surrounding our legs.

"She used to get this wistful look on her face when she talked about springtime and butterflies," Steph says, like she can see our grandmother's face.

"Yeah, she did. It's like she was trying to prepare us for our winters. Think about all the shit butterflies have to go through just to get their wings, Steph." I pull her hand into my lap and look into my sister's eyes before continuing. "I think it's time we acknowledge we deserve our wings and I want you to be able to always wear yours close to you, to remind you how much you've endured to get here."

"We have been through a lot lately. Like, a lot 'a lot'," she says, biting her lip in deep thought.

"I think you need to add an extra 'a lot' to that."

Steph pulls me into a hug that resembles a death grip and a laugh mixed with a cry escapes her throat as we sit on my bed holding one another.

"Dear Hustler. There they were, the bride and her sister. I'd always dreamed of sisters." Tommy's voice draws a low, annoyed moan from Steph as she pushes herself away from me.

"You're a pig, you know that right?" she tosses the barb at him and I foresee the beginning of a verbal sparring match.

"I've been called worse," he quips from the doorway.

"You realize I'm marrying your brother and, if you hadn't noticed, am increasing in size because I'm carrying his child, right?" I point to my abdomen as I stand from the bed, turning to face him just as he claps his hands and rubs them together.

"Hadn't noticed one bit, but even better since I've heard pregnant fantasies are all the rage." His sarcasm and crooked smile make me laugh out loud while Steph stays seated on the bed looking like she might vomit.

Pointing at my sister, Tommy says, "I see my work here is done. Okay now, in seriousness, do you know where Brian is? I need to talk to him."

"You lost your brother? That's an awesome Best Man thing to do, Tommy," Steph says in response, her nose wrinkling like she just got a whiff of dirty socks.

"I didn't lose him. He's just temporarily misplaced is all."

Watching the two of them is like watching a nearly dysfunctional couple love each other. Or siblings. I'd rather think of them in terms of siblings because I just can't imagine my sister and Brian's brother ever being more than family in the most platonic sense.

"I haven't seen him since he left last night to go to the other house. Check the back of his workshop and if he's not in there, go check at the coffeehouse." It's Brian. It's a big day. He's either going to be working on something made of wood or something made of dough. "Let me know if you can't find him in either of those places, though."

"Yes, ma'am." Tommy's playful eyes have turned serious. I'm not used to seeing that expression on him and it makes me nervous.

"Tommy, is everything alright?"

"Nothing that can't be handled. You worry about getting down that aisle and I'll take care of everything else. I can't wait for him to see how beautiful you look today." Before I can say anything else, Tommy turns and rushes out of the room.

"What the fuck just happened?" Steph is staring at me as I'm staring at the door wondering the same thing.

M.L. Pennock

Brian

Chapter Thirty-Eight

"I checked the workshop. You weren't there. I went to the coffeehouse. Nada. Locked up tighter than a nun's habit. But here? This is where you are on your wedding day?"

I twist my neck to look behind me. I'm silent as I watch Tommy walk up to the swing beside me, grabbing the chains and lifting himself over and into the seat like he used to when we were kids.

Tipping my cup of coffee, I point to the gazebo across the lawn from the playground.

"That wedding Stell and I talked about back at Christmas? That's the gazebo it was in. I just wanted to come back here and remember how I felt watching her face that day," I say, pushing back and letting go to swing gently with the crisp April breeze.

"And how did you feel?" he prods.

"Like she was the only other person in the world I wanted to spend forever with." Tommy pushes off and matches my tempo. "Today I'm finally going to get that."

My brother and I swing quietly for a while. If anyone else were here, I don't want to know what they'd think — two grown men in tuxedos acting like children on the playground? Mental cases, probably. I don't care though. We pump our legs until we can't anymore and then glide gracefully to a stop.

Tommy clears his throat, breaks the silence.

"I ..." he adds in a few um's and uh's as he stutters and stumbles through whatever it is he's going to say before finally clearing his throat again. Reaching into his jacket pocket, I watch a white envelope appear. "I need to tell you something."

"If you tell me you can't stand up there with me, I will never forgive you, so it better be something like cancer. I can forgive cancer. Maybe. No I can't. What's up with the envelope?" I can't stop my mouth from saying stupid shit. He'd never not stand as witness to my marriage and if he had cancer, Tommy's not the type to tell me right before my wedding. "Seriously, T, what's with the envelope?"

"It's from Emily."

"Emily?" But she left. She left me and Britt and didn't even give me an explanation. "What do you mean it's from Emily?"

"Bri, don't get mad."

"It's a little late for that, don't you think?" At the sound of her name I dropped my coffee cup in the stones beneath my feet and began feeling the heat creep up my neck, flaming hot as the anger of her leaving our son hits me like it did the day she walked out on him. Not even me. Him. She left Britton and never so much as called to see if he was okay. I reach for the envelope, demanding, "Give me that."

Tommy pulls his arm back.

"Let me explain."

And I let him.

For nearly an hour, I let him talk as he explains that he was somehow able to convince my son's mother to stay in contact with him when she abruptly left Britt and me. For six years he's been giving her updates about us? He looks pained.

"More about him, and not all six years. I let her know what was going on with you simply because you were an extension of Britt," Tommy says. "Emily admitted to me that she wasn't in love with you, just like you weren't in love with her. You were with her for Britt, and she was with you for Britt, but neither of you were with one another. Not like a couple should be. She loved you because you gave her Britt, but she wasn't in love with you."

"But she loved him? It was so hard. She made it look like he was draining her of every ounce of her energy. I can't tell you how many times I wanted to tell her to just suck it up because that's what babies do. They drain you, but instead of dealing with it, she left," I yell. I yell it at my brother because he's the only one here and though our parents know what I went through, I never fully opened up to Tommy about the end of my relationship with Emily.

"She was sick, Brian," he yells back. Then quietly he says, "She was sick. It wasn't just emotionally and mentally draining her to be a mom. Emily left you and Britt and started chemo a week later because she was afraid to let her son watch her die. She moved back to Mississippi with her mom to start treatment for leukemia."

"You aren't making any sense. She wasn't sick. I would have known," I say more to myself than to Tommy.

"Would you have?"

Tommy is looking at me, sadness in his eyes like I've never seen before.

"I'd like to think I would have. How did I miss this?"

"You were tired. You were working, trying to make a relationship work that wasn't meant to work. You were a new dad, and it was exhausting. More than that, though? She hid it from you, as best she could anyway. Emily told me she had been in remission for a long time, since before you met her, but they found cancer cells when she had labs drawn when she was about six months pregnant," Tommy says staring at the gazebo. "It was routine blood work for her oncologist, to make sure she was still in remission. I found all this out after she left, Brian, but she swore me to secrecy. She could have undergone treatment before Britt was born, but she didn't want to put him at risk."

"Why didn't she tell me?" I can feel the tears start to seep out from the corners of my eyes and I can't stop them from coming. "I could have helped her. I could have been there for her."

"You needed to take care of the baby. You did what she wanted you to do — you took care of Britt. You hated her for it because you didn't know why she did that to him, why she left him," Tommy says quietly.

I sit in silence, contemplating what my brother told me.

"Why now? Why are you telling me all of this now? First I hear you have a letter for me from her, then you tell me she had cancer and now what? Is she going to pop out of the bushes and say hello and that she wants us back? Because that would just make my wedding day even more memorable." I feel, rather than hear, my voice rising again until I'm yelling, my chest vibrating with the anger.

Tommy looks away and I barely notice him brush his hand against his face.

"No, Bri, she's not going to be popping out of any bushes," he reaches over and grabs my shoulder. It's in that moment, in the look in his eyes, that I understand my son's birth mother will never attempt to see him. She can't. "She passed away shortly after Britt's second birthday. The envelope has a letter in it for you, and one for Britt for when he's older. There's one for you and Stella to read together. It's everything she wanted to tell you and whomever you deemed worthy enough to be Britt's mom. Emily never told me exactly what the letters say, just that on the day you found *her* I was to give this to you."

Tommy looks back at the gazebo as he silently passes the envelope to me.

"I waited until today because I got to know Em enough in those two years she was fighting the cancer to know those letters contain nothing more than her blessing. I know things weren't always great for you guys when she was pregnant, but she was really trying to keep it together, which I think also meant pushing you away so you wouldn't look for her after she left," Tommy says, sorrow muffling the sound of his voice. "She loved you so much simply because you gave her the chance to be a mom, even though she gave it all up. I think she knew you needed to have a purpose, too, and that purpose was my nephew. So I'm going to leave you to absorb all of this for a little while and I'm going to go find some alcohol. I've been holding this in for four fucking years and I just ... I need a beer."

Tommy gets up from his swing, grabbing one of the chains and pulling it back as he walks off behind me, leaving me all alone on the playground.

I stare down at the envelope in my hand — it's tattered and the corners are worn and I can only imagine it's from Tommy taking it out to look at it before pushing it back in a drawer somewhere while he waited for the right time to give it to me. My name is scrawled on the paper in blocky cursive writing. There's no denying Emily's penmanship. It demands to be recognized like she's screaming at me from beyond the grave, telling me to tear the damn thing open and read her final words to us.

"I can't open this." I know no one is here, no one is within earshot, but I'm not talking to anyone physically here. "Emily, why would you do this to me? I could have handled the truth, I could have dealt with this. I could have helped. At least you would have been able to see him take his first steps and hear his first words. You deprived yourself of all of those moments."

And I let myself cry for the girl I loved but wasn't in love with.

Stella

Chapter Thirty-Nine

"Tommy what the hell are you doing?"

He's leaning against the refrigerator, tipping back a bottle of beer at 12:30 p.m. and the wedding hasn't even happened yet.

"If anyone in this house needs liquid courage, it's me. Since I can't have any, you certainly can't have any yet. What is the matter with you today?" He pulls the bottle away from his mouth and his bloodshot eyes catch me off guard. He's quiet and contemplative. "Earth to Thomas Stratford. Hello? What's gotten into you? What happened?"

Instead of answering me, he tips the bottle again and drains its contents before reaching into his tuxedo jacket pocket and pulling a full beer from within. I resign myself to the losing end of this battle and lean against the counter to watch him cautiously as he wallows in whatever pain it is lurking in his blue eyes.

"You're just going to stand there watching me drink beer?"

"You look like someone kicked your dog. Yes, I'm going to stand here and watch you drink your beer," I say, crossing my arms over my chest. "When you're done with that one, though, I want you to talk."

Tommy nods.

We understand each other.

The wait is over quickly and he deposits both empties on the counter next to me and turns to lean against it.

"I hate being the bearer of bad news —" he holds his hand up to stop my mouth. "It's nothing to do with the wedding or Brian. It's the reason I needed to find Brian, though."

"Spill it. What's going on? You don't just down one beer right after like that, not even on a let loose and party kind of night." I've only ever seen Tommy party once since he moved up here and that was shortly after Steph was attacked because he was drinking his feelings. Even then it wasn't like he was mainlining the liquor. I've heard the stories about his wild past, though, and the word "epic" doesn't do him justice from what Brian has told me.

A deep breath and then, "After Britt's mom left them, I was able to stay in contact with her ... until she passed away about four years ago. I needed to clear my conscience and tell Bri."

I know I didn't just hear him correctly.

"Emily's dead? I know Brian hadn't talked to her since she walked out, but ..." my voice trails off. I couldn't fathom a mother willingly giving up all rights to her child, but to learn she's dead now? "Was she on drugs?" It's the only logical explanation I can come up with, but I have a limited frame of reference for what she was like other than the little bit Brian has told me about her and the trouble she had adjusting to parenthood.

"I wish. I wish it had been that simple, Stella. Emily had leukemia, was in remission for quite a while and then it came back when she was pregnant with Britton. That's why she left, why she signed over her rights." Tommy shoves his hands in his pants pockets, playing with a set a car keys in one and loose change in the other. The sound is obnoxious, but at least it isn't silence. "I think she knew this time was the last time her body would be able to handle treatments and she didn't want Brian to feel stuck or let Britt grow up watching her die. It's sad to think about it, but she made the right decision leaving."

"So, why tell Brian?"

Letters. Tommy says there's one for me, too. She wrote me a letter.

"I haven't read them. She sent them in sealed envelopes and I promised her I wouldn't snoop. When I got the package, I read the note she sent me and that's it. The other letters were already in an envelope with Brian's name on it so they went right into my dresser where I knew he wouldn't find them."

He reaches up and pulls my hand away from my face, ending the little chew fest I'm having with my thumbnail.

"I wasn't done with that," I whine.

"You're going to chew right down to the bone. You need to stop."

He's holding my hand and staring at me like he has the answer to my unspoken question, so I find my resolve and ask. "Why is there a letter for me? Brian and I weren't even together when she died. Tommy, he hadn't even moved back up here at that point."

He sighs. A deep, strangled sound, like it's been stuck in his lungs for far too long. "She knew someday Brian was going to do the fall in love and get married thing. Brian doing those things meant a woman in Britt's life, too. I think it's Emily's way of saying she trusts you to raise her baby, because she couldn't do it." Tears threaten to break through, and when Tommy blinks, they begin coursing down his cheeks. "She might have made a poor choice not telling Brian what was going on, but in the end, she wanted nothing more than for him, for you, for Britt to know you all have her blessing to love as a family."

I wipe the tears from his face and whisper "thank you" as I pull him to me, and then I silently mouth it and pray somewhere Emily can hear me.

I hug Tommy and let him cry into my shoulder until his tears dry up and our quiet moment of gratitude is shattered.

"Uh, Stella?"

I freeze at the sound of his questioning voice. This can't be happening.

On my wedding day.

Nope. I'm going to keep hugging Tommy and ignore the fact I just heard my lying, cheating ex-husband's voice say my name.

So instead, I close my eyes, take a deep breath, and count to ten.

I'm on three when Tommy pokes me in the ribs and whispers in my ear, "Who's the douche?"

"The voice sounds like my ex-husband. Tall guy, dark hair?" I say quietly.

"Yup. And he looks like a douche." Unlike me, Tommy talks at his normal volume and I cringe slightly, pinching his arm and pulling out of his embrace.

"What are you doing here, Keith?" I say as I turn to face him.

I notice his eyes sweep down my body, and on the return visit to my face his gaze lands on my abdomen.

"I ... I came by after stopping at your house and some lady there told me you were here and ... are you pregnant?" He stammers through the question. He never was a very good communicator. His eyes grow wider as he waits for the answer. "Is that a wedding dress? What the fuck is going on?"

I look down at my belly, a smile lighting up my face, but notice out of the corner of my eye that Tommy's flexing his hands and balling them up into fists. He's got that "don't mess with my sister" glare down pat and it's aimed directly at my former husband. Reaching out my arm, I place a hand on his bicep as a gentle reminder to Tommy that I'm a big girl.

"I don't think you have a right to ask questions, Keith. Just so you don't have to try to satisfy your curiosity elsewhere, though, yes. To the first two questions. As for your third question, you're barging into my soon-to-be husband's house on our wedding day and causing a scene," I say, trying to keep my voice even. I look behind me and see both my parents, my sister,

Caryn and Greg hovering at the kitchen doorway that leads onto the deck at the back of the house. I hold my hand out and continue, "See? A scene. I find it hard to believe you have the audacity to stand there with your accusatory glances and shameful of me expression when you're the one who stepped out on our marriage. You got a girl pregnant while you were still married to me, remember? You can pretend to be the victim right now, because I can see you want to be the victim, and ask questions like you have a right to ask them, but I'm still not even sure why you're here. Why are you here, Keith? Our marriage was over long before our divorce was final. We have nothing to say to one another. Ever again, actually."

I've kept my composure so long, my shoulders thrust back and standing up straight, I feel like my spine might crumble, but he walked into my house — my home, where I'm going to start my family — and I want answers.

I hear his voice before I see him standing behind Keith in the doorway leading to the front of the house and my Kevlar-strong façade falls away as a grin takes over my face.

"The lady asked you a question. Correct me if I'm wrong, but, my mama always taught me to speak when spoken to and that goes for being asked a question, as well," Brian says, a sternness in his voice that relieves and terrifies me all at once.

Keith turns his back to me and comes face-to-face with the man who had my heart long before he did, the man who will have it long after this blip on our happiness radar.

"You? She's marrying you?" he scoffs. "Aren't you the coffeehouse guy? I saw her with you at the mall. That's classic. Stella the workaholic marrying a barista. It's like a damn fairy tale." His snide laugh twists the knife he put in my heart so many months ago.

I've seen Keith like this before. He thinks he's going to be able to talk down to Brian, as though the money in his safe is worth more than everything Brian and I have invested in one another. I wasn't aware our successes were measured by the padding in our bank accounts, the fancy clothes in our closets. If that's the case, Keith may win every time, but the reality of the situation is money doesn't make a man a real man.

"I may make coffee for a living, but I got the girl." His smile lights up the room, my heart, my soul. His smile ... is everything. "She's mine. I want you out of my house before I call my buddy, Max. Not sure if you've met him, but like me he provides a service for his living. His comes with handcuffs."

Keith turns on his heels and faces me again. "You'd let him have me arrested?" he asks, his tone incredulous, as though he doesn't believe I'd give Brian my approval to make the call. As though I owe him something.

"Why wouldn't I? You've been asked to leave. Now … you're trespassing, Keith." I try to hide my smile.

"The baby isn't mine. She lied to me." He blurts it out like it will make all the difference and fear seeps into his features, the stoic mightier-than-thou demeanor evaporated. "Beth left me. I wanted to ask you if I can buy the house back. I have nowhere to go. I'm desperate."

I hear Steph gasp behind me. She and Tommy have already signed a rental agreement with me. They're roommates as of yesterday. I'm sure her reaction is an attempt to quiet her disgust.

"The house isn't for sale," I say, matter-of-fact, as I tamp down the desire to hurt for him, for the lies she told him. I remind myself, she isn't the only liar; he lied to me. He hurt me. My anger flares. "You made your bed. Go lay down in it, Keith. You have no business here."

His mouth opens, then closes, and opens again.

"Get the fuck out of my house," Brian says from behind him. "And if you bother my wife again, I will have you arrested for harassment."

Keith turns his head and stares at Brian, who's leaning his shoulder against the doorframe, his ankles crossed and hands in the pockets of his tuxedo pants. He looks like a modern day nerdy James Bond with his perfectly messy blonde hair and black frame glasses.

He takes a step backward toward the door Brian's standing in and, dropping his head, Keith says quietly to me, "If you change your mind about the house, call me. Please?"

"Won't be happening any time soon, Keith. You may as well just look elsewhere," I say and turn away from him, walking swiftly to the bathroom and, closing the door behind me, I close the door on that chapter of my life.

I hear the front door slam. I hear the voices in the kitchen — a collection of "What the fuck was that?" and "He's lost his damn mind" — and feel the anxiety release me, the tightness in my chest loosen its hold.

I count to ten.

I count to ten again.

I give up and just count until I feel better.

M.L. Pennock

Brian

Chapter Forty

All I wanted to do today was get married.

Instead, I find out my son's birth mother was sick when she left us. I find out she died, making it impossible for Britt to ever know her now.

I read the letter Emily left for me, and I peacefully understand her reasons, but it doesn't change the fact she hid the truth from me.

Emotionally, I pulled myself up by my bootstraps and headed back to Stella's house to finish getting ready for the wedding I've been waiting my entire life for.

It was easy to change gears from the sadness I felt learning what Emily had been through to the joy of making my marriage to Stella official.

It was easy to get lost in the moment of standing in Stella's bedroom where I know we created the life she's carrying.

It was easy to ignore the doorbell when it rang because I knew Mama and Britt were both downstairs waiting for me so we could head the few blocks to my house. I knew Mama would answer it and whatever was needed from whoever was on the other side, she would take care of it.

I don't blame my mother for what I walked in on at my house. I just wish she'd called me downstairs so I could have taken care of it before it got to the point it did — before Keith even had a chance to finish asking Mama what the address was.

As Stella walks off toward the bathroom, Keith tucks his tail between his legs and heads out the front door of our house. I rub my hands over my face and look between them at my mama standing with Britt next to the front door.

She jumps as Keith slams the door on his way out.

"I should have just had him arrested," I mutter to myself.

Chaos takes over the kitchen, a slew of "fucks" flying out of every mouth in there, and I watch Mama cover Britt's ears at the first cuss word she hears.

"That was Stella's ex," she says more than asks.

"Yes, ma'am. That was him." I clasp my fingers together behind my head and lean back against the doorframe again, this time facing the front of the house and my mother instead of the back. "He's a real … let's just say he's the type of man you'd probably say 'oh, bless his heart' about if I told you too much about him, Mama. He did a real number on Stell."

"I gathered as much, Brian, but no point being kind about a boy like that," she says. Looking down at her hands still covering my son's ears, she candidly continues, "If he hurt Stella I'd probably just call him an asshole to his face. He's not worth a 'bless your heart.'"

I smile at her — a smile that reaches my eyes for the first time all day — and let out a deep laugh because … she's Mama and damn if she doesn't just cut to the core of things. In the midst of my laughter, she lets go of Britt's head and I catch him looking from her to me and back again, confusion crumpling his beautiful face.

"Hey, buddy, why don't you go check and make sure Grandpa doesn't need any help in the workshop," I say as he walks over and wraps his arms around my waist. I kneel down to his level and, putting my hands on his small but broad shoulders say, "We're getting married to the girl of our dreams today, Britton. Do you know how long I've waited for this day?"

"A real long time," he says. I hear the question in his voice, but it's only slight. Hardly noticeable.

"Yeah. A real long time. Since I was around your age. That's how long I've been in love with Stella." He smiles, a shot going straight to my heart when I see parts of his mother in him I hadn't noticed before and I feel conflicted. My love for Stella is unwavering; my love for Emily, because she gave me our son, is enough to cause a lump to form in my throat when I realize it's her nose Britt has, her chin.

"Did you love mommy?"

I blink, caught off guard by the question and feeling the smile on my face fall a little. He's rarely asked about Emily. It's always been us boys and Mama, and while I've talked about his mom, we've never had in depth conversations about the feelings that went into our relationship.

The answer, though, is simple. It's simple because I've been admitting it to myself all day, and now it's time to share that with him.

"Absolutely I loved her. I don't think I loved her like I love Stella, but she gave me you, the chance to be your daddy, and I will love her forever because of that." I can feel the tears burning behind my eyes as Britt and I somehow change roles and I find myself being held by my child on my wedding day as he comforts me in the wake of a pain I will someday soon have to explain to him.

But not today.

"Good. Because she told me she loved you, too," he says, a smile lifting his lips as he leans in and kisses me on the forehead before running out of the room calling for Whiskey.

"Mama. What just happened?" I'm still kneeling on the floor, frozen in place, when I feel a draft pushing cold air through the room and shiver.

And she laughs at me. I raise my eyes and see her openly laughing at me.

"Oh, Brian, you have so much yet to learn about children. You just wait until this next baby is born. I bet there'll be more drafts in this house than you thought possible." The smile is glued to her face. I shake my head, not understanding. "If I hadn't had the chance to know Stella's grandmother, I would think that child is talking gibberish. But that's not the case. I did know Nana Barbieri and she was a very, very wise woman."

"You're talking about how she always knew things, aren't you?"

"She had a gift, Brian," she responds, her voice gone stern. It's her lecturing tone. "She swore up and down that children have it, too, but because of the close minded people doing the raising, they forget they know the dead. They forget how to talk to them and start shutting them out. That child, he's just that. Britt is a child and he's still pure and open minded."

"Mama, you're not saying ..."

"I'm saying, keep an open mind where your children are concerned, Brian. Keep an open mind where your wife is concerned. She's cut from the same cloth."

"The same cloth?"

"Oh the things you've tucked away in your memory, locked them away," she clucks at me. I actually hear the tsk tsk she sneaks in. "Think about all those times you two almost or could have gotten in trouble. What stopped you from going down certain paths in the woods? That time you almost fell through the ice on the pond. What saved your ass, Brian?"

I think back to when we were little. It was always Stella. She'd tell me we couldn't ride our bikes down a certain road and I wouldn't question it because she just knew a better way.

"She grabbed my jacket and pulled me back," I say thinking back to that day. We'd been playing on the ice covered pond in a neighbor's horse pasture. I hadn't paid attention to the fact we'd had a day of warmer temperatures. I hadn't paid attention to much of anything other than impressing Stella. "I'd walked out onto the pond and she followed me.

Before I knew what was happening she was pulling me backwards and running."

"Had you even heard the ice start to crack?"

"No. We got back to solid ground and I remember wondering what had gotten into her ... and then I heard the pop and the center of the ice split wide open. Right where I'd been standing."

My eyes are on Mama, but she's smiling and watching something behind me.

"You okay, Bri?"

At the sound of Stella's voice, I turn.

"You saved me." She did. She saved my life more than once.

"Once or twice," she says shyly, lacing her fingers together beneath her belly, atop the white satin of her simple and beautiful gown. "It was a long time ago. So, Britt and I just had an interesting chat about his mom and now I've walked in on this, so I'm assuming we're all on the same page."

"Which page is that, sweetie?" Mama asks.

"The page where we don't dismiss our son's friends, imaginary or otherwise. I don't want to be one of those closed minded people Nana always warned me about," she says, lowering her voice like she's afraid someone might actually think she's less than open minded. Mama and I both nod. "Okay, now that that's settled, let's go get hitched. This day has been exciting enough already, don't you think?"

Mama walks toward the kitchen, stopping to lay a hand on Stella's belly and pull her in for a quick hug before disappearing through the doorway. I smile when I hear her shooing outside anyone still standing around and telling Tommy not to argue with her.

When I'm certain we're alone, I speak up. I have trouble letting sleeping dogs lie. "Stella, your grandmother, she could see things?"

Taking a deep breath, Stella grabs my hand and pulls me to the living room. Pushing me down on the couch, she sits in front of me on the coffee table — a few months ago this is where we discovered together that we were going to be parents and I get a sudden feeling we're on the cusp of something amazing being back in this place.

"Absolutely she could see things. Daddy likes to play the skeptic sometimes, but he grew up with her and he knows better than me how much she could see. When I was younger, she told me things that tore away at old wounds, things that brought feelings back to the surface that I had buried when you left. Feelings I think I buried along with that open mindedness she adored so much." I watch her take a shuddering breath.

"After your family moved I was devastated, Brian. I was still a little girl, but I had understood something about life that was so much bigger than us. When you left, I stopped understanding all of those things and focused on hating that you were gone. We could write, we called once in a while, but for the most part I felt like half of me was missing. You were missing."

I watch her curiously. I don't dare interrupt; I know the answers are coming.

The vein in her neck is pulsating rapidly as she wrings her hands together, wrestling with what she has to say to me.

"When I was seventeen, Stephie and I had a conversation with her. It was one of our normal heart to heart talks. We had them all the time. But something about this one was different. She basically told me despite how I thought I felt about Keith, you'd come back. I didn't want to believe her. I was a kid still. Shit, I was a kid still nursing the broken heart left in your wake. I couldn't believe her." She pauses. I hand her the handkerchief in my pocket and watch her dab her eyes, careful not to ruin her makeup. "But then, there you were, years later. And there I was standing in the rain. And I believed in fate again. ... I believed in her again."

"I was made for you, Stella. I was handpicked from the stars, just for you," I say quietly and hear her gasp at the sound of her grandmother's words being repeated back to her.

"I can hear her voice saying it," she says through the fingers covering her mouth, her eyes fluttering closed, the long lashes dusting her cheekbones. "But how did you know?"

"She told me, too. Before we moved. I had just walked out of your parents' house for what I feared would be the last time. She was sitting on the porch and said to me, 'Young man, we need to talk.'" I feel the tips of my ears burning. I'd never thought twice about what she'd said to me all those years ago, but now? It felt like putting the last piece of a puzzle in place. "We just fit together, Stell. We always have. It doesn't matter what your past is, it doesn't matter who gave birth to Britt, it doesn't matter if we live in this house or that one or a God forsaken cardboard box. We. Fit. Together."

Stella opens her eyes and looks into mine and I see nothing but love shining through.

"We do." Her eyes grow wide. "I do. Oh my God, Brian, we're getting married today. Why are we sitting in here talking about this when we're —" her head whips around to look at the clock on the wall "— officially late for our own wedding. We're late for our own wedding and it's in the backyard."

She grabs my hand and, laughing, we run through the house.

Stella

Chapter Forty-One

Dad takes my arm and wraps it around his while I still have my eyes closed. Today has been filled with highs and lows, and it's barely 2 p.m.

But it's been filled nonetheless.

With family. With their voices and their words and their love.

With friends. With their hearts and minds and kindness.

With hurt and happiness, memories and the ability to make memories.

Now I stand here on the cusp of our new beginning, at the edge of the doorway to Brian's workshop-turned-church and reception hall. He's over there waiting for me.

Still, I can't seem to open my eyes for fear this ... all of this ... is a dream.

"Daddy?"

"Yeah, Stell."

"This is real right? He's really here and I'm really marrying him, right?"

I feel him shift next to me and then a hand on my face. "Stella, open your eyes." I do. "He's here, and he's waiting for you. It's time."

And it is.

M.L. Pennock

Epilogue

Stephanie

I have a sister and in one fell swoop have acquired a brother, his brother, and a nephew.

I keep waiting for my Prince Charming to show up, but he won't. I don't plan on him arriving anytime soon.

This is not my fairy tale. It's Stella's, and she's deserved every damn moment of it.

It's not my turn.

So here I sit, in my sister's new home at her new-to-her dining room table in my new bridesmaid's dress drinking wine and dulling the ache in my leg, the ache in my heart. I'm trying to fill the void in my soul.

"Is this seat taken?"

My hair falls around my shoulders as I tip my head back to look at Tommy. My new brother-in-law's brother. My new roommate. The un-love of my life.

"Whatever, dude." I let my eyes roll back, wishing a little that I could disappear. "It's your brother's house. You can sit wherever you like."

He looks at me suspiciously before pulling the chair out and sliding into the seat. He reaches out and touches my hair, the soft curls long gone from an afternoon of mingling with Brian and Stella's guests.

Despite the small list of family and friends attending, the party has gone well into the evening and if I were to wander out to the workshop I'm sure there are still stragglers hanging out — like my parents, Brian and Tommy's parents, and probably the local police chief and his wife.

Because 'round here, we're all family.

I'm sure no one has put Britt and Whiskey to bed, either, because I can hear them running around upstairs. The click-clack of that pup's nails might have me on edge if it weren't for Tommy's fingers working wonders.

He keeps touching my hair and it's made me sleepy. He needs to stop.

"Stephie, if I didn't know better I'd think you were enjoying yourself," Tommy says, his voice quiet and rough from a night of singing along with the music and talking to everyone. I don't think I saw him sit and be quiet once all evening. Damn social butterfly. "If you weren't practically my sister I'd think it was kind of hot."

"And you, Thomas, are a pig. I should tell your mother on you. She'd have a conniption and you know it. Besides, hitting on the bride's sister? Isn't that beneath even you?"

I like to pick on Tommy. He's a couple years older than me, but he's easy to get riled up. I like to keep the men in my life on their toes, even the ones who won't ever be a relationship prospect.

"If you're getting drunk tonight, you need to let me know. I don't want you trying to take advantage of me."

The "picking on" goes both ways, obviously.

"Yes, Mom. Doubt I'm going to get drunk. It's pure exhaustion leading the charge tonight, though, so you may still have to carry me to bed. Promise, I'll keep my hands to myself." I lift my head back up, pulling my hair from his reach, and turn to face him. "When's it going to be my turn?"

I hate the pity in his eyes, and despite the fact he pulls his reaction back as quickly as it surfaced ... I still saw it. He thinks I'm a sad human. His face, for a moment says, "let's all feel bad for Stephanie. She's had a tough time." I hate it.

"I thought you were hell bent on finishing school, finding your way, figuring yourself out," he says, because he knows. I am determined to finish school. One semester off to heal and prioritize was enough to make me realize I've worked too long and too hard to give up. If I don't go back and complete this last semester and my research project so I can get my degree, I'll have gone through all of this for nothing.

Tommy knows better than most how I've been feeling. That's what being roommates does to you. You get to know each other; you get inside their head. This is just a slip, a shift in my armor that I need to put back in place. His voice is softer when he says, "What happened to Super Feminist Steph? The girl I found curled up on the couch the other night claiming 'I don't need a man to complete me'?"

I glide the tip of my index finger along the rim of my wine glass while I consider his questions. What did happen to her? In the last year she went from lonely to feeling loved to abused to stalked and attacked. And now? "She's lonely again, Tommy. She's scared of men and afraid of the dark, but lonely."

"I'm here, princess. You don't need to be afraid of the dark. I'll be just down the hall. You don't have to be afraid of men. Brian and Greg and I will be sure to scare them all away until you tell us to stop," he says, reaching out to tuck my hair behind my ear. "You're family. We aren't going to let anyone hurt you again."

I lift my eyes to watch his as I say, "But what about my heart? What if that gets hurt? You can't protect me from that."

He's quiet. Contemplative. Protective.

"We can try, though."

Something catches his attention, and I hardly realize Tommy's getting up and leaving the room before I hear his voice.

Max's voice.

"Steph?" he says from across the room as he watches Tommy get up and walk away. "Do you need a ride home?"

I do, but I don't make a move. I just stare at him and wonder ... what if I do?

The clock on the wall ticks. The little boy plays. The puppy yips. Laughter escapes from the kitchen.

A peacefulness winds its way through my sister's home, its heaviness settling in as life silently prepares us all for what's to come.

The end

M.L. Pennock

Acknowledgments

I'd like to tell you I spent months mapping out this book, having pages and pages of character developments, but that would be a huge lie. I have some handwritten notes in a legal pad. There are a ton of electronic notes in Evernote. This book has been a lot of flying by the seat of my pants. It's 93,000-ish words of, "I wonder what Brian's going to tell me he wants to talk about tonight?" Stella spoke to me through her anger at the situations I put her in, as well as the moments where I made her smile and laugh.

While this may be a work of fiction, it's all from my heart ... even the hardest parts. We learn nothing of ourselves unless we are removed from our comfort zones. Step outside yours. You just might find strength where before you only saw weakness.

My husband, Ron, has shamelessly listened to my rambling about fictional people for more than a year while working on this project and hasn't presented me with divorce papers, so he deserves many thanks. He suffered right along with me as I was writing some of these chapters, but ultimately it's been his love that gave me the courage to follow through. This has been a scary process.

This book would never have been completed without the support of my friend, Jen Krider. She worked with me in multiple capacities, from reading every possible version of the first draft to helping me choose which cover I really wanted since I couldn't possibly use them all. Thank you for reminding me when things got tough who I shouldn't let in my head and for helping me turn some of my less developed ideas into pieces of the most beautiful prose in the book.

Trista Ward, Melanie Maheu, and Sandi Sullivan — I don't know if I can ever say thank you enough for beta reading this beast for me. I'm so happy to have been able to share early copies of this story with you. Your love for these characters is endearing and gives me hope others will fall in love with them as you did.

Amanda Crans-Gentile — You are an amazing visionary and artist. The cover you created pulls the entire story together. I hope readers will be able to jump right into downtown Brockport along with the characters because of your keen eye for detail and ability to conceptualize and realize.

I want to also thank my parents, Kathy and Rich Vagg, and my sister, Krissie, for giving me room to play and create when I was a child, not getting mad at me when I wrote on my bedroom walls as a teenager, and not even batting an eyelash when I decided veterinary medicine would take a backseat to an English degree. This is a project that has been in the works for decades when we really think about it. I wouldn't have achieved all I have without your love, encouragement, and discipline ... because, let's be real, I'm a handful.

About the Author

Miranda L. Pennock was born and raised in Western New York. She attended Alfred University where she graduated with a Bachelor of Arts in English and communication studies and went on to earn her Master of Arts in communications from SUNY College at Brockport.

After a handful of years working as a reporter and editor in the newspaper industry, Miranda left the news world to care for her children and begin working on creative writing projects.

Miranda and her husband live in Central New York with their two daughters and black lab.

This is her debut novel.

Made in the USA
Middletown, DE
17 May 2021